A NOT-SO HOLIDAY PARADISE

GRACIE RUTH MITCHELL

To anyone who feels broken, defective, or unworthy of love. Do not believe the lies your mind tells you when life has made you tired. You are wholly, perfectly yourself, and that is all you need to be.

AUTHOR'S NOTE AND TRIGGER WARNING

From the very beginning of my publishing career, I knew I eventually wanted to write a character with epilepsy. I was diagnosed with epilepsy at the age of thirteen, and although I'm used to the way I live now, it's a condition that impacts my life in a major way. Despite being in my thirties, I don't yet know how to drive, and I have a fear of deep water that I imagine stems from the caution I've always had to exercise around pools, lakes, and oceans. I take medication in the morning, at midday, and in the evening, and the medications I take and have taken over the years have presented their own challenges and side effects. My children have a one in ten chance of developing epilepsy as well, and that's perhaps the most terrifying thought of all. Don't get me wrong; I'm well-adjusted, and for the most part I simply don't know any differently. I've lived this way over half of my life. But I'd be lying if I said it wasn't inconvenient at the very least.

As I was getting to know Molly, my main character, I realized that she was the right choice for the epileptic character I had been waiting to write. It fit with her arc, and it fit with the plot. I'm so glad I'm able to represent this condition, especially because I don't see epilepsy represented very often, and even less by people who've experienced firsthand what it's like to actually have a seizure.

I will admit, at first I was worried about the way I portrayed epilepsy; was I treating it with respect? Was I treating it with dignity? But then I realized something: there is nothing dignified about having a seizure. And it felt wrong, somehow, to romanticize that experience. I've handled the subject matter extremely accurately, based on my own firsthand experiences— and that's a scary thing in and of itself, putting so much of my vulnerability on the page—but this also means that I have not sugar-coated anything. What you are getting from this story is my raw, honest truth.

However—however!—more than anything else, I want to say this: just because seizures look undignified does *not* mean they are something to be embarrassed about or ashamed of. My body simply works a little differently, and that is *okay!* The woman with a headache is not ashamed; the man with a broken leg is not embarrassed. Whatever differences your body may have, whatever health challenges you may face, remember that: *you are not defective.*

If an on-page seizure will be upsetting or triggering for you, please skip the end of chapter 17. As always, with all of my books, please take care of yourself when reading, and feel free to put it aside if you're bothered by what I've written.

With much love and concern for your well-being,

Gracie

Christmas Escape Bingo

Read all seven books in the series to get a Christmas romance blackout!

Broken elevator	Sleigh ride through the mountains	Allergic reaction	Snowstorm Power outage	A walk down main street
Candlelit house tour	Define the boundaries chat (multiple answers)	Ice Skating on a frozen pond	Mint hot Chocolate	"Highway to Hell" ringtone
Boat ride	"Fresh" chocolate milk	FREE SPACE	Reindeer Attack	Miniature Christmas Tree
Hot chocolate at a Christmas market	Trip to Ikea	Burning hot chocolate	Home Alone movie night (multiple answers)	Listening to Bing Crosby
An angry dachshund	Blanket fort	Snowy Beach	Mandalorian pajamas	Snowmobile ride through the mountains

ONE
MOLLY

ONCE UPON A TIME, MANY MOONS AGO, I TRIED TO DYE MY hair purple—"tried" being the operative word. I was not particularly beauty-savvy. I was not particularly good with a curling iron or a straightening iron or anything else. And I guess I was not particularly smart, either, because none of these things crossed my mind at the time.

What you need to understand, in order to get the full scope of this fiasco, is that my hair has a mind of its own. It's a bright, vivid orange, a stark contrast against my pale, freckled skin. It can never decide if it wants to be curly or wavy, and so it usually goes with a little of both: wavy on the sides, curly in the back, and happy to misbehave at any time. It's taken a while, but I've made my peace with that now. I've even learned how to tame the beast, as it were, with the right conditioner and anti-frizz serum.

But in high school? Well, no peace had been made, and no beast had been tamed. The beast still very much ran wild, and I had not the slightest clue what to do with it. Which was why, my sophomore year, I believed—I *genuinely believed*—that purple hair was the right move for me.

Purple. Hair.

I blame it on Pinterest, honestly. It was showing me all these pictures of girls with beautiful lilac hair, and I *wanted* it. I wanted long, shiny hair in the palest of lavenders. I was going to be edgy yet elegant, an ethereal Fae queen gracing the halls of Logan High.

There's nothing edgy, elegant, or ethereal about me—nothing about my yellow backpack and white Keds that screamed "fairy goddess." There wasn't then, and there isn't now. I don't know why I thought that was the case.

And to be fair, maybe it would have worked out if I had gone to a salon. I'm inclined to think it would have gone badly no matter where I went, but hey—who knows. It's a moot point either way, because I didn't go to a salon. I went to my parents' bathtub. Just me, a canister of purple Kool-Aid, and a whole lot of unearned confidence that this was going to work.

It did not work.

It was a disaster. A complete disaster, and I walked around for the next two months looking like a dumpster fire of a human being, with reddish-purplish-brownish streaks in my already conspicuous hair—not to mention a halo of purple around my hairline, because I forgot to protect my skin from the Kool-Aid dye. It was my most humiliating look to date—

Until now.

Because this?

This might be worse. Go ahead and call me a drama queen if you want, but in roughly one hour I'm going to see Beckett Donovan for the first time in years, and my face is covered in splotchy, pink hives.

I look like a red Congo pufferfish, *Tetraodon miurus*, swollen and grouchy. Only unlike the puffer, who likes to

2

wallow in the sand and ambush unsuspecting prey, I would very much like to wallow in bed and ambush my unsuspecting Netflix queue.

"Whoa," comes a voice from behind me, and I jump, whirling around. My older brother, Wes, is standing in the doorway of my ocean liner cabin, looking both amused and concerned. "What happened to you?"

I groan, covering the lower half of my face with my hands and throwing myself onto the little bed tucked against the cabin wall. "I tried some of the fresh tropical fruits at the breakfast buffet, but I think I'm allergic," I say.

"You're *definitely* allergic," he says, inviting himself inside. The cruise ship we're on is pretty big, but my room is not, and Wes only has to take three steps before he reaches the bed. "How's your airway? Your tongue? Let me see," he says, sitting down and moving into nurse mode. "Move your hands."

"No," I grumble, covering my face more intently. "I can breathe just fine. I'm staying like this forever."

Wes rolls his eyes. "Come on," he says. He tugs at my hands, and I reluctantly let them fall away, exposing the rest of my face to him.

"Is it terrible?" I say, my voice little more than a whisper. Maybe I was overreacting before, or maybe it was just the lighting. Maybe it's not *that* bad—

"Oh, yeah," he says with a snort of laughter. "It's bad. Like the girl in the Willy Wonka movie? The one who turned into a blueberry? Only you're turning into a strawberry—"

"Wes!" I wail, giving him a solid *thwack* on the arm. "What am I supposed to do?"

Wes's eyes soften as he ruffles my hair, like I'm a child instead of a twenty-four-year old woman. "Calm down, Moll," he says. "I'm just teasing. We can run down to the infirmary and see if they've got some prednisone."

3

"We could, except we need to meet Mom and Dad," I point out, looking at the small digital clock on the bedside table. "Like...five minutes ago, we needed to meet them. And Beckett is gonna be waiting for us when we get off. We don't have time."

Wes doesn't seem nearly as concerned about this as I am, and I don't appreciate it one bit. If he could show even a fraction of the panic I'm currently experiencing, that would be nice. But all he does is shrug. "You can wait for the hives to go away on their own, or I can call everyone and tell them you need a minute."

I swallow, peeking hopefully up at him. "You think that would be okay?"

I know my parents are really looking forward to this port excursion, and I don't want to stand in the way of anything. They've been planning this Christmas cruise for the last year; my mom grew up in California, and she hates the winter. So my dad's Christmas present for her last year was a cruise this year over the holidays. And while I do love looking out the window on Christmas morning to see snow, I also won't be mad about singing "Jingle Bells" while reading a book on deck.

"Yeah, it will be fine," Wes says, waving my concerns away. "Go down to the infirmary. I'll call Mom and Beckett and explain."

I have no response to this—not if I don't want Wes to know that I'm depressingly in love with his best friend. So I simply nod, resigning myself to my splotchy, red fate for the next few hours at least.

Maybe Beckett won't notice. Maybe the hives will disappear by the time we get to him. Maybe it will just look like a bad sunburn.

Maybe, maybe, maybe.

DON'T ASK me when I fell in love with Beckett Donovan, because I don't even know.

It's not something I'm proud of, being head over heels for my brother's best friend. Because it's turned me into *that* girl— the one with a string of unmet dating expectations and standards that are way too high.

Despite the past purple-hair mishap and the current facial rash, I don't have a horrendous time getting dates. And I've tried to go out with other guys. I really have. All kinds of guys, too. Tall and short, introverted and extroverted, cheerful and solemn. I have gone through the dating buffet and tried a little of everything. Some of those guys have been nice. Some of them have been funny.

None of them have been Beckett.

And in the end, that's all my stubborn heart can focus on: that none of these men have measured up to Beckett Donovan.

Which is absolutely, categorically ridiculous, by the way. It's not like he's a god. He has flaws. Not to mention I haven't seen him in person for years.

Like, actual *years*. Roughly nine of them. So it's a little frustrating that my heart refuses to see sense and move on already.

But no. I fell in love with him when my young brain was still fragile and impressionable, and like the snippet of a commercial jingle you just can't forget, he's been living in my head ever since.

So when *exactly* did I fall for him? I don't know. Was it during one of the countless driveway basketball games I watched him play with Wes? Maybe. Was it one of the many times he offered to do dishes after having dinner with my family? Also possible. All I know is that it happened. He was always smart, always gracious—if not a little grumpy, even

5

then. He was always around, and I was always paying attention. I paid attention to his flush of embarrassment when my mom sent him home with containers of leftovers, because she knew his mom had left them and his dad worked late. I paid attention to the rare, reluctant smile that never once made his eyes crinkle at the corners. I paid attention to everything he said and did—and even more frequently, the things he *didn't* say or do.

I paid attention to him, and he never, not once, paid attention to me.

Oh, he wasn't rude, or anything. He just was three years older than me. I was Baby O'Malley to him, mostly invisible, from the day he first met Wes in elementary school to the day they both graduated from high school when I was fifteen.

But no longer will I be invisible.

No longer, Beckett Donovan.

I just need to take care of this little allergic reaction first, or I'm going to be making an impression in all the wrong ways—and that's not in the plan. I've been preparing for this moment for a long time. I have my favorite swimsuit ready to go, and in the last few years I've finally become comfortable with my five-foot-two, very curvy body. I want to impress him with my brain and my (sometimes) winning personality and my possible beauty...just not my skin rash.

I don't know how Wes is going to explain this delay to Beckett, though, and I don't ask. I'm not sure I want to know. There's nothing embarrassing about allergies, but still...hives. So instead of sticking around to hear Wes's phone conversation, I just nod silently at him, trying not to grimace as I catch sight of myself in the mirror again. I gesture to the door, indicating that I'm heading out. He nods back, his phone already pressed to his ear.

I'm beyond grateful that by the time I get back from the

infirmary thirty minutes later, he's face down on my bed, clearly done talking to Beckett and my parents.

"What did everyone say?" I say anxiously.

"They're all fine, just like I told you they would be," he says, his voice muffled. He doesn't look at me; he just stays with his face buried in my pillow.

"You better not be getting your spit on my bed," I say, eyeing him. "So everyone was okay?"

Wes finally rolls over, flopping from his front to his side to his back, only narrowly avoiding falling off the bed. "Yep. Mom and Dad are going to go ahead and meet up with Beckett, and we can join them when you're ready. You wanna wait a bit to see if your hives go away?"

I raise my brows at him, sitting on the foot of the bed. "Don't you want to see Beckett? He's been working on a tiny island for the last *eight months*. And it's been several years before that since you've seen him, hasn't it?"

Wes shrugs, sighing contentedly as his eyes flutter closed. "He's still the same old Beckett. Besides, I know you're embarrassed about the hives. And this bed is comfortable, and I'm not a morning person."

"Ah," I say, grinning. "The ulterior motive appears."

"Just thirty minutes," he says, his voice already drifting away as he takes off his glasses and folds them on his chest. "I told Mom we would be there in a little bit, depending on how you felt."

I shake my head, still smiling. I'd rather just get going, but I guess I can wait. "Thirty minutes, you lazy bum."

Wes grunts, and then he's out. This is easily one of his most infuriating qualities, alongside his overprotective nature, his incessant flirtatiousness with every woman he meets, and his inability to think of me as an adult: he can fall asleep absolutely anywhere, and it never takes him longer than thirty seconds.

This is wildly frustrating for those of us who lie in bed at night replaying our most embarrassing moments on repeat until the wee hours of the morning.

Some people have all the luck.

While Wes snores lightly from my bed, I double-check my backpack to make sure I've got everything I need for the day excursion. Beckett is meeting us in port, and then we're taking a boat over to the island where he's been working on installing an astronomy research campus for the last eight months. This was part of what made my parents choose this particular cruise to the Virgin Islands—they love Beckett like a son, and they jumped at the chance to get to see him.

I'm excited to see him too, obviously, but I'm also anxious to check out the area because I'll be back here in a couple months. I've signed up for a work study that starts then; not on St. Thomas, but several islands over. It will be the perfect way to spend cold, dreary February.

"Sunscreen," I mutter as I dig through my bag. "Bug repellent, sunglasses..." I look up, biting my lip and glancing around my small room as I think. When my eyes snag on my snacks, I smile. "Sustenance," I say. "Yes."

I'm the kind of girl who likes to snack on familiar comfort foods when possible, which means I frequently bring my own. Mom did a bunch of holiday baking before we left, and I made off with some of the spoils: namely one small box full of miniature shortbread and gingerbread cookies in Christmasy shapes.

I open the box, smiling fondly at my cookies before grabbing one and biting the head off of a mini gingerbread man. Then I close the box again and shove it into my backpack. After a moment of deliberation, I also add my freezer bag of crunchy granola bars. I probably won't eat them; it's mostly just to help me feel better about bringing the very unhealthy cookies.

Also the canteen of Dr. Pepper. That's coming too. Because

like Wes, I am also not a morning person, and I need caffeine. Wes and my parents both have giant water bottles that they've been lugging around the whole trip so far; if I need a drink of water, I can get one from them.

Once all my food is packed, I grab the medicine bottle on the nightstand and take out one pill from my bottle of seizure medication, placing it in a sandwich baggie and then zipping it in an inside pocket of my bag. That will be enough for my afternoon dose. I was first diagnosed with epilepsy when I hit puberty; it's been a long road with a lot of setbacks, but I've finally found a medication that works well for me and has minimal side effects.

"Meds, food and drink to take them, sunscreen, bug spray, sunglasses..." I say as I run through my mental list. Then, glancing at the time, I go to my suitcase and pull out my clothes.

As I'm changing into my swimsuit in the bathroom, I'm pleased to note that my hives are starting to fade from a mottled red flush into a lighter pink. I grab my phone and do a quick search, which informs me that the allergic reaction could take up to several hours to disappear. Looking at my face, though, I don't think it will be that long—maybe another hour.

After this my google search gets derailed, and twenty minutes later I find myself looking at the mole on my right thigh to determine if I have skin cancer. It's only when a text from my mom comes through that I'm pulled back to the real world—the world where my mole is just a mole, although it's always wise to keep an eye on your skin.

MOM: *How are you feeling?*

· · ·

9

OOF. How am I feeling? Like I've just reappeared from the rabbit hole. I scramble to finish getting dressed, pulling my shirt and my shorts over my swimsuit before texting my mom back.

ME: *Better. I'll get Wes and we'll be there soon.*

"WES," I call as I exit the bathroom. "Get up. It's been longer than thirty minutes."

We're going to pretend that's not because I was learning the ABCDEs of malignant skin lesions—*Asymmetry, Border, Color, Diameter, Evolution*—but because I was simply feeling generous.

"You lost track of time, didn't you?" Wes says as he stretches.

Welp. So much for that. "Uh," I say. "Yes. Look, though." I point to my face.

Wes sits up, squinting as he looks at me. He puts his glasses back on, and then his expression clears. He nods. "A lot better. If I didn't know you, I probably wouldn't notice anything wrong."

"Perfect," I say happily. "In that case, let's go." There are tidepools for me to examine...and one brother's best friend for me to gaze longingly at.

Is anything going to happen between me and Beckett? No. Of course not. We're seeing him for one day, accompanied by the rest of my family. But if I could just manage to make a good impression? I'd call that a win. And who knows—maybe after this I'll even be able to move on. Maybe seeing him again will be just the closure I need.

Maybe, maybe, maybe.

TWO

BECKETT

I'M NOT A PARTICULARLY SOCIABLE GUY. Don't get me wrong—I love my best friend and his family. Heck, I'm probably closer to them than I am to my own family. It's kind of hard to bond with a mom who walked out and a dad who was always working. But just because I love them, just because I'll be happy to see them, doesn't mean I'm looking forward to a full day of socializing.

I've been happily working on a remote island for the better part of a year. It's safe to say I don't mind being on my own.

My less-than-social nature, though, doesn't dampen my happiness when Mr. and Mrs. O'Malley appear in my line of sight, rushing down the pier toward me with giant smiles and enthusiastic waves. Wes and Molly aren't with them yet; apparently Molly had some sort of allergic reaction at breakfast that needs to die down, and then they'll come.

It's been years since I've seen my best friend in person and even longer since I've seen the rest of his family. That never stops his mom from sending me care packages a few times a year, though, or from calling me up every now and then just to check in. I'm loathe to say I *need* anyone in my life—I've always done fine by myself—but I do enjoy having the O'Malleys around.

It's early in the day still, but I can already tell it's going to be a hot one. I stroll up the pier at a leisurely pace, my hands in my pockets, watching Wes's parents move closer and closer. When we finally meet, Mrs. O'Malley pulls me into a giant hug like I'm her own flesh and blood. She's a short little woman, but her grip around my middle is tight, and I wrap my arms gratefully around her shoulders, smiling.

"Hi, Mrs. O'Malley," I say, looking over her shoulder and nodding my greeting to Mr. O'Malley at the same time. His bald head reflects the sun as he returns my nod, his face splitting into a wide smile.

"Let me look at you, sweetie," Mrs. O'Malley says, releasing me and taking a step back. She reaches up and holds my face still, peering up at me with the all-seeing eyes of a mother. Her gaze skates over my face for a second before she tuts.

"You're too thin, Beckett," she says, pinching my cheeks and then looking at her husband. "Does he look thin to you, Robert?"

I laugh, swatting her hands away. "I've been eating just fine," I counter. "I'm just working a lot."

The Charlotte Amalie cruise port bustles around us, the pier full of tourists in sunhats and fanny packs, and I steer Mrs. O'Malley to the side so that we don't get run over. Mr. O'Malley follows until the three of us are off on our own.

Mrs. O'Malley looks around, though, and points down to the end of the pier, where the paved thoroughfare turns a sharp corner around the port terminal. It's a unique-looking building, blue with three massive archways and a red roof. "It seems busy under there," she says, her eyes fixed on the shadowed archways. She looks around some more and then nods to the large, white awning off to one side. "Let's go wait there, shall we? There are seats," she says, casting an anxious look at Mr. O'Malley. He's got a bad knee, and I know she worries about him walking long distances.

"Sure," I say, because I'm not about to get in the way of a wife worrying about her husband. She's right, anyway; a decent-sized crowd is congregated in the shadowed terminal area, so we'll have better luck waiting comfortably somewhere else.

Mr. O'Malley texts Wes as we head in that direction, and when we pass into the shade, I'm just as grateful to be out of the sun as they are.

"This is much better," she says when we reach one of the last unoccupied benches, looking at Mr. O'Malley. "Isn't this better, Robert?"

"Much better," he agrees with a nod. "We can save our energy for later today."

They settle themselves on the bench, while I look with faint amusement at the batch of tourists that walks by in a steady stream. I'm a big people watcher, and tourists are always fun to observe. There are red faces and tanned faces, tired faces and energetic faces. People of all races and nationalities swarm to the island like ants to an anthill.

"So, Beckett, tell us about work," Mr. O'Malley says as he settles into his spot on the bench. "How's the research facility coming along?"

"Pretty well," I say with a nod. "We had a few delays with equipment getting to us, so I've been here a little longer than I expected to be, but that's fine. I don't have anywhere else to be, and I like the weather."

I'm an employee of the University of Florida, and my current project involves overseeing the placement of a small research campus on a tiny, speck-on-the-map island here in the

U.S. Virgin Islands that we call Van Gogh Island. The island is uninhabited, and that's what we liked about this location. Because the facility will be used primarily for astronomy field research, the university wanted to avoid all sources of light pollution. It's the perfect place.

I tell the O'Malleys about work for a while longer; Mrs. O'Malley is particularly interested in the mundane details, like what everything looks like. Then she begins asking me about my life here on the island. She wants to make sure I'm eating enough, sleeping enough, taking care of myself well enough; so we chat for a good forty-five minutes while we wait for Wes and Molly, and I try to answer all her questions.

"And are you seeing anyone, sweetie?" she says now, a gleam of interest entering her eyes.

"Nope," I say. It's the same answer I give her every time she asks this question.

"No girlfriend?" she presses. "Don't have your eye on anyone?"

"No," I say firmly. "No girlfriend, no one I'm interested in."

She nods, looking thoughtful. "Well, I'm excited to see everything you've been working on," Mrs. O'Malley says, rubbing her hands together. "I want to see all the things you've been up to—oh," she says suddenly. "Look, there's Wes!"

I spin around, following her gaze, and I grin as soon as I catch sight of my best friend. He looks the same as he always has, for the most part—the tallest one in his family by far, with reddish-blonde hair, pale skin, and square glasses perched on the end of his nose. As far as I know their Christmas cruise only started two days ago, but Wes is already sporting an admirable pink glow on his cheeks and forehead—much like the one on his dad's bald head. He doesn't appear to have seen me yet, and he's waving and smiling over his shoulder, talking to someone still hidden by the steady stream of people. Molly, maybe? I assume she's around here somewhere.

I take the opportunity to jog toward him, leaving his parents on the bench. By the time I reach Wes, he's just turning to face my direction again. He laughs when he sees me approaching, looking over his shoulder one last time before meeting me in an affectionate—but very manly—hug.

I laugh too as we embrace, my smile widening when I catch a glimpse of the woman he must have been talking to—not Molly but a curvy redhead wearing sunglasses. Her head is turned in our direction.

I shake my head, still laughing as I step back. "Same old Wes," I say. "You've been on vacation for two days and a woman is already chasing you down." I give her another subtle look, my appreciation growing. She's one of the more attractive women I've seen him with over the years, but she's not his normal type at all. He usually goes for tall and toned, very athletic—there are a lot of volleyball and basketball players in his past—but at first glance this girl doesn't appear to fit that description. She's too short, too curvy.

My eyes swing back to Wes, and I grin. "She is *way* out of your league. If she decides she's tired of you, pass my number on, yeah?" It's a joke, of course; I don't do much dating, and Wes knows that.

He doesn't laugh like I expect him to, though; his smile has faded, and he scratches his head. "What are you talking about?" he says. He frowns at me, looking confused, before turning around to follow my gaze. Then his head swings back in my direction. "You idiot," he says, rolling his eyes. "That's Molly."

Oh. *Oh.*

Oh, *crap.*

I'm not proud of it, but my jaw actually drops as I look back to the woman.

Because no. There's no way. There's *no way* that's Baby O'Malley. I mean, granted, I don't have social media, so I don't see her there; and while Mrs. O'Malley does call me and send me packages, she doesn't include family photos. Still, I gape at the woman, trying to see what Wes could possibly be talking about—

Until a sharp elbow connects with my gut, causing me to double over.

"Eyes off," Wes says under his breath, frowning at me as I rub my stomach.

"They're off," I mutter, and I grimace as I stand up straight again. "Sorry. I didn't—I didn't realize. I didn't recognize her."

Except as she finally reaches us, pulling off her sunglasses and placing them on top of her head, I begin to see the proof.

The last time I saw Molly O'Malley was...what, ten years ago? Nine years ago? When Wes and I graduated from high school. I didn't return home more than once or twice during my college years, since I didn't feel much need to see my dad—but even when I did go, I didn't see Molly. She was a clumsy little shadow back when Wes and I graduated, always present but usually silent except when she was knocking something over, scrawny and short with bright red hair and a face full of freckles.

The freckles are still there, I notice, and still starkly visible against her milky skin. Her hair, too, is the same color as it was all those years ago, though it's longer now, and she seems to have tamed it, weaving it into a loose braid that's tucked over her shoulder to one side.

It's her eyes, though, that convince me. I remember those eyes peeking up at me from her pale face, warm and lively and intelligent. That gaze was one of the key features that made the

O'Malleys' house feel like home. Because home is a place where people actually want you around, and although I never encouraged the hero worship I saw in Molly, it did make me feel welcome. She was always watching, even when she pretended she wasn't. And she's watching now, too, her eyes not darting away even when our gazes clash.

Everything else about her is different. Wes is showing signs of wanting to jab me again, though, or maybe gouge my eyes out, so I look away instead of cataloguing the other changes the years have brought. I don't need to be noticing anything more.

I pick a spot over her left eyebrow and direct my attention there. "Hey," I say to her forehead, forcing a halfhearted smile onto my face. I take a quick breath, hoping to get rid of this jitteriness that's sending adrenaline through my veins. I feel... shaken, I guess, and I don't like it. I don't like it one bit. But I'm still getting over the shock of checking out a woman only to realize it's Molly O'Malley. It's that same feeling you get when you take a drink, expecting water, only to taste flat, day-old soda instead—a wrong-footedness that makes you shudder.

"Hi," Molly says, smiling up at me. It's a gorgeous smile—familiar, but new, too. There's none of the shyness I remember, and none of the shining adoration. It looks like her puppy love crush ran its course a long time ago. "It's been a long time," she goes on. Then she holds out her hand in the space between us.

I look down at it, surprised, and then look back up at her.

"What?" she says, glancing at her hand. "Is that weird? Should we not—"

"No," I say, cutting her off and shoving my hand forward to shake hers. I'm being stupid. "Not weird. Sorry." My voice sounds wooden and stiff, even to my own ears, but I can't help it, and I'm not sure I want to get chummy with Molly anyway. Still, to be polite, I force out, "How have you been?"

"I've been good," she says slowly. "You?" And even though

I'm staring at her forehead, I can see the expression she's wearing—lips turned down, a tiny crease in her brow like she's confused about my behavior.

And look. I don't mean to be cold or rude or anything. But I'm not good at faking it, either. I'm not the sort of person to pretend at a warmth I don't feel—or in this case, to spend energy on a relationship I don't want or need. It's nothing personal. Molly and I will just be acquaintances for a day; I'm not going to put myself through the draining process of pretending it's anything more than that, especially since I don't want to send her the wrong signals.

I give her a short nod, answering her. "I'm good, thanks." Then I turn to Mr. and Mrs. O'Malley, who've made their way over from their spot on the bench and are now watching our exchange with interest. "Should we get going?" I say.

"Yes, let's go," Mr. O'Malley says, rubbing his hands together excitedly. He doesn't seem to notice anything strange or off about my interaction with Molly. I sneak a peek at Mrs. O'Malley, but she too simply looks anxious to get started on our day.

A sigh of relief slips out of me. Good. This is good. Everything in its place, everything normal. Just a normal outing with the people I consider family. Nothing awkward, nothing forced, no weird feelings or realizations.

Good. All good.

IT DOESN'T TAKE TOO long for all of us to move through the checkpoint in the port terminal. We emerge into what's essentially a large outdoor shopping center—perfectly placed for tourists to spend money, of course. It's a paved courtyard, bustling and chaotic, punctuated with palm trees and cased by colorful shops and restaurants. We pass a tall, dreadlocked man with two tiny monkeys on his shoulders, and Molly stops to coo at them. I might do the same if I hadn't already met both the man and his animals; his name is Nilson, and the monkeys are Alfonso and Señorita. Alfonso is fine, but Señorita has only ever pulled my hair and stuck her creepily long fingers in my ears, so I stand back and wait, nodding at Nilson when he spots me.

"Hi, baby," Molly says in a soft voice as she runs her hand down Señorita's back. "You're pretty, aren't you?"

"You want to hold her?" Nilson says, adjusting Alfonso on his other shoulder while he reaches up for Señorita.

It's on the tip of my tongue to warn Molly, but I keep it in. She probably wouldn't listen anyway, judging by the way her eyes light up.

"Oh, yes!" she says, smiling. She shrugs off her backpack and sets it on the pavement before patting her right shoulder. "Here?"

Nilson smiles. "Sure. This is Señorita."

And Señorita goes straight from Nilson to Molly without a fuss. She settles comfortably on Molly's shoulder, not pulling her hair, not sticking her finger in her ear. She's a perfect passenger, and Molly is clearly in love.

Señorita, that little she-devil. It must just be me she likes to torment. I glare at her, and she stares back, her beady little eyes taunting me.

I pull my eyes away from Señorita when Molly's attention turns to me. "Have you ever held these before?" she says, her hand gently holding the little monkey in place.

I nod, stepping closer. I try to keep my gaze neutral as I look at Señorita. "We're acquainted, yes," I tilt my head. "Though she didn't like me as much as she seems to like—"

But I break off at the flash of motion I see, and I'm hit with

19

that same spike of adrenaline you get when a baseball flies straight at your face—my eyes squeeze shut, and I flinch away—

But it's too late.

Not half a second later I feel something warm and furry pressed over my nose and mouth, something writhing, with arms banded around the back of my head.

A monkey.

A *monkey*.

Hanging off my face, using me like her own personal jungle gym.

"Oh!" Molly says as her body collides with mine, and I realize with a start that Señorita's tail is still curled around her neck.

"Get—*off*—" I mutter, except it's more of a mumble because of the monkey-over-face situation, and my mouth snaps shut immediately lest I get a taste of fur or something else equally as disgusting. I claw at Señorita—she should *not* be this strong; that is giving her far too much power—not bothering to be gentle as I reach up and uncurl her arms from around my head.

"Señorita, naughty girl," Nilson says. His voice is no more than gently chiding—I need *outrage,* Nilson—while off to the side, Wes is bent double with laughter. Nilson moves closer and uses one giant hand to pluck Señorita off my face.

"Ow!" I yelp as she leaves me with her parting gift: one long finger, jammed into my ear with unnecessary force.

Violence against animals is wrong, I tell myself as I glare at the she-demon now settling happily on Nilson's shoulder. *Violence against animals is wrong.*

"A pleasure as always," I say through gritted teeth to the little monkey.

"Sorry about that," Nilson says, glancing back and forth between me and Molly.

Molly just laughs—she *laughs!*—and gives Señorita an affectionate look. "That's okay," she says.

It most certainly is not okay.

But I'm clearly the only one with problems being mauled by devil monkeys, so I don't say anything else. I just give Nilson his tip, passing a neatly folded bill into his hand, before gently redirecting the O'Malleys. Wes is wiping tears of laughter from his eyes, but he calms down as we make our way further into port.

It ends up taking us longer than I expected for us to flag down a taxi. Several come and go, but someone else always gets there before us. Thankfully the vehicle we finally claim for ourselves is a large, clunky van that seats all of us comfortably. I direct the driver to the ferry pier about ten minutes from the port terminal, and from there it's a twenty-minute boat ride to our destination. The first thing I do when we board the speed-boat is find the stash of disinfectant wipes and give myself a sanitizing wipe down. I get some of the soapy residue in my mouth, and I'm honestly not even upset. In fact, if anything, I feel better. I need to remove all traces of monkey from my person.

Then, once I'm satisfied that I'm clean, we're off to our destination.

Van Gogh Island is an underwhelming two square miles, roughly. What it lacks in area, though, it makes up for in beauty. The waters are a clear turquoise color, the sand golden, the vegetation a lush, greedy green. It's the kind of place that ends up on postcards and screensavers—lazy palm trees, dazzling sunsets, warm nights under a crystal-clear sky.

It's that crystal-clear sky I'm the most interested in, of course. My colleagues and I have been working hard to install a top-of-the-line research campus here, but it hasn't been without its setbacks. Parcel delivery out here is spotty, with anything we need being delivered to St. Thomas and then transferred to Van Gogh Island ourselves. Installing a research-grade telescope and dome enclosure, as well as building a 70,000-square-foot facility, requires a lot of moving parts to come together. It's going well now, though, something we're all grateful for.

The speedboat we're using technically belongs to the University of Florida, but it's one of my favorite places to be out here. The wind in my face and the sounds of the ocean are far more relaxing to me than the presence of other people. I ferry a group of life-vest-clad O'Malleys across the water, with Wes perched next to me and the others toward the back. I glance over my shoulder to check on them every so often, but the view never changes: Mr. and Mrs. O'Malley resting, looking happily around, and Molly halfway out of her seat, red hair whipping in the wind, her face a picture of utter delight.

I direct my eyes back ahead of me and keep them there for the remainder of the journey, until we reach our destination.

The "port" on Van Gogh Island is only a port because we call it that. In reality, it's little more than a few meters of planked wood and several posts where we can secure our speedboats. It's almost empty now—Christmas is less than a week away, so most of our employees are home or traveling to see family—save for a couple of the guys on the general contractor's crew. They'll be heading out a bit later today, though, from what I remember, and I'll head back to St. Thomas tonight when we're done here. We'll all resume work after the new year.

The O'Malleys and I spill onto the port deck one by one, the breeze tugging at our clothes and hair as we move. It's only once we've reached the sand that I stop, gesturing at everything from the ocean to the beach to the dense greenery.

"Well," I say, "welcome to Van Gogh Island."

Mrs. O'Malley claps her hands like I've just given a speech, and Mr. O'Malley nods, the sun glinting off his bald head. Wes is already bounding ahead.

Molly, though, smiles up at me from a few feet away. "Oh!" she says. "Van Gogh Island—I get it."

"Get what?" Wes says over his shoulder.

She turns and looks at him. "Van Gogh. Vincent Van Gogh. He painted *The Starry Night?*" She twirls her finger around to encompass our surroundings. "And this is an astronomy research facility." She turns to me. "Right? Or am I way off?"

"No," I say, stunned. "That's exactly right. That's where we got the name."

She nods, looking satisfied. "I thought so." Then she's off, trailing after Wes, her braid falling apart where it hangs down her back.

I take a deep breath, letting the ocean air fill my lungs. That briny smell is probably part of my cellular composition by now —salt crystals in my veins, sand in the nooks and crannies of my internal organs. I don't mind. I let the air out again, a slow, controlled exhale.

One day. I can be open and social for one day. I love these people like my own flesh and blood. So for them, I'll make this the best day I can.

Just no more monkeys.

THREE
MOLLY

IN WARM, TROPICAL WATERS LIKE THOSE OFF OF BRAZIL, the West Indies, and the southeastern coast of the United States, there lives a fish called the longspine squirrelfish—*Holocentrus rufus. H. rufus*, or Rufus, as I will now call him, is a funny-looking little guy. This is mainly due to his eyes; he has these big, dark, buggy eyes that look unnaturally large on his little fishy body.

All things told, Rufus appears fairly innocuous—a silvery-orange, goldish-striped body with a pronounced dorsal fin and a long third spine on the anal fin. Despite his looks, however, Rufus is actually a poison-secreting, meat-eating fish that hunts mainly at night.

And it's this poison-secreting, meat-eating longspine squirrelfish that first popped into my mind when I held my hand out to Beckett; when he just stared at it, frozen, wide-eyed. I think I first noticed his reaction—suspicious, like I was trying to poison him with my handshake—which then led me to think of which poisonous fish I might be, which led me to Rufus, due to our similar reddish-orangish coloring.

Yes. If I had to be any poisonous fish, *H. rufus* would be a top contender.

As it stands, however, I am *not* a fish—poisonous or otherwise. Which means I have to wonder why Beckett's reaction to me was so strange.

My reaction to *him* should win awards. The man is gorgeous. Deep brown eyes with absurdly long lashes; a stubborn chin and square jaw; a lean, muscular build encased in blue swim shorts and a white linen button-down. Despite his appearance, though, I did not drool. I did not stutter. I was cool and calm and collected, a pinnacle of chill, and for the rest of my life I will hold this up as one of my main achievements. You got your PhD in rocket science? That's all well and good, but *I* managed not to trip over my own feet in front of my unrequited love. So who's really winning here?

Trick question: we're both winners!

"Molly," Wes says from next to me, pulling me out of my head.

I look over at him, my feet sinking into the sand as I walk. "Huh?"

"You're talking to yourself."

"Oh." I blink and try to think back, but I don't remember. "Am I?"

He nods, putting one hand on my elbow to steady me as I trip over the beachy terrain. "You said, 'We're both winners!'"

"That's embarrassing," I say with a sigh. "But..." I trail off, thinking. Then I nod decisively. "I stand by it. We're both winners, Wes. And don't you forget it."

He grins, and I laugh. It's a giddy sound, but I'm just so excited to be here. Here on this island, here with Beckett—all of it, even if something about Beckett's behavior is bugging me.

"Let's wait for them," Wes says when we've almost reached

the line where sand turns into rock-studded soil. He stops in place, turning around, and I follow suit.

We aren't the only ones on this beach; there's another guy wandering around a second boat, loading things in, securing them, and whistling loudly the whole time. I name him Whistling Wally in my head. He stops Beckett as he passes.

"You gonna be long here?" he says to Beckett, scratching the top of his head.

Beckett shakes his head and gestures to my parents. "Just showing them around for a bit. We'll head back later this afternoon."

Whistling Wally nods. "All right. I'm here until about two, and then I'm gone. If you need me, find me before then."

Beckett just gives him a jerk of his head that I think is supposed to be a nod; then he resumes his path with my parents by his side.

I could take this time to clear the sand out of my sandals, but there's absolutely no point; it will accumulate again in two minutes flat. So I wait instead, watching as Beckett and my parents make their way toward us. Beckett is holding onto my mom's elbow the same way my brother was holding onto mine, helping her stay upright in the sand. Every few steps his eyes dart up to where I'm standing with Wes, but I notice they never linger; in fact, they jump over me altogether, like I'm not even here.

Like instead of a poisonous fish, I'm an invisible fish.

I pull back the sinking in my heart, burying that disappointed feeling deep, deep down where no one will ever look for it. Today is not about me; not really. Did I want to make a good impression on Beckett? Yeah, of course. I *really* wanted that. But just as badly I want to make sure he's doing well—that he's healthy and happy. He doesn't have to fall in love with me. He just needs to be okay.

That will have to be enough for me.

The problem is, I'm not sure he *is* okay. I don't know him now the way I used to years ago, and I'm not sure it's something I can ferret out over the course of one day. But I don't remember him being this closed off before.

Maybe I'm imagining things, but it seems to me that on his perfectly tanned forehead, hovering over his brows and deep brown eyes, there's a large *LEAVE ME ALONE* stamped in bright red ink—a flashing neon sign with a blaring alarm attached. It's the vibe he gives off—to me, anyway. He hugged Wes and has been chatting comfortably with my parents, so maybe it's just me he's uninterested in talking to.

That's a great feeling, let me tell you.

I sigh, pushing that thought away. I distract myself instead by checking out our surroundings. It's not midday yet, but it's getting there. The sun is hanging overhead, and the warmth surrounding us is thick and muggy, pulling an unpleasant clamminess to my skin. It's only the breeze coming off the water that makes it bearable. I can feel my hair whipping this way and that, escaping its braid and doing its own thing as per usual, so I pull it over my shoulder and remove the hair tie, combing my fingers through it to get rid of what's left of the braid. Then I stand with my face to the wind, so that it's pushing my hair back where I need it to go, and pull all of that orange up into a floppy bun on top of my head.

I smile when I feel the wind on my neck; it chases away the clinging dampness, kissing my skin like a promise. "Much better," I say happily, smiling to myself. I close my eyes, tilting my face toward the sun.

I soak up the rays until my parents and Beckett catch up to us, and I know they've caught up to us because my mother does not do anything quietly.

"And how much longer do you think you'll be out here? I worry," she says from a few feet away.

My eyes pop open just in time to see Beckett's half-amused, half-affectionate look as he answers, "I'm not sure, exactly. But if everything goes to plan, we'll be able to wrap up in about six weeks."

"Oh, that's not bad," my mother says. Her cheeks dimple as she smiles at him. "And then what will you do? Come back to the States?"

"Technically this *is* the States," I point out. "These Virgin Islands are U.S. territory."

She doesn't even look at me; she just swats a hand in my direction. "He knows what I mean," she says.

"I'll probably go back to Florida then, yes," Beckett says. "Keep working in the lab at the university." He stops walking, and all of us gather around him—sheep circling our shepherd, waiting for his direction.

"So as you can see, there's a bit of a path here, but it's not paved." He points to the tree line, where a narrow dirt path appears to wind through the dense greenery, disappearing from view. "We'll take that for a little way, and it will open up to a wider dirt road. There's a paved road we laid down on the other side of the island, but I thought you guys would like to see the stuff we've left mostly untouched."

He's right; choosing between a paved road through paradise and a path so narrow I can spread my arms and touch trees on each side, I'll take the narrow path. Pick me up and drop me in the wild; as long as I have the necessities, I'll love every second.

Speaking of necessities...

I pull my backpack off, clutching it to my chest. It's old and faded now, a buttery yellow instead of the sunshine it once resembled, and it's so worn that the zipper is smooth and silent when I open it.

"Here, Dad," I say after a second of digging, pulling out my jumbo bottle of sunscreen. "You didn't wear a hat."

"I put some on already," he says, reaching up to touch his shiny head.

"The stuff you and Mom brought?" I say. "That's SPF 30. This stuff is SPF 70." I wiggle the bottle at him.

"I already—"

"Just take it, Robert," my mom says, tutting at him. She grabs the sunscreen from me and forces it into my dad's hands. "You're miserable when your head burns, and it looks funny when it starts to peel. Put some more on."

I try to hide my smile at this, but I'm not sure it works. "Anyone else can use that if they want," I say. I personally already smell like a walking Coppertone ad, but I'll apply another layer in an hour or two. Skin cancer is no joke—as I am now intimately aware, thanks to this morning's rabbit hole dive about cancerous moles.

My dad grumbles under his breath as he slathers a big blob of white all over his head, which increases the shininess factor by probably fifty percent. We're not quite talking disco ball level, but it's still a phenomenon I can't leave unexplored.

"Whoa," I say, standing up on my tiptoes so I can see better. I tilt my head, examining the greasy sheen and the way the sunlight is bouncing off. "I bet I can see my reflection—"

"No need," Wes says with a smirk. "You're just as ugly as you were before we left."

"Wes!" I smack him hard on the shoulder, and he darts away, cackling like a maniac. I force a laugh too, though, as I say, "You jerk. I look fine now!"

"I don't know," he says, pointing at my face. "I think I can still see some pink—"

"Children, children," Beckett intones with exasperation. "Let's act our age, shall we?"

29

"Yes, Father," Wes says, grinning.

I roll my eyes. "Yes, Father," I repeat. I snatch my sunscreen from Wes, who's about to squirt some into his open palm. "You've lost your SPF 70 privileges." I shove it back into my bag, swinging the whole thing back over my shoulder and then marching forward. I pass Beckett, who's mouthing wordlessly and sputtering.

"Don't—I'm not—your *father*," he finally gets out, speaking to Wes. Wes just cackles again.

"I'm not sure about that," I say with an innocent shrug. "All this sun seems to be making you crotchety."

"You two are incorrigible," Beckett says, pointing between Wes and me. Then his gaze turns to my parents. "Where did you find them, Mrs. O'Malley? What dumpster did you dig your children out of?"

"I know," she says with a sigh while my dad laughs. "They're hooligans."

"The hooligans should get moving, yeah?" I say, looking at Beckett. "We want to make good progress before we hit the hottest part of the day."

Beckett nods, but he doesn't look at me.

And all at once, it hits me—what's so strange about how he's acting. I've been trying to put my finger on what seems off, and watching Beckett's eyes dart away from me, I've finally got it.

If he didn't pay attention to me at all, that would be sad, but it wouldn't be weird. What *is* weird is that he tries to make it *seem* like he's looking at me—when really he isn't. Instead of meeting my gaze, he looks at my forehead. When he's looking in my direction, his eyes are aimed just over my shoulder.

He's actively avoiding me but trying to be subtle about it. That's the only conclusion I can draw from the evidence I've observed. What's up with that? It's odd, isn't it? Especially since he's *pretending* to pay attention to me? That's weird, right?

It feels weird.

It also feels like a challenge.

I set my jaw stubbornly. It's not like I'm asking him to marry me. He should at least be friendly, though. I don't think that's too much to ask, is it? It's not an unreasonable request that he treat me like he's treating the rest of my family? I meant what I said—this trip isn't about winning him over. I know that's not going to happen. But I'm getting the sense that he's already made up his mind about how he wants to treat me, without giving me a chance to change his mind.

That...doesn't sit well with me. If you're going to write me off, do it *after* you've gotten to know me and decided I'm not your cup of tea. Because I might be a delicious cup of your very favorite tea, for all you know. So don't just *assume* that I'm not worth knowing.

As Beckett brushes past me, giving me an awkwardly wide berth, I roll my eyes. Then I turn and follow him, along with the rest of my family, my mind churning with thoughts and ideas and snippets of plans.

My breath escapes me, though, as we step into the lush forest. The trees are thick and green, the air heavy on my skin and in my lungs. I'm grateful that my hair is up off my neck, although I can't help but think that that bun on top of my head is going to make a prime nesting area for any little buggy critters that fall out of the foliage above.

The five of us follow the narrow trail, Beckett in the lead with the rest of us trailing behind. I can hear my mom and dad talking, but they've lowered their voices enough that I can't understand what they're saying. I understand the impulse to whisper; there's something about a forest that feels sacred. It's teeming with life but suspended in time, a coming-together of old and new—a baby bird chirping in its nest, tucked safely into the lush greenery of an ancient tree.

It's too humid for the dirt beneath our feet to kick up in puffs of dust, but my sandals are still gritty with sweat and sand. Despite the shade there are little pockets of perspiration all over my body—behind my knees, in the creases of my elbows, in between my toes—and the worst, under-boob sweat.

"Ooh," I say as we pass a vine-like plant with white and yellow trumpet-shaped blooms. I stop, leaning in to look closer. "Pretty. Beckett?"

He slows down, turning to face me, and lifts his eyebrows.

"Can I pick this?" I say, pointing to one of the flowers.

I get one short nod in response before he's turned away again. That's as good as I'm going to get, I guess, but I'll take it for now. I pluck the flower carefully off of its stem, inhaling deeply and then tucking it behind my ear with gentle fingers. I smile once it's in place, hurrying along to resume my place on the path. Beckett and Wes are in front of me, carrying on their own conversation, and my parents are behind me, their *oohs* and *ahhs* punctuating the air every now and then.

The trail has been widening gradually as we walk, and after a couple more minutes we emerge onto a dirt road, just wide enough to fit one car. The sun is once again beating down on us, hotter than I expected it to feel. It's the humidity, I think; like a big, damp, sunny blanket.

I find my eyes glued to the back of Beckett's head as we tromp along. It's stupid how good-looking he is from behind. It's also stupid how quickly our chance to reconnect is slipping away. But the man will barely even *look* at me—so what does a girl have to do to get a decent conversation around here?

I'm going to get one, I decide as I narrow my eyes in the vicinity of his shoulder blades. I'm going to get him to have a conversation with me. If that's all I can accomplish today, then so be it—but by the time we leave the Virgin Islands, I will be able to call Beckett Donovan a friend.

FOUR
BECKETT

"Unfortunately we can't go inside," I say. "Not everything is up to code yet, and I don't have all the keys anyway."

The five of us are standing at the bottom of the drive, looking up at the fruit of my labors for the last eight months. I raise my arm, and the O'Malleys look as one in the direction I'm pointing. "But you can see the dome up there; that's where the telescope is. And then the rest of this"—I gesture to the remaining stretch of building—"will be lab space and a small dormitory."

It's not a particularly pretty building. Rather it's utilitarian; built to last and to remain functional, so that students and researchers will be able to work here for years to come. Part of our goal was to use as little space as possible so we could minimize the effect on the land; we wanted to leave as much natural growth undisturbed as we could. The trees and wildlife crowd the facility on all sides, greenery bleeding into the red brick.

"Oh, neat!" Mrs. O'Malley says. One hand is shading her

eyes as she takes the building in. "How many students will be able to stay there?"

"Capacity will be something like forty," I say. "It will be the field study portion of the senior astronomy course, and the grad students will use it too."

Mrs. O'Malley turns to Molly, who's gazing up at the astronomy dome with interest. "It's too bad you couldn't have taken that class," Mrs. O'Malley says. "You could have come to the Virgin Islands and gone stargazing every night."

Molly blinks at her mother. "I'm not studying astronomy."

"I know that," Mrs. O'Malley says, waving her hand.

"I'm not even at U of F—"

"I know that!" Mrs. O'Malley says again, more vigorously this time. "I was just *saying*. It would be neat, that's all. But you'll be back in February."

"Not *here*, precisely—" Molly begins, but Mrs. O'Malley cuts her off.

"Molly is getting her master's degree in fish," she says to me.

"In fish," I repeat faintly, raising my eyebrows at Molly.

"A master's degree in fish," she says with a roll of her eyes. "It sounds stupid when you say it like that. Call it *ichthyology*. Or fishery science, or marine biology."

"It sounds stupid because it *is* stupid—" Wes begins, but Molly silences him with a *whack* to the back of the head. "Ouch," he mutters, rubbing the place she's just cuffed him. "Violence is not the answer, Moll."

"Why ichthyology?" I say, turning to Molly.

She looks at me with surprise—like she wasn't expecting me to speak to her. And, I realize with a twinge of guilt, she probably *wasn't* expecting it, considering how I've been acting. But she doesn't say anything about that; she just tilts her head and looks at me curiously. The motion causes her bun to flop dangerously to one side on top of her head, the sun glinting off the red and showcasing a spectrum of colors everywhere from coppery orange to strands of gold. Then she crooks one finger at me, beckoning me closer.

I freeze in place like a dang coward. That finger crook, and her accompanying smile, give off flirtatious vibes that make me want to run in the opposite direction. But her family is here, every one of them watching our interaction; she wouldn't try anything, and anyway my pride won't let me flee. So I step toward her, swallowing down the sudden nerves that are crowding my throat. I have to crane my neck even closer to her in order to hear when she talks.

"Why ichthyology?" she says, looking amused.

I already regret asking, but I nod anyway—one short jerk of my head.

"Because," she whispers, "I strongly suspect I was a clownfish in my previous life."

Wes snorts loudly, muttering something about "ridiculous" and "nutjob." But I can feel my eyebrows climbing my forehead.

"Are you serious?" I say. The words escape without my permission, and they sound undeniably rude.

The corners of Molly's lips twitch, her eyes dancing with laughter. *Hot chocolate,* I think out of nowhere. Her eyes are the exact color of my favorite mint hot chocolate, the kind I have to special order, the one my colleagues tease me about drinking in the balmy tropics.

"No," she says, looking more amused still. "I just don't feel like telling you the truth."

What? She doesn't feel like telling the truth? How am I supposed to respond to that—do I laugh? It wasn't really that funny. But if she's waiting for me to laugh—

Except no; she's not waiting for me to laugh. She's not

36

waiting for me at *all*. She turns right on around, giving me her back. Her hair flops to the other side as she tilts her head again, lifting one hand to shade her eyes as she begins chatting with her mother about who-knows-what.

Fish, probably.

I think most of our group would be perfectly fine to get moving again after this glimpse of the building, but Mrs. O'Malley is having none of that. She wants to see it from every angle, and she looks so eager and interested that I don't have the heart to tell her no. Wes puts up a fight, complaining loudly, but Molly doesn't seem to think it's worth it; she just nods with tired acceptance when Mrs. O'Malley asks if she'll please come along. So while the O'Malley men stay back, fanning themselves and clinging to their patch of shade, I lead the female O'Malleys around the perimeter of the building—even though there's no footpath.

"It's still going to look like a brick building on the other side," Molly mumbles as she trails behind us. "With a dome on top and a lot of trees."

"I know that," Mrs. O'Malley says. "I just want to see, that's all." She stops and turns around, putting her hands on her hips. "You could've just stayed with your brother and father back there. There's no need to be here if you're just going to complain."

Molly stops too. "You asked me to come with you," she says.

"Well, yes, but you could have said no if you wanted."

I see Molly's lips move as she answers, but I can't hear whatever she says. Her disgruntled facial expression makes it pretty clear, though, that she's wishing she *had* said no. I can sympathize, Mrs. O'Malley is hard to say no to. She doesn't really ask for bad things, so you rarely have a good reason to deny her requests, and she wheedles you if you initially turn

37

her down. She'll respect your answer if you stand firm, but very few people have the nerve to do so.

I know these things because I spent just as much time at her house growing up as I did at my own. She's like a mother to me, always sincere, always warm and welcoming, so I'm willing to indulge her. I don't see her very often anyway.

When I've finished walking Molly and Mrs. O'Malley around the perimeter of the building, we return to where Wes and Mr. O'Malley are waiting for us. They're exactly where we left them, red-faced and hands fanning.

"You said there was a waterfall around here, right?" Wes says, his cheeks pinker than ever. A sheen of sweat has settled on his skin, and the hair around his hairline looks damp. He could clearly use some cooling off.

We all could, for that matter. The sun is high in the sky now, and even though it's December, I'd guess we're sitting at a very humid eighty degrees right now. Hiking in this is like wading through a sauna. So I nod to Wes.

"Yeah," I say, pointing to the paved drive coming from the direction opposite the way we came. "If we head that way I can get us there."

"A waterfall?" Molly says, smiling—first at Wes, then at me. It's another one of those smiles I don't need to see, beautiful and brilliant. Every now and then you'll meet someone who smiles not just with their face but with their whole body; that's her. Her lips stretch, but her nose also crinkles and her eyes squint. Her shoulders rise up toward her ears and she claps her hands together, dancing on her tippy toes a little.

Like I said: a full-body smile. It's the kind of thing I'd normally find adorable on a woman, but that's not an option here. So I just nod at her before looking away, turning my mind to other things.

"Is everyone set to go?" I say.

I get a chorus of assent in varying degrees of enthusiasm. Molly and Wes seem particularly excited, but even the quiet Mr. O'Malley is rubbing his hands together and looking interested. Mrs. O'Malley is already pressing forward on her own, power walking like it's Thursday morning at the local mall, her arms swinging impatiently at her sides.

I better keep up. Can't be outstripped by my best friend's mom.

The paved road is more comfortable to walk than the dirt path through the trees. I'm accustomed to setting the pace and people following my lead, but I keep having to remind myself that Mr. O'Malley has a bad knee—something Mrs. O'Malley visibly reminds herself of as well. She's initially gung ho to get to the waterfall, until I notice her look over her shoulder at all of us, her eyes softening when they fall on her husband. After that she slows down considerably.

It takes us about ten minutes to get to the point where we branch away from the road and move into the trees again, and another fifteen minutes of hiking from there to get to the waterfall. The nice thing about a small island, I guess, is that no matter how slowly you're moving, it still doesn't take terribly long to get anywhere.

And I've been here multiple times now, but it never ceases to catch me off guard when I arrive. You're enmeshed in the trees one second, and the next—*boom*. Waterfall, right there. You step out into the clearing, the ground fading from dirt into rock beneath your feet, to find yourself looking up at the cliff face. It's covered mostly in tangled, choking vines, but the overhang creates a little cove where the water laps at your toes and then gradually deepens to a few feet at the base of the waterfall. The only warning you're about to stumble upon any of it is the sound of rushing water, white noise in the background that sneaks up on you.

Wes exclaims loudly as we step out of the trees, and Mr. and Mrs. O'Malley do the same. Only Molly is silent; I watch as she looks around, her eyes wide, her jaw dropped. She seems to be speechless, and even though growing up she didn't say a lot, I get the feeling that silence is no longer her natural state.

I glance around too, because this sight isn't something I'll ever get tired of or take for granted. The spray of the water, the rich green surrounding, the sun overhead, beaming down in rays like golden spotlights...it's perfect. Paradise on earth.

And nature favors Molly, it seems, because several of those spotlights hit her perfectly, working magic with her skin and her hair—milk and fire, rosy lips, freckles like constellations. I watch for a second as she continues to gape at the scene around us, her feet aimless and absentminded as she moves.

"Careful," I murmur when she steps into the water without looking. My arm shoots out to grasp her elbow just in time as she slips, the wet rock dangerously slick.

"Whoa," she says, her eyes flaring as her other arm flails. She regains her balance and then says, "Thank you."

"Pay attention to where you're going, please," I say stiffly.

"Yeah," she breathes, staring at her feet, still looking shaken. "Sorry."

And yet—*and yet*—not ten seconds later, off she goes again. Plunging recklessly into the water, wading further out, her arms outstretched as she airplanes for balance. It looks a little silly, but it's probably for the best; I can already tell that balance is not this woman's strong suit.

Neither, apparently, is listening.

I shake my head, forcing myself to turn away. I don't need to be worrying about her. She's managed to survive this long; she'll be fine.

"Watch your step," I say to Mr. and Mrs. O'Malley—yes,

maybe a little louder than necessary, but it's just so that Molly will hopefully overhear and be careful.

Mr. O'Malley nods, slipping his Chacos off and lining them up neatly on the rock. Mrs. O'Malley takes her shoes off too—a pair of glittery sandals that are far less sensible than Mr. O'Malley's shoes—and puts them next to his, though neither as neatly nor as carefully. Together they step into the water, shuffling forward until their ankles are submerged. I hesitate, wondering whether I should say anything, when Wes speaks up.

"Should we keep our shoes on?"

He's smart to bring it up. Molly, I can't help but notice, didn't even *need* to ask; she already knew the answer. I saw her shoes earlier in the day, yellow Chacos similar to Mr. O'Malley's, perfect for when she walked into the water.

"I would," I say. "If you've got the right shoes. Mr. O'Malley, you can keep those on"—I point to his Chacos—"and they'll protect your feet in case you step on anything. Mrs. O'Malley..." I grimace. "You're better off barefoot. If your shoes get wet, they'll just make you slip."

Mrs. O'Malley looks sheepishly at me, but I just smile. Then she and Mr. O'Malley move back to where their shoes are sitting, and she crouches down, helping him get his feet into his sandals as they whisper back and forth.

"I told you last night to wear good shoes," Molly calls to them, and I look at her. She's waded far enough that the water hits just above her knees; now she looks down at her clothes, seeming to debate with herself, before turning and heading back in our direction. "It's gorgeous out here, isn't it?" she says as she moves, speaking to no one in particular. "So dreamy and romantic. This is the perfect place to fall in love."

"I wasn't aware there are perfect places to fall in love," Wes says from next to me as he dips one foot into the lapping water.

"Well," Molly concedes. She's only a few yards away from us now, and still wading closer. "I guess there aren't any *bad* places to fall in love—"

"Uh, yes there are," Wes says, blinking at her. "There are *tons* of bad places to fall in love."

"Absolutely," I echo, frowning.

"Prison," Wes says.

"Rehab," I add.

"Family reunion." Wes again.

"Hospice—"

"Fine!" Molly cuts me off, fisting her hands on her hips and frowning at us. "Fine. I was wrong. There are bad places to fall in love. But *this* isn't one of them." She waves her arms, gesturing at the waterfall and the lush greenery around us. The movements are awkward and uncoordinated, the kind of hand-waving that would make me nervous if I were standing right next to her.

I look at Wes just as he looks at me, and we grin. Teasing Molly was always high on the to-do list when we were younger.

I turn to check on Mr. and Mrs. O'Malley, but they seem to be doing just fine. They're still talking amongst themselves, their whispers low, as Mrs. O'Malley rubs kneading fingers in circles over Mr. O'Malley's knee. That makes me a little nervous, but I guess I'll just trust them to know their limits. I'm distracted, anyway, when I hear Wes speak again.

"Molly, what are you—for the love. Stop taking—Molly!"

My head jerks back to him, but he's looking at his sister with an expression of outrage. I follow his gaze, just in time to see Molly shimmying her shorts down her legs. Her t-shirt is already off, draped over her shoulder, revealing one of those retro-looking swimsuits that looks like a sailor's outfit.

"Molly!" Wes says again.

"We're swimming, Wes," she says, rolling her eyes as she

finally gets her shorts down to her ankles. She's still standing in a few inches of water. "What do people wear when they swim?"

Wes folds his arms stubbornly across his chest but doesn't answer.

"Swimsuits, Wes. They wear swimsuits," she says. I watch nervously as she steps out of her shorts, half expecting her to lose her balance and fall, but she doesn't. She manages to stay upright, tossing her shorts and shirt over to where her parents are standing so that she's left looking distractingly like a pin-up girl from the 1950s.

"I'm not taking my shirt off," Wes says, pointing to his chest. "We have company." He jerks his chin in my direction but doesn't look away from Molly. "So can you please stay decent?"

Molly frowns at him. "Keep your shirt on or don't, but don't project your insecurities onto me. I look good and I feel great, so I'm going to stay exactly as I am."

"Unbelievable," Wes grumbles as she turns and walks away, heading back into the deeper water. "She took a few psych courses years ago, and she still thinks she can analyze me."

Personally I think she's spot on, but I'm wise enough to keep this to myself. Also kept to myself is my appreciation of her curves—because good grief, those curves are *flawless*—and sexiest of all, the way she handles herself with complete and utter confidence. Not once does she look around to see who's watching her; not once does she seem unsure. It's...well, it's attractive. Really, really attractive to see a woman—and as much as I hesitate to think of her that way, Molly is all woman —who's happy with herself.

I sigh, pulling my eyes away from her. Maybe in another life, where she wasn't Wes's baby sister and where I actually had the desire to date or fall in love. It's not worth thinking about now, though. Especially since I need to be paying attention to more than just Molly. I know this isn't *my* island, and I know no one has signed disclaimers or safety waivers, but I still feel responsible for getting this group back to their cruise ship in one piece this evening.

Which is why, some thirty seconds later when Mr. O'Malley takes one wobbly-looking step into the water, my gut twists anxiously. I don't know how bad his knee is, and I don't know how to ask, but these rocks are slick. He takes another step, and then another, and I fight the urge to go stand next to him so he'll have something to hold onto.

"Wait for me, Robert," Mrs. O'Malley calls to him from where she's tentatively trying to find her footing.

Yes, Robert, wait for her, I think. *Go back to your wife and please, please don't get hurt on my watch.*

But maybe the universe is feeling spiteful; maybe Mr. O'Malley is simply impatient. Whatever the reason, he doesn't slow down, and the nature that so favored Molly turns its back on her father.

I watch with horror and paralyzed limbs as Mr. O'Malley steps further into the water. I see the flash of surprise on his face, his arms flying up at his sides. And I watch as he goes down, pitching face-first into water that's not deep enough to cushion the fall, as all of his weight lands on his knees.

FIVE

MOLLY

OF MY TWO PARENTS, I THINK I'M MOST LIKE MY FATHER.
The rest of the world would probably disagree, and at first glance it's easy to see why. In looks I resemble my mother; we share the same coloring and similar heights. My mother is a decidedly round woman, while I'm somewhere between curvy and plump, but even then we look alike. It doesn't matter that she keeps her hair short and I keep mine long, or that she swears by Crimson Kiss red lipstick while I've never worn lip color in my life. She is a picture into my future, a snapshot of what I might become some thirty years down the road.

But there are two kinds of people in this world: *bulldozers* and *bulldozees*. And while my mother is firmly in *bulldozer* category, my father and I are not.

It sounds bad, the term *bulldozer*. I guess a better way to put it would be someone who doesn't back down versus someone who does. It's not always a negative trait. Sometimes that's just the way things are, that push and pull between people as they interact.

My mother pushes. And my father lets her.

She doesn't mean anything by it, and my dad isn't a weak man. It's just their dynamic; he's happy to concede if it's not going to hurt anything, and she prefers things to go her own way.

Which is why, twenty minutes after my father has slipped and fallen on the rocks at the waterfall, my mother is convinced it's time for him to go back to the ship. And she won't hear a word against it, no matter how my father protests that he's okay.

To be fair, he doesn't *look* okay. His knee is red and swollen where he came down on it, and his usually unruffled expression is instead twisted into a grimace. It's my default setting to side with my dad when my mom is being pushy, but this time...I think she's right.

"Mr. O'Malley," Beckett says, rubbing the back of his neck. "I mean, it doesn't look good."

"It's fine," my dad says stubbornly. He managed to limp out of the water with the support of Beckett and Wes; now he's seated on a medium-sized boulder while the rest of us huddle 'round, holding court over his left knee.

"Look at it," my mom says, gesturing to the knee. "It's all *red*, Robert. And fat. It's getting puffy."

"Swollen," I interject.

"He knows what I mean," she says with a wave of her hand. "You need to go to the infirmary on the ship, Robert."

I nod. "I'm no doctor, but they'll probably need to wrap this." I tap lightly on his leg.

"Well, I'm kind of a doctor," Wes begins, "and—"

"You're not a doctor. You're a nurse," I cut in, grinning at him. "You wear a little nurse's cap and apron and let the doctors boss you around all day—"

"I do *not*," Wes says hotly, "and you know it. Nurses are *just* as smart as doctors—"

46

"Why aren't you a doctor, then, if you're just as smart?" I send up a mental apology to all the brilliant nurses out there who I've just insulted in order to aggravate my brother.

"*Children.*" The word comes from my mother, my father... and Beckett. All three of them are looking at Wes and I with exasperation, their facial expressions so similar they could've planned it beforehand.

I look at Wes. He looks at me. And then we burst into laughter at the same time. He clutches his sides as he doubles over, and I throw my head back, feeling the sun on my face.

As much as the two of us bicker like an old married couple (*ew*), laughing with him is one of my all-time favorite things to do.

"You're the worst," Wes says to me as he wipes tears of laughter from his eyes.

"And you're the cutest little nurse in all the land," I say, reaching over and pinching his cheeks. He swats my hand away, and I just laugh again.

He's more serious when he addresses our dad again, though. "I'm sorry," he says, "but I really do think we need to call it a day. You need to get this looked at, Dad. If you keep walking on it, you're only going to make it worse."

When my dad looks at me, pleading in his eyes, I shake my head sadly.

"I think they're right," I say, my voice soft.

"You were my last hope," he says to me, his mouth tugging into a painful approximation of a smile.

I smile back, patting him on top of his bald head. "I know. And I'm sorry. But I don't want you to get hurt. An explorer always remembers—"

"Safety first," he finishes with a sigh.

It's a mantra he was forced to come up with when I was just a kid, striking out recklessly on my own to discover and investigate and eat up the world in greedy, voracious bites. I wanted to experience everything, and it got me into trouble—falling out of trees, taking ipecac after nibbling unidentified mushrooms from the woods behind our house, getting stuck on the roof.

It was and is one of the main reasons I think I'm more like my dad than my mom. I get my admitted carelessness from her, that enthusiasm that leads me to act before I've thought everything through, but my insatiable desire to learn comes from my dad. And it's one of my most defining qualities.

And I'm not *so* careless, really. I'm not stupid. I know my limits. Plus, I would argue that a calculated risk is different from recklessness.

"What to do, what to do," my mother says, cutting into my thoughts with her fretting. She presses one hand to her mouth as she looks around the group of us. "I feel terrible, Beckett, sweetie. You planned this nice day on the island for us—"

"I didn't do *that* much planning," Beckett interrupts, rubbing the back of his neck again. "It's really not a big deal."

"And we so wanted to spend more time with you," my mom goes on, as though he hasn't spoken at all. Her eyes narrow thoughtfully as she thinks. "I suppose..."

I don't like the way she trails off. And I *really* don't like the way her eyes light up when they land on me.

"No," I say immediately.

"Oh, stop it," she scoffs. "You don't even know what I'm going to say, Molly-doll."

My cheeks heat at the nickname, but I keep my eyes firmly on my mother rather than letting them stray to Beckett. It's not like he's never heard me called that, anyway; it's a pet name that my parents have been using since I was a wee lass.

"Still—" I begin, but my mom cuts me off.

"Here's what we'll do," she says, nodding resolutely.

"Beckett, sweetheart, I hate to think that all your planning has gone wasted. Why don't you show Molly around a bit more? Wes and I will get Robert back to the ship, and Molly, you can meet up with us tonight for dinner on the ship. How's that?"

"It's bad," I say blankly. "That's a bad idea."

My mother's face as she looks at me is just a *touch* too innocent to be believable. "What's wrong with that idea? Beckett's okay with it, aren't you?" She looks at him.

"Don't you need help getting Mr. O'Malley back to the ship?" he says weakly.

"Not at all," my mom says. "Wes and I can manage. So you're all right with this?"

"I'm—I mean—yeah," Beckett says finally, sighing. "That's fine with me."

"What about me?" Wes butts in, looking annoyed. "Why aren't you asking if I'm okay with this plan?"

"Because you don't have a choice," my mom says, tutting at him. "Molly and I couldn't very well move your father on our own. I need your muscle."

"And how are we supposed to get back to St. Thomas?" Wes counters, still looking annoyed.

My mom's head swings back to Beckett, who looks very much like he's about to be fed to a vat of barracudas. "Your colleague said he was leaving around two, right?" she says.

Slowly, looking pained, Beckett nods.

"Well, then, that's settled. Let's go catch him before he goes."

"Mom..." I begin, but she stops me with one raised hand.

"Molly, is there any reason you specifically don't want to stay here with Beckett?" she asks pointedly.

As if I can answer that, much less while everyone is watching and listening. What would I say? *I have a hopeless, immature crush on him, but he doesn't seem too crazy about me. I don't want to impose where I'm not wanted.*

I look at Beckett, and his eyes meet mine. What follows is a completely wordless battle of wills in which he jerks his head at my parents while I shake my head and shrug helplessly.

"No," I say, my voice small. "No reason. This is fine."

My mother's nod is sharp. "Good. Take lots of pictures, please, sweetheart. I want to see everything."

"Yeah," I say, picking up my backpack and hoisting it over my shoulder. Somehow it feels heavier than it did before. "I will."

And that, in short, is how I end up watching my parents and brother sail off into the sunset while I remain on shore, accompanied by one grumpy, gorgeous man.

Except they don't actually sail off into the sunset; it's only early afternoon. The sky is a clear blue, fading to a less saturated color at the horizon. It's a bit breezier than it was when we arrived, and a bit cooler, but still nice. The work colleague we met earlier is a little *too* helpful, in my opinion—would it kill him to tell my parents that their daughter should accompany them?—going on and on about how my mom doesn't need to worry, that Beckett is a great tour guide who will make sure I don't miss any of the tiny island's must-see spots. This alone seems to kill what little fight was left in me; Whistling Wally, whose real name I learn is Carl, sells the experience so thoroughly to my mother that she's practically beaming from ear to ear as she helps my dad onto the speedboat.

Wes needs to be getting on too, but he heads in my direction instead. "Look, Moll," he says, grabbing my arm and tugging me toward him. His voice is low, like he doesn't want to be overheard. "Don't...you know. *Try* anything. With Beckett, I mean."

My jaw drops as I gape at him. "Are you serious?"

"Yeah, of course I am," he says impatiently. "I don't like this. I don't like leaving you two here. I know you've got a thing for him. And he's obviously my best friend. But Beckett is not the man for you, Moll. He's terrible with women and socializing, and he has a lot of baggage—"

"Get out of here," I say, whacking him on the arm. I'm not sure why I'm suddenly so irritated; he's not saying anything I don't already know. "Go." I swallow, trying to ignore my cheeks heating. "Nothing is going to happen." I can't believe he's known this entire time that I like his best friend. Maybe I was more obvious than I let on.

Wes's eyes search my face from behind his square-rimmed glasses, and then he gives me a nod. I turn away when I see him approach Beckett; I don't want to know what he says, and if it turns out he's warning his best friend away from me, I'll die of mortification. I'd just as soon remain ignorant.

A few seconds later, Wes bounds away from Beckett and me, leaping into the speedboat with all the ease of a tall man.

"Carl says you'll have a blast!" my mom yells from the boat just before the engine revs to life.

"Carl can suck it," I mutter, waving at her. My irritation is directed more at her than at the situation, but I'm still feeling sour all the same.

There's a snort of laughter from behind me, and I whirl around, surprised. I stumble back a few steps when I see how close Beckett is, tripping and falling flat on my bum. The wet sand soaks my shorts right through; when I stand up there will probably be two perfect cheek imprints left behind, including the stitched outline of my back pockets.

"How old were you when you learned how to walk?" Beckett says, looking at me with raised brows. He puts his hands on his hips. "And do you think it's safe to say you still haven't mastered that life skill?"

Rude.

"I can walk just fine," I say. I stare at him expectantly, waiting for him to offer his hand to help me up, but he doesn't. He just keeps those hands on his hips.

"Fine," I huff to myself, because what's with this guy? "I don't need help."

And it's mostly true. I do manage to get back up. There's some awkward body-contorting that goes into it, since I get overly ambitious and try to wipe the sand off my bum while in the process of standing, but overall it goes just fine.

So there, Beckett Donovan.

I spend about thirty seconds staring at the little speck on the horizon that is my family speeding away, and during that time I do a quick analysis of the situation—because it requires some analyzing.

Maybe I should be excited, getting this time with Beckett. And those feelings might come in a little bit. But right now I'm still feeling the buzz of embarrassment and irritation that arose from being strong-armed into staying behind. I hate being put on the spot, and I hate that I can never seem to say no to my mom. Maybe most of all, I hate that I'm such a clear imposition to Beckett. There's nothing worse than being where you're not wanted, and my mom has forced me into that situation. It's humiliating.

Because I didn't expect to have a handful of hours alone with my lifelong unrequited love. But with the way Beckett has been looking at me...well, I'm not overly hopeful. I wanted to become friends with him. But is it worth it to put in the effort to be charming? Is *charming* even in my wheelhouse?

The adrenaline is pumping through my veins, partly because I'm flustered, partly because I'm embarrassed. It's the embarrassed half of these feelings that convinces me: charming *isn't* in my wheelhouse. Not today, anyway. And I've been waiting for this opportunity too long to fill it with regret by attempting to flirt and then striking out.

I never expected anything to happen with Beckett. That much hasn't changed, even though I suddenly find myself with some unexpected one-on-one time. So I'm not going to start sucking up to him now.

Which is perfect, because I have feelings about this situation.

I turn to Beckett, putting my hands on my hips in a mirror of his pose. "Why didn't you tell my mom no?" I demand. "You don't want to be here with me. You should've said no."

Beckett's stupidly perfect jaw drops as he looks at me. "Me?" he says incredulously. "What about *you?* You didn't fight it either."

"Yeah, because she never listens to me," I say. "But she probably would have listened to you."

"No," he says, shaking his head. "I can't argue with your mom. I'm not family. She doesn't have to forgive me if she gets mad. She can just hold a grudge forever."

An unexpected pang of sadness twinges somewhere around my solar plexus, and I rub the spot uncomfortably. Is that really what he thinks? How do I even respond to that?

"Of course you're family," I say, because I don't know what else to offer. It's true, anyway. Then I glance around. The beach stretches away from us in both directions, and the water is lapping invitingly at the sand. I take a deep breath and give Beckett my full attention. "Look. You don't want to show me around, and I don't want to impose. Should we just hang out on the beach until it's time to go back to the main island? I think I'd prefer that."

"I—yeah," he says finally, sighing. "That's good." He still looks way pricklier than he needs to, though, not quite meeting my eye, his hands shoved into his swim trunk pockets. And he was always a little standoffish, even when we were growing up, but it never felt personal before.

Now, though, it seems different. And I'm left wondering if I've done something to offend him. But as much as I try, I can't come up with anything. I've just been my normal self. Is Normal Molly offensive? I don't *think* she's offensive. She maybe refers to herself in third person sometimes, but she's far from contentious.

Maybe he just thinks I'm annoying. He wouldn't be the first.

I sigh, plopping down in the sand and staring tiredly at the water, the waves a wild hypnosis that lull my mind into a continual round of questions and musings.

This day is not turning out how I expected it to. Not at all.

SIX
BECKETT

Bro Code Rule Number One: Always leave at least one urinal between yourself and another bro when going about your bodily business. I have no problem with this rule; in fact, I'm a big fan. There's nothing about another bro that I want to see in my peripheral vision when I'm taking care of things. I need space, they need space; we're all good with that.

No, it's Bro Code Rule Number Two that's sloshing around in my brain at this precise moment, causing all sorts of problems.

Bro Code Rule Number Two: Never mess with your bro's sister. Not ever. Don't check her out, don't hit on her, and *definitely* don't touch her.

I haven't touched Molly O'Malley. Don't plan to. I haven't been hitting on her, either. In fact, I've been pretty standoffish.

But if I'm completely, absolutely, 100 percent honest with myself? My eyes have wandered her way a few too many times for it to be natural or accidental.

It's possible—not definite, but possible—that I maybe, kind of, *might* be checking her out.

Maybe.

She's lounging in the sand right now, her hands behind her head as she lies on her back, one leg propped up, the other stretched just far enough that the waves lick the soles of her feet. She's got her shorts and t-shirt back on, a boon for my sanity, but there's still plenty to appreciate. Her chin is tilted up, her lashes fanning over her cheekbones, a full smile on her lips. Her hair is still piled on top of her head, mingling with the sand, red against gold.

And it's strange, looking at her. She evokes something oddly...well, I don't know. I'm not sure what word to use. *Visceral,* maybe. She evokes something visceral in me. She's not a classic beauty, with traditionally attractive proportions. She's too short, too curvy, to be model-like or statuesque. No, the thing that's so captivating about Molly is that she experiences her surroundings so openly, so sensually. There's nothing reserved about her delight or enjoyment. She's probably the kind of woman who makes borderline obscene noises when she eats her favorite foods, and she likely thinks nothing of it. That's just how she lives: with an almost embarrassing amount of pleasure, with greed for the world.

"This is nice, isn't it?" she sighs happily. She stretches a bit, arching her back, and I look away.

"Not particularly," I mutter, scooting sideways to put a bit more space between us—not that it's necessary, since we're already separated by a healthy three feet of sand. But I don't care; both my body *and* my thoughts will stay far away from Baby O'Malley—even if it's painfully clear that she's not so little anymore.

Figuratively speaking, anyway. Physically, the woman probably has to stand on her tiptoes to reach the top shelf of the refrigerator.

Molly rolls her head sideways, one hot chocolate eye

squinting open to look at me with definite attitude. "Are you always this grumpy, or do I just bring out the best in you?"

"A little of both," I say, a grunted admission that she might not even be able to hear over the sounds of the wind and the ocean. Her family only left an hour ago, but in that time it's cooled off considerably, and the breeze is a refreshing change from the muggy heat of this morning.

"I guess you and Wes can balance each other out," she says, rolling her head away again so that she's once more looking at the sky. "Him with his happy-go-lucky shtick while you just glower in the background."

"Probably," I admit. "That's how it usually was in high school."

"I remember," she says.

I'm tempted to ask her how *much* she remembers, because she was so easy to ignore back then. She didn't force you to pay attention to her without even trying, the way she does now. I would hazard a guess that she remembers a lot more about me than I do about her.

Although maybe that's just my ego speaking. I have no desire to sit here and reminisce with her, anyway, so I don't say anything. I just study the darkening horizon. I've been keeping an eye on the shadows that are rolling in from that direction; I'm not worried at the moment, but the weather can turn on a dime out here.

"You should try to cheer up," she says with another happy sigh. "It's almost Christmas, but you're riding the Scrooge Express. You live on a gorgeous island doing work that you love. Smile a little."

I'm silent at this, because how do I explain that I'm normally more friendly than I have been toward her? And how do I explain that while I'm maybe not the most open person, I *like* the way I am?

"I smile," I say instead, threading my fingers through the sand on either side of me. But I look over when Molly gives a snort of laughter, unladylike and loud, and find her eyes on me once again.

"Do it," she says, a challenge in her voice.

I blink at her. "Do what?"

"Smile," she says. "Do it. Smile. Right now."

My lips pull down as I stare at her. "What are you—"

"No," she says, shaking her head. She sits up slowly, brushing the sand off of her hands and back. Then she turns her whole body toward me and points at my face. "That's a frown," she says. "That thing you're doing with your mouth. It's a frown. When you smile, your lips go *up*."

I glare at her. Where did all this sass come from?

"Nope," she says, and she shakes her head again, gesturing at me. "That's even worse. That's a glower."

"I can't just smile on command," I say.

"Sure you can," she says. "Everyone can smile on command. Look, see?"

And then she pulls out a smile, blinding and bright and genuine. She points to the corners of her mouth.

"They turn up, see?" she says around that smile. "And it's nice if some teeth show too"—she points to the row of white teeth visible between her lips—"but I won't strictly insist upon it. I've seen some very nice closed-lip smiles."

I will not be doling out any smiles on command, closed-lip or otherwise, and I make this very clear using the expression on my face. We enter into a weird stare down, her smiling maniacally, me glowering, our eyes locked. With every second that passes she forces her smile wider and wider, and with every second that passes I frown more severely. I don't let myself get caught up in details like the color of her eyes or the tendrils of red that have escaped her top knot. I just stay laser-focused on winning, taking note as her crazy smile becomes more and more genuine, until finally a real, loud laugh bursts out of her.

She tilts her head back, laughing to the sky, and I can't stop my reluctant smile either. I'm not sure when I last had an honest-to-goodness staring contest, but it feels good to let my guard down a bit as my lips twitch.

"Fine," Molly says as she wipes her eyes. Then her smile transforms into a little pout. Her bottom lip juts out, and if her dad were here, he'd warn her that a bird might land there. "I guess I can't force you to smile." She looks around and sighs. "You're worse than Leonard."

I stare blankly at her, taken aback by this sudden change in topic. "Who's Leonard?"

"He's from the aquarium I work at," she says. "Everyone loves him, but he's completely antisocial."

I frown. "Why do they love him if he's antisocial?"

She shrugs. "I personally just like him because he's cute, but most people like to touch him. Kids especially. He's bigger than average for sure, so they think that's cool."

My eyes widen at the picture forming in my head: a morbidly obese man being poked and prodded by children all day, just because he's large. It's horrible. I'm not one to judge people on their parenting—I can only imagine how hard it is to raise kids but letting your child invade the space of someone just because of his size? It's dehumanizing—

And then a sudden thought hits me. "Wait a minute. Are we talking about a person or an animal here?"

"Who, Leonard?" Molly says.

I nod.

"He's a cownose ray," she says. "*Rhinoptera bonasus.* Completely adorable." She pauses, glancing at me. "Oh! You thought I was talking about a person?"

I nod again, and she laughs again, tilting her head back.

The air around us eats the sound up, but it still lingers in her smile as she looks at me.

"Sorry, I should have specified. Leonard is a ray," she says. "We do not let children pet our employees, no matter their size."

I huff a little laugh. "Good. That was concerning."

"It would be, yes," she says with a nod. "But no worries." Then she tilts her head, casting her gaze like a fishing line to the tide lapping in. "We should do something Christmasy."

For the love. I can't keep up with all the subject changes. How fast must her brain be moving for her to have jumped from a ray named Leonard to Christmas?

"Yeah, let's do that," she says before I have a chance to respond. I'm not sure what I would say, anyway.

"Pass" is what I come up with. Original, I know. Eloquent. Expressive.

"Fine," she says. "I'll be holly jolly on my own. You can sit there and sulk at the sky or whatever it is you like to do in your free time." Then she moves forward a few feet, so that she's sitting in the wet sand. She seems to have given up on keeping her clothing clean, and it's probably for the best anyway; you can't come to the beach without getting sand on everything you own.

I watch as she digs her hands into the sand, like a child with greedy hands plowing into a birthday cake. At first I think she's going to attempt a sandcastle, but as she begins scooping and patting and building, something different takes shape, vaguely conical.

A Christmas tree. I think she's building a Christmas tree. And—I strain my ears to listen—she's singing "Deck the Halls" under her breath. Slightly off-key, dreamy in its faintness.

I can't help my smile, but I do rub my hand over my mouth so she doesn't see. Although she's so absorbed in her work—now using her finger to create a garland pattern—that she's not paying me a lick of attention.

I lie back, settling myself comfortably in the sand as I watch her. She's lost in her own little world, and she seems happy there. This woman is a complete enigma to me, a question mark in the void.

She's still singing to herself when my eyes drift shut.

I WAKE to the feeling of something wet and cold. It's a disorienting way to re-enter consciousness, and for a second I'm convinced that a bird has just pooped on me. When that wet coldness is followed by more wet and more cold, though, fat droplets that splat against my skin, I realize it's raining.

My eyes fly open, and I come to three rapid conclusions:

1. A storm is at our doorstep, and judging by the size of the rough, choppy waves, it's too late to return to the main island,
2. We need to find shelter, immediately, and
3. Molly O'Malley was made for sleeping on the beach.

She shouldn't be so captivating, not while she's just lying there. And yet, I can't look away. Because she's got a little smile on her face as she sleeps, the slightest tilt to her lips, and her hair is no longer in a bun on top of her head. It's loose now, spread out in the sand around her, and her chest rises and falls slowly as she breathes. She's completely out, apparently oblivious to the trouble we could be in very soon.

"Molly!" I shout, scrambling to my feet.

The clouds on the horizon—*much* closer than when I

stupidly fell asleep—are dark and angry, and even as I stand here, they move, the rain picking up.

"Molly!" I shout again, moving toward her with long, tense strides. "Molly, we need to go."

She finally begins to stir, stretching her arms above her head and arching her back. She sits up slowly and looks around, blinking. I lean down and grab her by the wrist, pulling her to her feet amidst stuttered protests. I tug her behind me, letting go only when she twists her arm away from me.

"I'm coming," she says, speaking loudly to be heard over the wind and rain. "Chill. I'm coming."

"We need to get off the beach," I say. "Come on; quicker. We need to move."

She picks up the pace behind me without complaint, which I appreciate. "Where are we going?" she says as she scrambles along. "Didn't you say—"

"I don't know," I snap, holding up one hand. "I'm thinking. Hang on."

The observatory is locked. I know this for sure, and I don't have keys. They left the island with Carl.

"Okay," she says, and I jump when I feel her small hand on my arm, pulling me to a stop.

"We need to *move*, Molly," I say, rounding on her.

"I know that," she replies calmly. She pulls her hair over her shoulder as she speaks, her fingers weaving it deftly into a sand-studded braid. "But first we need to figure out where we're going. So just stop for a second and breathe. You're too frazzled."

"No, I'm not," I shoot back.

Except I am. She's right. So I suck in a lungful of air that smells like rain, my eyes still on the sky and the waves. I take another deep breath, and then one more.

"All right," she says, her voice completely conversational. "What are our options? Lay them out for me."

"There's a hut," I say immediately as my mind whirls. "It's no storm shelter, but it's a roof. There may be something vaguely cavelike up near the waterfall, but no guarantees there."

"Whoa. You *live* on this island? In a *hut?*"

"Of course not," I say. "I have a place on the main island. We use the hut for storage."

"And the facility is locked?" she says.

"Yes." I push my hand through my now-wet hair. The rain is starting to get a little meaner, hitting sharply against my skin.

"How bad is this going to get?" she says, gesturing at the sky.

"Bad," I say immediately. "Look at the clouds."

"Cumulonimbus. Pretty dark," she agrees.

What's with this girl? Does she study clouds in her spare time? And *how* does she still sound so calm?

"And getting darker. And look at the waves." I have to force myself not to worry about the remaining speed boat; all I can do is cover it with the tarp and hope for the best. "Let me just..." I trail off, already running to the boat. I climb in and dig around until I find the tarp, securing it in record time before jumping out and moving back to Molly.

Molly points at the boat when I reach her. "And we shouldn't just head back to the main island in that. Right?"

"Correct," I say. "The waves are too rough, there's lightning, I'm not a particularly skilled sailor or whatever—"

"Right," she says, cutting off my rambling. "No boat. In that case," she says, "you need to decide. We can go up to the research facility and break a window. That's the safest shelter, but we risk not being able to break in, and you might get in trouble. Or we can go to your hut thingy, but we risk not being

63

completely safe. I think we should nix the cave idea; better to stick to definites."

"Yes. Okay." When she lays it out like that, the solution is clear. I don't know why I didn't think of it.

And maybe it's a weird time to notice this, but it hits me all at once how *smart* this woman is. It's not just evident in her random intellectual facts, either. I see it more right now than I have thus far as she stands here thinking, her face twisted into an expression of concentration—eyes narrowed on the horizon, brow furrowed. There's something captivating about watching her mind work.

I nod. "Let's go break a window."

"They're not barred? Or reinforced glass or anything?"

"It is tempered glass," I admit. "But I can try to break it."

"Tempered glass is roughly four times stronger than regular glass," she says, biting her lip.

I huff impatiently. "If not, we can still use the building as a wind break."

Just then a particularly loud roll of thunder vibrates through the air around us, and out over the water, a web of lightning crackles down. Molly winces at the sight, or maybe at the noise, turning her back to the ocean. It's the first time I've seen any hint of distress on her pale face.

"Sorry," she says quickly. "The lightning. I shouldn't look at flashing lights."

It takes me a second to work through what she means, but it's not until I see her fiddling with the silicone bracelet around her wrist that a vague memory resurfaces, prompted by the tiny medical alert symbol I spot—the one with the snake curling around the staff.

"Oh, you have—you have seizures, right?" I say, casting her a questioning look. I think that's what she's talking about.

She nods. "They've never been triggered by lights before, but...well." She shrugs. "It feels stupid to test it out now."

"Agreed," I say, a new sense of urgency overcoming me even as I realize that no matter where on the island we go, there will still be lightning. Crap. "Let's get moving."

One thing at a time. All I can do is one thing at a time, and that's all I have the mental capacity to worry about. So instead of letting myself spiral into my worries, I shove everything out of my head except for the path to the research facility. The boat, Molly's seizures, the cruise ship she needs to be on when it departs this evening—I get rid of them all, dumping them behind a door in my brain that I won't open until Molly and I are out of immediate danger.

"One thing at a time," she says to me, and I blink at her, startled to hear her echo what I'm thinking. "Just focus on one thing at a time."

"Yeah," I say faintly. I don't really like relying on other people; I don't like letting them too far into my life. But at this exact moment, it seems I don't have any choice. So I guess all I can do is suck it up. "Let's go." Then I grab her hand and tug, and together we disappear into the trees.

SEVEN
MOLLY

BECKETT DONOVAN IS NOT A TALKER.

He's not a talker, and I *am* a talker, and this presents some very obvious logistical problems.

And to be fair, I get why he's not exactly feeling chatty at the moment. I wish I weren't feeling chatty either. It's just a sort of nervous habit I have; I'm scared and tense and so I'm talking his ear off, babbling on and on.

About fish.

Which I can tell he's really thrilled about.

The two of us are huddled against the side of the research facility, the red brick sturdy and anchoring. We're facing each other but looking at our feet, our arms folded over our chests as we attempt to make ourselves as small as possible.

We did try to break one of the ground floor windows, but it wasn't as easy as they make it look in action movies. They chose tempered glass for this building precisely for this reason: so it wouldn't shatter in severe weather.

Good call on their parts. Those windows aren't going anywhere anytime soon.

I can't help but think of the soft, fluffy snow that's probably falling at home as I huddle here, being pelted by bruising rain, talking feverishly about the mating habits of the common goldfish. My backpack is hanging like dead weight off my back, my mind only half intact as I speak.

And I hate it.

I hate the way my voice sounds to my own ears, laced faintly with the anxiety I'm trying to outrun. I hate the twisting in my gut, the adrenaline rushing through my veins as the sky is revealed time and time again through the flashing lightning. I mastered my fear of water a long time ago; why am I still affected by lightning like this?

"But you know, the common goldfish is actually considered an invasive species in North America," I babble, my voice growing louder as another roll of thunder sounds around us. "They compete with local populations for food, and their feeding habits reduce the clarity of the water which then affects plant growth because of the lack of light that reaches the bottom—"

But I break off when Beckett speaks for the first time in probably ten minutes.

"For the *love*," he says, quietly enough that I barely hear him. Then he steps closer to me and, in a move that completely obliterates my personal bubble, clamps one hand over my mouth.

Over. My. Mouth.

My jaw would be gaping open if it weren't being held closed by Beckett's warm, work-roughened hand. I glare at him, reaching up to pull on his wrist, but it's like trying to break that stupid window all over again. No matter how I tug, he doesn't budge—because while one hand is over my mouth, the other is at the back of my head, holding me in place.

"There was this kid your brother and I were in school

with," he says to me, his voice low. There can't be more than six inches between us, and for a moment I just watch in fascination at the way his lips move when he speaks.

"And this guy was nice enough, I guess, but whenever we were about to take a test, he would start running his mouth about all the things he'd studied. It was like a compulsion; he couldn't sit quietly. He did this thing where he tapped his fingers on his desk too. It made your brother laugh, but it drove me nuts. All that nervous energy made me feel twitchy."

I pull my eyes away from his lips just in time to see his brown eyes boring into me.

"So I know you're scared, Baby O'Malley," he goes on, and his voice is gruff, though not unkind, "but I need you to calm down. Okay? Please."

I stare up at him, stunned, at a complete loss for words. He stares at me expectantly, though, his hand never moving. I can just smell him over the scent of the rain, now that he's so close; something fresh and clean, a sharp, soapy scent.

Because he's still looking at me, still seemingly waiting for my answer, I nod once.

"Good girl," he murmurs in a low voice.

My stomach flips at his words, which is categorically stupid, but I gave up trying to control my responses to him a long time ago. I wince, though, when another shock of lightning laces the sky overhead. I flinch into his hand, which is still over my mouth, and he lets it fall away.

Except he doesn't move his other hand from the back of my head. No, he uses that hand to pull me closer, and I stumble forward as my head collides with his chest.

I shiver as I hear another crack of lightning, and his hand tightens in my hair.

"I—yeah," he says, sounding resigned. "Just stay there for a bit. Don't look at the flashing light." His chest rumbles against my face as he speaks, his shirt wet against my cheek. The thin linen is plastered to the planes of his chest—something I've done very well not perusing up until this moment, thank you very much. But now that my forehead, nose, lips, and chin are all squashed up against him...well. I can't help but notice.

Along with the muscle, though, I am also keenly aware of how stiff his body is, tense and coiled. He's clearly uncomfortable having me this close. I don't blame him, I guess; he hasn't exactly been acting like my biggest fan. I would move away, except his hand is still holding my head to his chest. Not to mention...I do feel a little better having my eyes shielded from the lightning.

I wasn't lying to him earlier; I've had seizures for years, since I was thirteen, and they've never once showed any response to flashing lights. I've done several EEGs—a neurological test that involves dozens of little sensors attached to my scalp with goopy glue, while I'm exposed to different triggers—and strobe lights have never affected the electric signals my brain is putting out. The only thing that seems to trigger my seizures is sleep deprivation. So it doesn't really make sense that I'm so wary of lightning or strobe lights or anything like that.

It doesn't make sense, but it happens anyway.

I used to be afraid of water, too; a bit more understandable, perhaps, but still something I wasn't happy about. So when I went to college, I started my own form of desensitization therapy. I swam with friends in the university's pool. I learned cool stuff about the ocean and marine life. That's what led me to ichthyology. It wasn't because I was a clownfish in my past life —although hey, who knows?—it was because I spent so much time trying to get over my fear that I ended up falling in love with that world.

When will I fall in love with the stormy sky?

I don't know how long we stand like that, my head buried against Beckett's chest, the rest of my body awkwardly keeping its distance. It's a weird pose to be in, uncomfortable and comforting all at the same time. He never relaxes, not once, even as the minutes drag on for what feels like forever.

At some point the storm picks up even more, turning downright violent. I've never seen rain or winds like this, except for one time when we were visiting family in the midwest during tornado season. Now is when Beckett and I finally give up trying to keep our distance; although we don't say anything—I don't think we'd be able to hear each other over the roar of the elements—we both move at the same time, our bodies colliding as I step into him while he simultaneously pulls me closer. He yanks at the straps of my backpack, pulling it off of me and tossing it to the ground beside the wall. Then he shuffles us around so that my back is to the brick, shielded almost completely by his body. I'm soaked to the bone, and he is too; I can feel him shivering just as violently as I am.

"Can you breathe?" he says, his voice muffled as he speaks into the top of my head.

I can only barely make out what he says, but I nod against his chest once I've figured it out. "Are you okay?" I say—or yell, more like.

"I'm fine," he says. "Just stay where you are, please."

I tilt my head up, so that my chin is resting on his chest instead of my whole face being squashed into it. "I can't just let you take the brunt of this—"

"Yes, you can," he says. His voice is tight, tense, his lips barely moving against my forehead as he speaks. "Now please stop talking. I can't focus on conversation right now."

That's fair, I guess. My teeth are starting to chatter, anyway, making speaking difficult.

And something hazy starts happening with the world

around us then. I'm awake, I'm aware, but it's also like we've entered a weird new dimension where time passes both impossibly quickly and impossibly slowly. Like we're stuck in one moment, a moment that drags out infinitely, and yet at the same time everything around us is hurtling by. Maybe this is the theory of relativity in action.

Or maybe I'm just really, really cold and really, really worried, and my brain has lost the capacity to compute anything but those two facts.

My hands are both pulled tightly to my chest, my wrists curled at awkward angles, and they've long since gone numb. Beckett's drenched shirt is still wet against my face, but it's not the cold kind of wet anymore, now that I've been pressed up against it—small mercies, I suppose, and the warmth his body exudes is more than welcome.

So I burrow in a bit more. And although Beckett tenses even further, it's only for a second; I can feel the exact moment he gives in to what this situation calls for. Until now he's had one hand at the back of my head, one on my shoulder; now, though, his whole body sags, and then his arms are wrapping tightly around me, holding me so close it's almost hard to breathe. They band around my shoulders and my back, separating me from the brick wall.

And even though it's stupid to feel this way, even though his actions mean nothing except that he doesn't want me to die on his watch, I still can't help the little smile that spreads over my face.

TIME PASSES.
The wind roars.
The rain lashes.

We stay exactly where we are.
And we wait.

MAYBE IT'S NOT possible to sleep while standing up in the middle of a tropical storm, but it is possible to doze fitfully if your body and your mind are so utterly spent that they have no alternative but to shut down. When I become more aware of what's going on around me, I notice that although Beckett is still holding me close, both of us have slumped against the wall. He seems to be leaning on me pretty heavily, and in a strange way, I'm glad; I'm glad that I can do *something* for him, however inconsequential. If holding up his weight is all I can manage, I'll do it happily.

I'm not sure if he's awake or asleep or somewhere in between, but I get my answer a few short moments later, when Beckett's arms loosen their grip.

It's the change in volume, I realize, that caused me to snap back to what's going on; the storm is finally dying down. The wind has lessened, and the rain that was painful before now feels more like a pleasant shower. He's clearly realized the same thing; although he doesn't let go of me completely, his hands come to rest on my shoulders, and he shuffles his feet, standing up straighter. I follow his lead, doing the same, not quite able to look up at him. This is a strangely intimate thing we've just lived through, and I'm not sure what to do with that yet.

"Beckett?" I breathe, because even though I'm not ready to look at him, I do need to know if he's okay.

He grunts in response but doesn't say anything else.

"Are you all right? Are you hurt?"

"I'm fine," he says.

He doesn't sound fine. But I wouldn't either, in his situation. I'm just glad he's conscious and coherent.

"Okay," I say. "Just checking."

"I'm going to let go of you now," he says gruffly. "I know it's still raining, but I've been keeping an eye on the sky. I haven't seen lightning for quite a while—"

"That's fine," I say quickly, because he's done more than enough for me already. "I'm fine. I'll be okay."

I feel him nod, the last movement to touch me before he steps away, his arms falling limply to his sides. Now that we're not pressed together, I can look him over; I avoid eye contact, but I let my greedy gaze take him in, searching for any injuries. I circle him like a shark circling its prey, and although he frowns at me, he doesn't say anything about it.

The backs of his legs are red and splattered with mud, and every inch of his clothing is plastered to his body. I notice a few scratches on his legs and the back of his neck that might be new. There's nothing life-threatening, though, and I breathe a sigh of relief.

I jump when I hear another roll of thunder a few seconds later, and I resume my place next to Beckett; not in his arms, but right by him, huddled in the inefficient shadow of the building.

"You gonna start talking about fish again?" he says, casting me a wary glance.

I rub my hands up and down my arms, trying to distract myself from what's left of the storm. "No," I say defensively. "I'm not."

"But you want to," Beckett says, his brows raised at me.

"Only because it helps keep my mind off all this," I admit, gesturing to the sky.

He nods slowly, looking utterly spent. "All right," he says, his voice tired. "Tell me why ichthyology, then. The real reason."

Huh. He's still interested in that; I wouldn't have expected him to care, or to have given my earlier answer anything more than a passing thought.

And maybe he doesn't care. But it's been a long time since anyone asked this question, and even longer since I answered truthfully. I know he's asking as a way to help me, so...I'll answer.

I take a deep breath, then say, "I used to be scared of the water."

Beckett turns his head toward me. "Because of the epilepsy?"

I shrug. "Maybe? Probably. My fear never felt like it was related to the idea that I would drown if I had a seizure while in the water, but I also don't remember being afraid before I was diagnosed. So, yeah—I think it's probably a subconscious epilepsy thing." I've thought a lot about it, and this explanation makes the most sense to me.

Beckett turns the rest of his body toward me, shifting his position against the wall so that it's pressed up against his side instead of his back. "Okay," he says. "So you were scared of water."

"Yeah," I say. Something about having his full attention is nerve-wracking, and I find myself fidgeting with the end of my braid as I speak. "I was scared, but I didn't want to be. So I started going swimming a lot, tubing with friends, stuff like that. And then I sort of realized—well." I break off, feeling heat creep into my cheeks.

"What?" he prods, and wow—he's looking at me like he genuinely wants to hear what I have to say.

"Well, humans walk around every day breathing oxygen, right?" I say. "And it doesn't even occur to us to be afraid of the air we breathe. So I sort of realized that for fish, water is the same way. And if all these different creatures swim around in the ocean, completely trusting of the water..." I shrug. "I wanted to study that and learn more. So I started reading about ocean life, and I got hooked."

Beckett doesn't say anything, even when I'm silent for long enough that it's clear I'm done speaking. I both want to look at him and don't want to look at him, but in the end, curiosity wins out. I'm not normally self-conscious, but...this is Beckett. The guy I've been dreaming about for years. And I've just told him something very personal.

What does he think about that?

It's hard to tell at first. We're facing each other, but he has his head ducked. The rain has turned his hair a few shades darker, and I watch as droplet after droplet after droplet rolls down his forehead all the way to the tip of his nose.

When he finally speaks, I've become so engrossed in the rain trailing down his face that I jump, startled.

"That's pretty cool," he says, tilting his head up so that he's looking at me.

"What's cool?" I say. "That a grown woman is afraid of the water?"

"You're not a grown woman," he says. "You're a kid, Baby O'Malley."

"I'm twenty-four," I reply hotly. Who does he think he is, acting like he's so much older than me?

"Are you? Crap," he mutters. "So young. But that's not what I meant." He swallows—I watch, fascinated, at the bobbing of his Adam's apple—and then says, "I meant it's cool that you turned your fear into a strength. That's all."

"Oh," I say, surprised. I never really thought of it like that, but..."I guess you're kind of right."

"Of course I am," he says gruffly. He stretches one hand

out, palm upturned as he looks at what little of the sky is visible through the trees. He watches the rain for a moment, then turns his head back to me. "Got anything else to distract yourself in there?" he says, nodding to my backpack, which is still propped against the brick wall.

"Maybe," I say, biting my lip as I eye the bag. It's wetter than it's ever been in its long lifespan, of course, and I find myself wondering if my cookies are still safely sealed in their container.

I lean over and unzip the backpack, digging for a second with no particular goal in mind. The contents are a little damp, but hopefully there's nothing in here that's been irreparably damaged by water. I pause when I feel my tube of body lotion, grabbing it and pulling it out. I flip the cap open and stick the tube right under my nose, inhaling deeply—vanilla peppermint swirl, my favorite holiday scent—before squirting a big blob into my palm and then dropping the lotion back into my bag.

Beckett watches me silently, until it finally seems he can't hold his tongue any longer. "That's not what I meant. This isn't the time for pampering, Molly," he bites out.

"Wanting to moisturize doesn't make me pampered, *Beckett*," I shoot back. I rub the lotion more vigorously over my hands and arms. "Good skin care is always relevant."

He pinches the bridge of his nose and exhales slowly, his eyes closed like he's praying for patience.

Well, go ahead and pray, Beckett Donovan. Go ahead and pray, and while you're at it, have the Good Lord send us a miracle. A boat-shaped miracle, preferably.

Because I'm starting to worry that that's the only way we're going to get off this island in time for me to board the cruise ship with my family. Otherwise...I'm stuck. Left behind and stranded.

On a desert island.

With Beckett Donovan.

EIGHT
BECKETT

ALL TOLD, THE WORST OF THE STORM LASTS PROBABLY about two hours. My phone is toast, so without asking Molly I don't have a way to tell what time it is, but I've spent enough time on this island now that I've got a vague sense of things.

I've *definitely* got a vague sense that we're not getting out of here tonight, for example. There's no way. I don't know what Molly's going to do about the cruise ship, and I don't know if her family will realize she's gone in time, but I guess we'll just do what we can on our end.

Which basically amounts to staying alive.

The rain that's falling now is sporadic and light, and since Molly and I can't possibly get any wetter, we finally abandon the research facility and head toward the hut. It's where we're going to have to stay tonight, assuming it's still standing. I'm eager to get moving, partly because every second I stand here next to Molly—who now smells like peppermint and something sweeter—is another second I'm remembering how it feels to have her pressed up against me.

It's not that it was a particularly enjoyable experience,

holding her close. I didn't have the presence of mind to be very affected by how near she was. But I'd be lying if I said I felt *nothing*. And since I would very much *like* to feel nothing, I think it's best if we relocate.

She was just so...soft. So soft and small, shivering in my arms, her hot breath warming my chest where her face was pressed. I really had no choice but to wrap my arms around her; we were both cold, both trying to shelter each other. And even though I didn't want to be impressed when she told me about how she came to study ichthyology, I couldn't help but feel admiration at the way she changed her life. Most people just learn to live with their fears, myself included, but she didn't.

I have to respect that, even if the last thing I need is more emotions involving her.

She walks in front of me now, at my insistence, mostly because she's dead on her feet and I don't trust her not to trip and fall or even just faint. The path to the hut is slick with mud, and it's not going to dry out any time soon. Out here one bout of rain can last for days.

In spite of these conditions, Molly hasn't complained at all. In fact, I've even caught her turning to look at me more than once, as though she's worried *I* might not be okay. I can tell she's having a hard time, though, and I don't blame her. Both of us need to get warm and then sleep for a solid twelve hours.

We pass through the trees, all of which seem impossibly green and teeming with life, and the closer we get to the hut, the more apprehensive I become. What kind of shape is it going to be in? We built it when we first started so that we'd have a place to store tools and odds and ends, but once the research facility was functional, we didn't have much reason to go there anymore.

At least we had the foresight to build it on higher ground—something that's making this trek a bit of a pain, but ultimately a good thing—and we did what we could to reinforce the roof at the time. Molly and I half walk, half stumble our way there, both of us silent, until finally I spot the bend in the path that will open up to a tiny clearing. I pick up the pace, coming to walk next to Molly instead of behind her, then moving on ahead. And by the time the hut is in my line of sight, I'm jogging to get there, my nerves on high, my mind zooming as I play out all possible scenarios.

Because I don't know what we're going to do if this place is trashed. I really don't. We need warmth and rest. And if the walls and roof have been destroyed...

"Oh," Molly says from behind me as we approach. "Wow. So this is like...a *hut* hut."

"Yes," I say, circling the small shelter as I take everything in. I'm trying to keep a tight leash on my hope, trying not to get too excited, but the truth is, I'm just *so* tired. I would kill for somewhere to lie down, and I need this little shack to be that place.

To my immense relief, nothing major jumps out at me. There are a few spots on the roof that need to be patched—I'll have to do that tonight—but it's still standing. The walls, made of rope-bound wood, are all in decent shape. The door is hanging a little sideways, but that's okay.

So it's really just the palm-frond roof that needs the most attention.

"What can I help with?" Molly says, stepping up next to me. When I look over at her, she's inspecting the shelter with a critical gaze. Then she tilts her head, her eyes narrowing as she points to the roof. "Or is it supposed to look like that?" Her head swings toward me, and I force my attention elsewhere when she bites her lip. "Confession," she says, "I can't really tell. I'm not super knowledgeable about huts."

The thought of Molly clambering up onto that roof sounds like a nightmare, so I quickly say, "No. I mean, nothing."

Rubbing the back of my neck, I add, "There's nothing you can do. So if you need to—I don't know. Check the stuff in your bag, or whatever, do that." I'm just grasping at straws. She already dug through her backpack earlier, but it was brief, and if she's up on that roof with me, I'll only be able to focus on making sure she doesn't fall.

"Yeah," she says with a sigh. "That's probably best."

We're speaking more loudly than we'd normally need to, but it's still raining. I'm in desperate need of space, so I jerk my chin toward one of the larger trees next to the hut. It won't provide a ton of shelter for her, but it will be better than nothing.

"Sit over there," I say. "Or stand, whatever. But just wait there while I work, and don't go wandering off. Okay?"

Molly nods but doesn't say anything; she just hoists her backpack a little higher on her back and moves in the direction I've indicated. There are strands of hair plastered to the sides of her face, her pale lashes darkened and clumped together by the rain. Her shirt clings to every possible curve—none of which I let myself linger on—and her feet in their sandals are caked with mud.

She looks rough.

"Yeah," I say, frowning at the tug of worry I feel. "Just...go sit. Here." I stride past her, clearing some of the branches and debris away from the base of the tree. "You're going to get more muddy, but—"

"A little mud never hurt anyone," she says tiredly.

I nod, grateful that I'm apparently not going to get any diva-like complaints from her. I watch as she makes herself as comfortable as possible, not moving until she's completely settled, her backpack resting in her lap, her head tilted back against the trunk of the tree, her eyes closed. Only then do I get to work.

The first thing I do is brave the inside of the hut to grab some bowls, cups, containers—anything I can collect rainwater in. It's not guaranteed to be clean, but out here it's a pretty good bet, and we need to secure drinking water as soon as possible. I end up with a large metal mixing bowl and a storage container that I empty of its contents right on the dirt floor of the hut. I set them outside and watch with satisfaction as they immediately begin collecting water. Then I move to the roof.

There's a peaceful kind of monotony in doing manual labor in the rain. It's a mental reprieve; the external stimuli of the rain and the work create enough physical distractions that my mind is able to go blissfully quiet. I don't think about being stranded, or about the cruise ship leaving in a couple hours, or about my best friend's little sister.

Just the rain, and the roof, and that's it.

I'd be lying if I said I don't check on Molly every now and then, though, just to make sure she's okay. She doesn't move from her spot by the tree, her head tilted back, her bag on her lap. I think she's making her very slow way through the contents, because one time when I look I spot a canteen next to her, and another time what looks like a freezer bag, but for the most part she just sits there, resting.

Until, that is, she moves.

I don't know how long I've been working without glancing behind me—twenty minutes, maybe. But when it occurs to me to check on her again, she's nowhere in sight.

I blink once, then twice, rubbing my eyes against the falling rain to make sure I'm not seeing things incorrectly. But I'm not —she's gone. Her bag lies abandoned at the base of the tree, propped against the trunk, and that's the only sign of her.

And it's stupid, the way my fear spikes. She's not a child, and she's certainly not dumb. I don't need to worry like this. And yet, I scramble down from that roof faster than I ever have before, calling her name well before my feet drop with a *squelch* onto the muddy ground.

I've yelled for her twice when I hear a response. It's louder than I expected, and my head swivels this way and that to see where she is.

"Up here," she calls, and when I finally pinpoint the direction of her voice, my heart skips several beats. Because what I see of her—*all* I see of her—is a pair of pale, mud-crusted legs, dangling from up in the flimsy branches of the tree she was sitting by.

I sigh with frustration, watching her flail around up there. Does she have a death wish? Where is her sense of self-preservation?

"Let's talk about survival instincts, Baby O'Malley, and how you don't seem to have any," I grit out. "What are you doing?" I then ask, raising my voice so she can hear me. I move quickly to the base of the tree, trying to follow the trajectory of where she'll fall when she inevitably tumbles down. "You're going—" I break off, forcing myself to take a deep breath. Before I open my mouth again, I do my best to get a grip on the strange anxiety I feel watching her up there. "You're going to fall. Do you ever use your brain? What would possess you to climb a tree when you can barely walk without tripping?"

"My phone got a bit wet," she says. "It was off in my bag, so I climbed up here to turn it on and see if I could find cell service at all." Her brow furrows in concentration as she shifts, but infuriatingly, she doesn't look frightened or concerned about her situation at all. "And I think you're overreacting," she goes on. "I'm capable of climbing a tree just fine."

I shake my head, disbelieving. Because while I have a strong suspicion that this woman's mind could run circles around mine, her coordination has so far shown itself to be lacking—especially in our current physical circumstances.

I rub my chest, frowning. Why am I so agitated right now?

"Just get down," I bite out, once again speaking so that she can hear me over the rain. "Now, please. Forget about the phone. It won't work out here anyway." I move closer to the base of the tree, my arms outstretched. The tips of my fingers just barely brush her muddy sandals.

"Drop here," I say, waving my hands a few times. "Right here."

Molly's head peeks out further from the limb she's on, and she frowns at me. "Are you gonna catch me?" she says.

"Yes," I say impatiently. "Come on."

"And are you sure you can carry me?" she says, looking more dubious still. She casts a glance over her body. "I'm not a little one-hundred-pound girl like you're probably used to."

For the first time in hours, I actually laugh. It's crazy to find any humor in this situation, but I can't help it.

"You have no idea what kinds of women I like in my arms," I say, shaking my head. "But I'll tell you this: they aren't a hundred pounds. So just come down, okay? I'll catch you."

And crap. *Crap.* What's going on in her mind that has her eyes trailing over me like that, her teeth digging into her bottom lip, her cheeks turning pinker than normal?

My breath hitches in my chest as something electric spikes in my veins. She is absolutely checking me out right now, blatant and unabashed, and the color in her cheeks tells me she likes what she sees. She *likes* the idea that I prefer my women curvier, softer, rounder—

"Molly," I bark out before my thoughts can stray to places they shouldn't go. "Focus."

"Yeah," she says, her voice breathy. She clears her throat and repeats, "Yeah. Okay. Should I just—"

"Just let yourself drop," I say. "I'm right here. Make sure

you're not going to get caught on anything—good—no, put your left foot a little closer to the trunk, good, now—*jump*."

And to her credit, she does exactly what I tell her to. Not one second later she lands in my arms, her breath escaping her in a *whoosh* on impact...

And then escaping her again when I promptly spill her out of my arms and onto the ground.

"Beckett!" she says, looking up at me in shock. "You—you dropped me!"

"I put you down," I correct.

Her eyes narrow, and against my will, I find myself fighting a smile. It's just that she's so covered in mud at this point; there's more brown visible than skin tone. She looks like a little piglet that's been rolling in the dirt.

It's weirdly, bizarrely...*cute*. She's *cute* glaring up at me, covered in mud.

"Beckett," she fumes. She holds her hand out to me, and it takes a second to realize she's asking for help standing up.

Except based on her expression, she's less *asking* and more *demanding*.

I take her hand and give her a pull, and she jolts up toward me, wobbling a little before steadying herself.

"You shouldn't have said you could carry me if you were just going to drop me," she says, her eyes fixed somewhere over my right shoulder. "That's kind of super embarrassing."

"I'm not embarrassed at all," I retort, raising one eyebrow at her.

"Not for you," she says with a roll of her eyes. "*Me*. It's embarrassing for me."

I blink at her, feeling my forehead wrinkle as I frown. "How—"

"Because it makes me feel like I was so heavy that you couldn't hold my weight," she cuts me off, throwing her hands

up in the air. "And normally I'm pretty confident about all this"
—she gestures to her body—"but it's *you*, and it's been a weird
day, and—I'm tired," she sighs.

It's then that I notice how red her cheeks are, and how her
body has curled in on itself as she slouches. And even though
my only motivation in dropping her was to put space between
us, I suddenly feel like a jerk.

"It's not that at all," I say quietly.

And I must be mental. I must be absolutely nuts. Because
the last thing I should be doing is scooping this woman up into
my arms—and yet that's exactly what I do. One arm behind her
knees, the other around her shoulders, straighten up until I'm
holding her like a groom with his bride.

His very startled bride, who's covered in mud and staring
dumbfounded at him.

"See?" I say, lifting her slightly. "This is nothing. So don't
—" I break off, swallowing as I purposefully hold her away from
my body a bit. My voice is gruff as I finish, "Don't be self-
conscious, all right?"

"Yeah," she said faintly, still staring at me with that same
thunderstruck look on her face.

"I'm gonna put you down, okay?"

"Yeah," she repeats.

I don't let her fall this time; I settle her gently on her feet,
steadying her with one hand.

"Now," I say with a sigh, flexing my hands subtly to rid
them of the memory of her skin. "Let me finish the last bits of
the roof. You try..." I wrinkle my nose as I trail off, looking her
over. "Try to wash off a little. You're filthy."

She frowns at me—no doubt telling me that it's my fault
she's covered in mud—but nods and begins rubbing her arms
and legs, holding them out at an angle to get more rain on them.
I turn away, focusing on the task at hand.

It takes me about fifteen more minutes to finish up the roof. I give Molly her privacy during that time, purposefully not looking at her, because earlier I saw her pulling her shirt over her head from the corner of my eye. I can only assume she's trying to get her clothes clean.

Not sure what she's going to put on over her swimsuit in the meantime, but I'm trying not to think about it. I'm also trying not to think about our sleeping arrangements for tonight, or the fact that we're most likely going to have to get up close and personal to warm up after getting so waterlogged.

Nope. I don't think about any of that. I just focus on the roof...

Until I have no choice but to face my immediate future.

"That's as good as it's going to get for now," I call over my shoulder as I climb down from the roof, using a rickety ladder I found inside. "Let's go in."

I hear a vague response from Molly, but she's not loud enough for me to understand what she's saying. When I turn to look at her, she's got her soaked shirt and shorts draped over one arm, and she's shivering in just her bathing suit.

And though it's the last thing I want to do, I open the door to the hut, beckoning her to come inside.

Here goes nothing.

NINE
MOLLY

I HAVE SOME RESERVATIONS ABOUT OUR SLEEPING quarters.

"I'm not trying to be dramatic, but this is my worst nightmare," I say as I stare into the dark interior of the hut, not moving forward.

"Really?" Beckett shoots me a skeptical look before elbowing past me. Then he steps inside the hut, ducking as he passes through the doorway. He turns and looks at me over his shoulder. "So when you fall asleep at night and wake in a cold sweat, it's because you were dreaming of being stranded on a desert island with your brother's best friend? Stranded for a few days *tops,* with basic shelter and drinking water at your disposal? That's what gives you nightmares?"

Well. If he's going to be all *logical* about it.

"Fine," I huff. "No. This is not technically my worst nightmare." I swallow, pointing at what I can see of the hut's interior. "But what kind of little critters and bugs are in there? And are they going to crawl all over me in the night?"

"And here I was, relieved that you weren't going to act like a diva," he says under his breath.

I fold my arms over my chest. "I'm not! I like being outdoors. I like camping and stuff. But being concerned about contracting rabies or malaria does not qualify me for *diva* standing."

"Just get in here," Beckett says with a sigh before turning away from me.

All right. It's fine. True, anything could be lurking in there, and true, I've got a lot of exposed skin for little beasties and buggies to find, but...but...

Crap. I need an upside. Where's the upside?

The roof! There's a roof. That's a positive for sure.

Also a positive: the bug spray I brought along. I dig it out of my bag quickly and then coat myself in a solid three layers before chucking it back in and following Beckett.

I'm short enough that I don't have to duck through the doorway like he did. The fading light outside means it takes a second for my eyes to adjust, but once they do, I peer around with half eagerness and half dread at the interior.

This takes me less than three seconds, because it really is that tiny. I've always loved the trope in books about a couple who only have one bed to sleep in, but somehow I think it's going to be less romantic when both Beckett and I try to squeeze onto that pile of leaves in the corner.

At least I don't see any creepy crawlies.

"Oh, they're in here," Beckett says when I mention this. "I'm sure they're just hiding."

So that's not helpful at all.

There's a little whine of panic in my chest, a worry that's been growing since I went through the contents of my bag. It amplifies itself now, tendrils of fear twisting and spreading like ink in water, as my eyes take in all the places rodents and bugs could be hiding. There are boxes and crates stacked in the corner, prime real estate for rats, and cracks in the floor where there could be entire colonies of insects.

There are probably multiple breeds of spider in this hut, and they're probably plotting my demise right this very second. They will eat me in the night, like that movie where the girl's feet get eaten by rats, and when I wake I will be nothing more than a skeleton—

Nope. Can't think about that. Moving on.

I look at my shirt and my shorts, still hanging over my arm, still as wet as if they just came out of the wash. Then I turn to Beckett.

"I don't suppose there are clothes or blankets anywhere in here," I say. My arms and legs are covered in goosebumps, and there is way more of my body on display than is helpful in this situation. I'm fine wearing my suit while I'm swimming; it's totally cute, as it should be, since it was stupidly expensive. They don't sell high-quality swimsuits for large-bosomed women at department stores or malls. I have to order my swimsuits and bras from a specialty store online if I want proper support. So yeah—this suit was expensive, but it's a price I was willing to pay.

Sleeping in it, though? Especially next to Beckett? No. That's too much.

"There might be," Beckett says. And maybe I'm just imagining things, but I could swear that his eyes skate over my body before he says, "Anything we can find is yours, though."

I can feel my cheeks turning pink, but I just nod. "Thank you," I say quietly. "I'm feeling a little exposed."

Beckett grunts but doesn't say anything else as he begins digging through crates. He pulls out several musty-looking contraptions I don't recognize, followed by a few mesh bags that appear to hold utensils—like a meal kit you'd take camping, sort of—and then, finally, *blessedly*, a large, folded blanket.

I'm by Beckett's side in point-two seconds, one arm outstretched, the other still clutched protectively over the ladies, lest the swimsuit padding fails to do its duty. I'm trying to make the stance look casual, but honestly, I think it probably just looks like I'm holding them up.

Whatever. I can't bring myself to care about what Beckett thinks anymore. Not today, at least. I'll try again tomorrow, maybe.

He passes me the blanket, and my fingers clutch gratefully around the rough wool. It's going to be scratchy, but it's better than nothing.

"Shake it out first," Beckett advises, but I'm already in the process of doing just that. I unfold it all the way before airing it out. I snap the blanket again and again, doing my best not to let it drag on the floor of the hut, and watch as musty clouds puff into the air around us. Not sure how all that dust got there when the blanket has been folded in the bottom of a crate, but oh well. At this point I'd probably be happy to curl up in a barn if it meant I could cover up with hay and go to sleep.

The blanket is rough as I wrap it around my shoulders, but the wool is thick and warm, and I feel immediately better having a way to cover up a bit.

"Thank you," I say as I settle down on top of another crate, my legs tapping against the side of the wood as I examine the dark tartan of the blanket. "For everything." I swallow, then go on, "I don't think I actually said that before. But I appreciate—" Ugh. How do I even say these things to him? "I appreciate what you did during the storm."

There. It isn't eloquent. But it's the best I've got right now.

"You can repay me by not climbing any more trees," Beckett says as he starts on another crate. He rummages for a while, and I just watch. I try not to pay attention to the way the light in the hut is fading more and more with each minute that passes, but the shadows it casts on his biceps—because yes, I'm watching those too—grow fainter and fainter until it's impossible to deny anymore.

Night is falling.

I am still here.

And I've missed the cruise ship departure.

As though he's read my mind—or maybe just the worry on my face—Beckett says, "What are you going to do?"

"About what?" I say, and the forced cheerfulness in my voice makes me cringe.

Beckett clearly doesn't like it either, because he shoots me a glare that looks exactly like that emoji with the flat mouth and the flat eyes—completely unimpressed and begging me to cut the crap.

"I'm going to live it up on the island, apparently," I say, my voice still horribly chipper. "Maybe I'll just stay here forever." I point to the corner of the hut where the leaves have gathered. "Put a bed there, a desk along the wall—"

"Molly."

One word; just my name, spoken in Beckett's serious, quiet voice. He's stopped his rummaging, and though he hasn't stepped away from the open crate or approached me at all, my peripheral vision tells me that his body is turned to face mine, his eyes trained on me.

I blink rapidly against the tears that are trying to make an appearance. Because the truth is, this is bad. This is so bad. I'm stuck here, the cruise ship is almost certainly gone by now, and I don't have—I don't have—my—my—

"Molly." My name from his lips again, but with a start I realize that he's standing right in front of me now, and—oh. I'm crying. I'm *crying*. Great, heaving sobs tearing out of me like I'm a wet cloth that's being wrung out.

"Molly," he says again, his voice urgent. His hands hover awkwardly in the space between us as he stands before me and the crate I'm still perched on. "It's okay. We're going to be fine." My head drops as I give in to the weight of holding it up, and that's when Beckett finally seems to abandon his awkwardness. Just like he pulled me close in the storm, he pulls me close now, stepping forward and wrapping his arms around me. My head is planted somewhere around his ribcage as he pats my back, murmuring meaningless words that somehow soothe me all the same.

I'm not even totally sure why I'm crying. Or rather, I guess, there are a lot of things that could be causing these tears, and I'm not sure which one it is. All of them, maybe; being stuck, missing the ship, the things I have with me—and the things I don't.

"Breathe," Beckett says as another wave of tears hits me. His hand is firm as he rubs my back, but his voice is gentle. "Breathe. Come on. Take a breath with me."

I suck in a lungful of air, making a sound like a winded rhinoceros as I struggle. But Beckett doesn't comment on the noise; he just keeps rubbing my back.

"And again," he says softly. "Good girl. And another."

Somehow it's helpful to have him talking me through each breath, despite the fact that I've been breathing very well on my own for my entire life. His words are a gentle, repetitive mantra that steadies the turbulence raging inside, and several minutes later I'm almost back to normal.

"Look, Molly, we need to go to sleep, okay?" Beckett says. He sounds just as tired as I feel, and the halfhearted pat he delivers to my back only emphasizes it. He needs rest. We both do.

I nod, my forehead rubbing against his shirt, and then finally pull away from him, sitting up straighter.

"Yeah," I say, swiping at my eyes. "Let's do that." I take several deep breaths. "Where should we sleep?"

"I wasn't joking about the bugs and rodents being in here," Beckett says, stepping back and looking around. "So I think we should create a sort of wall with these crates. Like a kid would make a fort, kind of."

I nod. "Yeah," I say again, feeling relieved at this suggestion. I don't want rats to eat my feet in the night. "Okay. Good."

So together we move, pushing and dragging and arranging until there are massive trails in the dirt floor and we've cordoned off what essentially amounts to a tiny, rectangular room with crates for walls.

"Is this the only blanket?" I say, pulling mine a little tighter and praying that his answer won't be *yes*.

"Yes."

Great.

"You take it," I say quickly, unwrapping myself. "I've had it for a bit. I'm warmer now."

It's a lie; I still feel frozen to my bones, which I don't understand at all. It's not freezing outside the hut or within. We're maybe in the sixties. Is it psychological? Is that a thing?

"No," Beckett says, shaking his head. "Keep it. Or we can share; either way. But you need it too."

I blink at him, intending to thank him once again, but what comes out is "You're being really nice."

A snort of laughter, maybe a little bitter, escapes him. "Not really. Your brother would kill me if I let you die on my watch."

Ah. Right. That makes sense, I guess. But even though it's stupid, I can't help the small twinge of disappointment I feel. It's not like I was expecting him to confess his love or to say he cares more about my comfort than his own. I know that's not the case.

So why is my heart sinking?

"Tired," I mutter. "I'm tired." That has to be it. This has been a fantastically terrible evening, and even though night hasn't fallen in earnest yet, I'm wiped out. Of course my emotions are going to be iffy at a time like this.

"Get in," Beckett says, thankfully not bringing up the fact that I'm talking to myself. He nods at our makeshift sleeping chamber, and I eye the space warily.

It's going to be a tight fit. No starfishing tonight. And what if I do something embarrassing in my sleep, like snuggle up to him? What if I snore? What if I talk in my sleep?

"Should I put the blanket down first?" I say, because I need to stop psyching myself out.

"Oh," Beckett says, rubbing the back of his neck. He looks at the blanket in my arms and then at the dirt floor. "Yeah. And then we can kind of roll ourselves up in it."

Like two little island burritos.

"I don't guess there are any types of fish that sleep rolled up in leaves or whatever," Beckett says.

I blink at him, frankly shocked by the question. "Uh," I say. "Not quite, that I know of. But betta fish—"

"Those are the blue ones in aquariums a lot, right?"

"Not always blue, but yeah. They sometimes use leaves as little hammocks, sort of." I blink at him again. "Why do you ask?"

He shrugs, looking self-conscious. "Just seems like you like to talk about fish, so I thought...I don't know. You might want to tell me about it."

That's...unexpectedly sweet.

But he points to our little crate room before I can say anything. "Spread the blanket," he says.

You know," I say, leaning over the edge of the crate nearest me and spreading the blanket as neatly as possible into the space. "There's a specific group of fish called sand-sleeping wrasses that bury themselves to sleep. They sort of burrow into the sand."

"I'll stick to my bed."

The two of us clamber over the crates to reach the space in the middle, him gracefully, me less so. Then, not making eye contact with each other, we both lower ourselves to the ground and lie down. It's an awkward shuffle of muttered "sorrys" and knocking elbows and knees, but we make it.

And then we're just lying there, the two of us stretched out side by side like a couple of sardines staring at the roof, and my mind is speeding once more through all the ways this could go wrong.

I might snore. I might talk in my sleep—something I've never done before but am suddenly very concerned about. I might cuddle up to him or spoon him or something. I even read a book one time where these people *kissed* because they both thought they were dreaming. Crap.

"I'm sorry if I kiss you in my sleep," I blurt out, the words rushing from my mouth.

Silence.

Pure silence, broken only by the sound of the rain on the thatched roof.

Then...

"*What?*" Beckett says, his head jerking to the left to look at me.

"It's not going to happen," I say quickly, keeping my eyes firmly on the roof of the hut and cursing my stupid mouth. "I'm sure it's not. I shouldn't have said that. I was just thinking of all the things that could go wrong and that seemed like a possibility because I read this book one time where that happened and I wanted to let you know that—"

"No one is kissing anyone in their sleep," he cuts me off firmly. "On accident or on purpose. That is not happening. Do you understand?"

It's a warning he's giving me, unmistakable and clear.

I nod rapidly. "Of course," I say, the words spilling out of me, tumbling over one another in an effort to do damage control. "It's not like I *want* to kiss you. Obviously. And as far as I know I've never kissed anyone else in my sleep—"

"Molly," Beckett cuts me off again, his voice strained like he's speaking through gritted teeth. "I do not want to hear the word *kiss* come out of your mouth again. I cannot handle that. Go to sleep now, please."

"You don't have to be rude about it," I mutter, tugging the flap of blanket on my left up around my body as far as it will go.

"I'm not trying—I'm just—" But he breaks off with a sound of frustration, and when I look over at him, he's in the process of rolling onto his side, his back to me. And even though he's still right there, even though I can hear him breathing, it leaves me feeling incredibly alone.

Like I might be the only person in the world tonight.

The tears burn hot behind my lids as I squeeze my eyes shut, trying to bully my brain into shutting down for the night. I can feel the tracks those tears leave as they slide down my temples and land somewhere in my hairline, and as hard as I try, I can't seem to stop them. I guess it's a good thing, then, that Beckett has turned away from me. He already doesn't like me; no need to make him think I'm completely pathetic. Does a guy like Beckett even know how to cry?

Unbidden, a memory floats into my mind, hazy and worn around the edges. Beckett as a kid, maybe in second or third grade, hugging my mom fiercely and blinking tears from his eyes when she came to visit him on Parents' Day. He would have to have been at least that young, because I remember being with my mom, which means I wasn't in school yet. I didn't understand then why he was crying, but I get it now. With his mom gone and his dad devoting his life to his job, he must have felt so lonely and embarrassed to have no one come for him—and so grateful when my mom *did*.

Slowly, I let my head fall to the side. I take in what I can see of the man next to me—damp, messy brown hair; the tanned skin of his neck; one freckle I know to be near his hairline, though it's too dark to see that detail now.

He's so gruff, so much a loner, but how much of that is because that's what he's always known?

The tears continue to slide hot over my skin, and I turn to look back at the roof of the hut. I think Beckett is asleep already, but I try to be as quiet as possible when I sniffle, just to make sure. When he doesn't react to the sound, I breathe a little easier.

"Beckett," I whisper softly to his sleeping form. No movement—good. I need to get this out, need to admit it to myself instead of running from it, but it will only make Beckett worry. "I don't—" I manage before another wave of tears hits. I force myself to go on, to say the words that I've been hiding from. "I don't...have my medicine."

There. There they are, spilled from my lips and into the damp, musty silence. The one fact that I've been avoiding since I went through my bag a couple hours ago and realized the problem: I don't have my anticonvulsant. I brought one extra pill when I packed my backpack this morning, and I took that dose earlier this afternoon, thinking I'd be back to the ship by now—

"*Crap*, Molly."

I startle at the rough sound of Beckett's voice in the rain-spattered silence, shying instinctively away as he rolls back toward me.

"You're—awake," I squeak.

Beckett sits up without any delay, and it's clear that he hasn't just woken up; there's no grogginess or sluggishness to his voice or motions. He was never asleep.

I sit up too, mostly because it's awkward to be lying down next to someone who's sitting. I watch as Beckett rubs both hands over his face.

"What do you mean, you don't have your medicine?" he says, finally looking over at me.

Oh, look; more tears.

"I mean I don't have it," I say, wiping my eyes with the backs of my hands. "I had one that I took this afternoon, but that's it."

Night hasn't fallen completely yet, but in here it's dark enough that I can only barely make out Beckett's expression—stormy and frustrated.

"I'm sorry," I say, crying freely now and giving up on drying my eyes. "I'm sorry. I just thought I'd be back on the ship this evening." I wrap my arms around my knees and bury my head, the tears coming fast and steady.

This is what's been making me cry.

"How many pills do you take each day?" Beckett says. His voice is low, close, like he's speaking directly into my ear.

I let go of my knees with one hand and hold up three fingers. Beckett swears softly, a puff of breath against my right temple, before falling silent.

It's only a second or two later, though, that I feel his hand on my back.

"Come on, Baby O'Malley," he says, his voice heavy, that hand trailing up and down my spine. "Let's go to sleep. We'll talk about this in the morning."

"I'm not a child," I spit out, because it's just one more irritant piling onto my overburdened shoulders. I lift my head up and glare at him. "I'm a grown woman, Beckett Donovan."

"I'm trying not to notice," he says hoarsely—what is *that* supposed to mean?—and what little I can see of his face is closed off, a mask of neutrality. "Let's sleep, all right? Are you warm?"

"No," I sniffle, lying back down and closing my eyes so I don't have to look at him. "I'm weirdly cold."

I hear him sigh, hear him shift and adjust as he lies down too.

And then...one hand at the curve of my waist.

A tug that has me rolling onto my side, facing Beckett.

My eyes pop open in surprise just in time to catch the look on his face as he pulls my body into his: pained. Conflicted. Jaw clenched, eyes burning.

And then my front is pressed to his front, my head tucked under his chin, his arm draped over me. With that arm he grabs the tail end of the blanket on my other side and pulls it up until it covers me.

Warm. He's so warm. And he's holding me—honest-to-goodness *holding me* in his arms, like we're lovers.

We're not lovers. Not even close. But maybe...

"This makes us friends, right?" I murmur sleepily into his chest.

He's silent for so long that I think he really has fallen asleep this time. But then I hear him, so quiet I almost miss it.

"We don't need to be friends, Molly," he says, speaking into my hair. His voice is almost...regretful? "We just need to sleep."

I disagree. I want to be his friend.

But I'm asleep before those words can make it out.

TEN
BECKETT

HAVING MOLLY O'MALLEY IN MY ARMS AS THE NIGHT stretches on is a strange kind of torture. *Strange* because I shouldn't be feeling like this. My heart shouldn't be pounding violently against my rib cage. My mind should not be cataloguing every single curve I feel. None of this should be happening.

I should be vaguely indifferent at best. This should affect me the same way as if I were cuddling with a Golden Retriever.

Yes. That's it. From now on Molly will be relegated to Golden Retriever status.

Except...Molly has warm, soft *skin,* not fur. There's nothing remotely dog-like about the shape of her. And if she tilted her head up and licked my face...I have to admit, though only ever to myself and only this once, that I don't even think I would be grossed out.

That is how attracted I am to this woman. She could swipe her tongue up my cheek and instead of pushing her away, I'd have to stop myself from kissing her. Add in the fact that her personality is magnetic, a ray of sunshine cutting through all the defenses I try to keep in place, and I've got a recipe for trouble.

"Golden Retriever," I mutter under my breath. "Golden Retriever. Yellow fur and dog breath and about half her current IQ." Because Golden Retrievers might be smart, but Molly is smarter.

I'm not sure if Molly hears me, but her body curls further into mine at my words, her head nuzzling my chest. I quickly adjust the blanket so she's better covered. Then she shifts again, and I tilt my head away from her, my jaw clenched as I breathe deeply.

Golden Retriever, Golden Retriever, Golden Retriever...

Crap. It's not working.

This is not a dog. This is a woman. And she is inconveniently adorable with the most perfect curves and I want to take care of her and I am just going to have to *deal* with all of those things. I'm going to have to suck it up and *deal. With. It.*

I will tell absolutely no one about these thoughts and feelings. Not one single person. I will not even acknowledge them to myself after this moment.

So I lie there while Molly sleeps, my arms around her, and I try to drift off myself. I try counting sheep—which has never worked for me, by the way, so I don't know why I bother—and I try counting my breaths. But every time my eyes drift shut, they pop right back open.

Because the woman pressed up against me is seizure-prone and out of medicine, and whenever I think about the possibility of sleeping through one of her seizures and not being able to help her...something deep in my gut twists with a dread I rarely feel.

It's not entirely logical, this desire to stay awake; I know that. I desperately need sleep. But it's hard to banish the impulse to take care of her, to make sure she's safe.

Molly O'Malley is not my responsibility. I owe her nothing. I'm not her brother or her father or her boyfriend or even her *friend*.

These are the things I tell myself as we lie here, but they ring false. Because right now, I'm the only one here with her. There's no one else. Not to mention, she's Wes's little sister.

And...I don't know. There's something about her that makes me want to protect her. Which makes no sense at all; she's not helpless. But that's the impulse that seems to have developed over the course of this hellacious day.

No, I think furiously. Didn't I *just* say I wasn't going to acknowledge these feelings again?

I slam my eyes closed, squeezing them shut so hard I see starbursts behind my lids. I try to force my mind to quiet, pushing away all thoughts of the woman in my arms. This time as I attempt sleep, I count not my breaths but Molly's; it's this compromise between ignoring her and keeping watch over her that finally seems to work. My brain succumbs to the tired monotony of listening to her inhales and exhales, and sometime a few hours before dawn, I finally drift to sleep.

"BECKETT?"

Her voice is soft, little more than a murmur in my ear, but it pulls me to the surface of consciousness until I gradually become aware of my surroundings—hard ground beneath me, softness in my arms, the sound of gentle rain outside.

My eyes flutter open, squinting against the wan daylight that's starting to stream in through the cracks in the walls.

"Molly?"

"Hmm?" she says lazily, and her face pops into my field of vision. She props herself up on one elbow as the blanket falls away from her, and my eyes trace the curve of her neck, that perfectly kissable juncture of smooth, pale skin where the strap of her swimsuit disappears over her shoulder.

My view is obstructed as Molly leans closer to me, smiling sleepily, before dropping a tiny kiss on the tip of my nose. She seems amused by my reaction as she leans back again; her lips curve into a wide smile, her eyes dancing as she laughs.

"Look at that," she says, placing one finger under my chin and closing my gaping mouth. "Look at that face you're making."

"You—you can't—"

"Mmm," she hums, still looking amused. "Can't I, though?" She leans back in.

Soft lips on my neck.

Hot breath on my ear.

"Molly," I gasp in protest—even as my arms tighten around her.

"I was just thinking," she murmurs into the patch of skin below my ear. "We're stuck here, and I like you. I've always liked you. May as well enjoy ourselves, right?"

"No!" I get out. My brain is on the fritz, my blood humming with want, my hands itching to trace her curves. "No," I say again.

She pulls away, pouting, a ridiculous face with that bottom lip pushed out in a way that makes me want to nip at it. "You're no fun," she says, giving me the most pathetic puppy-dog eyes I've ever seen. "No fun at all..."

And then darkness.

"Beckett!"

I jerk awake all at once, my arms already pushing Molly away as the fragments of my dream linger.

"Beckett!" Molly says again. Her voice is close to my ear, like it was in that stupid dream, but there's nothing sexy or seductive about it. I'd place this tone somewhere in "squawk" territory.

"Ow, Molly, my ear," I groan, untangling my arms from around her.

"I have to pee, Beckett!" she yelps, pulling herself free and then bolting upright. "Like, *so* bad," she says as she dances from foot to foot. "Where do I pee?"

"Outside," I say, pointing in the vague direction of the door. "Obviously outside, Molly."

"Outside," she says breathlessly as she scrambles over the crates that surround us, stumbling her way to the door that's still hanging slightly off its hinges. She throws it open and bolts outside, disappearing from view.

And I honestly couldn't tell you why I start to laugh then. I truly don't know. Maybe it's that I'm feeling a little off-kilter after that dream, and Dream Molly juxtaposed with Morning Molly are so starkly different that all I can do is see the humor. I don't know. Either way, some of the tension bleeds out of me as I shift on the hard ground, bringing one arm up behind my head.

Probably gonna need a lobotomy to get all memories of that dream out of my mind, but other than that, I feel oddly light this morning. I must have slept better than I thought.

Molly comes barreling back in two minutes later. "It's still raining," she says unnecessarily.

"Yeah," I say, eyeing her damp hair and swimsuit. I push myself into sitting position before standing up. "I can see that."

"Also," she says. "I feel kind of awkward? Because I'm pretty sure I majorly invaded your personal space last night. Not to mention I was squashed right up against you." Her hand moves up to play with the end of her braid as she speaks, her cheeks turning pink as she tries and fails to hold my gaze.

"Not a problem," I say, because what else am I supposed to say? After that dream, I'm just glad *I* didn't try anything in my sleep. Molly's limbs tangled up with mine were less offensive than she would have found my subconscious's projections.

Now *there's* an intriguing thought, one that floods in before I can stop it. What would she think if she knew I'd dreamed about her? Would she be upset? Or would she like it, her cheeks turning the same pink as when she was up in that tree—

"Stop it!" I say to myself, swearing internally.

There's silence for a second, punctuated only by the sound of rain coming from outside. Then Molly speaks. "Um. Sorry?" she says, giving me a confused look.

"Not you," I say quickly, feeling like an idiot. "I was—not—not you. Sorry. Never mind."

Why do I even speak? Life as a mute might be worth exploring.

Ugh. I'm being stupid. This is just Baby O'Malley—something inside me twinges uncomfortably at calling her that, but I force myself to repeat the term several times in my head, just to remind myself how off-limits she is—so it's not like I need to impress her. It's not like she's someone whose opinion of me matters.

Yes. Exactly. Her opinion of me doesn't concern me. She could think I'm the world's biggest jerk and I wouldn't care. I wouldn't care at all.

Not one bit.

"So," she says, the word gusting out of her as she stands in the middle of the hut, hands on her hips, looking around. "What now? What needs to happen so we can get out of here?"

"Preferably it would stop raining," I say immediately,

because I've already been thinking about this. "And we need to see if there was any damage to the boat."

"Probably not. Right?" she says as she turns to me. "The damage to this little place was minimal, and it's not nearly as sturdy as a speedboat."

I shake my head. "It doesn't necessarily work like that. The speedboat is out in the open, whereas the trees surrounding this hut probably provided a lot of protection where debris was concerned."

"Hmm," she says, biting her lower lip as she thinks. "Like eyelashes protect the eyes."

I blink at the comparison. I hadn't thought of it like that, but..."Yes," I say. "Exactly."

She nods. "All right. Let's go check on the boat, then. I need to get off of this island."

The following silence holds all the words she's not saying: that she needs to get back to her medication, back to her family.

"But the seizures," I say, rubbing the back of my neck. I sit on one of the crates. "Sorry to bring it up, but just so I can be prepared—they're triggered by..."

"They happen when I'm in between sleep and awake," she says promptly, coming to sit next to me. She's short enough that her feet only skim the floor, while mine rest completely flat on the packed dirt.

"That's it?" I say.

She hesitates before nodding. "That's the only known trigger. Which is good, I guess—that they don't just happen out of the blue."

Despite saying it's good, though, she looks troubled, her gaze far away, the corners of her lips downturned.

I shouldn't pry. I shouldn't care what's putting that look on her face. And yet...

"But?" I say into the rain-saturated silence.

"But...I don't know." Her shrug is a halfhearted thing as she goes on, "I worry."

I can feel my brow creasing, but I don't stop it. I'm too busy focusing on her. "What do you mean?"

She sighs. "I mean, I *worry*. I worry when I go anywhere with flashing lights. I worry when I don't get enough sleep. I don't think it's anxiety, I think it's just normal worries. The mind is programmed to throw up red flags against things that could hurt us, right, and so even though I'm medicated and well-controlled, I worry."

I nod slowly. "Okay, yeah. That makes sense."

"The problem is, I can't really *tell* anyone I worry. Because then they freak out and start watching me like I'm going to drop dead at any moment."

I don't like those words coming out of her mouth. I *really* don't like them. But I don't say anything; I just let her keep going, because from what she's saying, it sounds like these are thoughts she's never spoken out loud. I have too many of those to deny her the chance to get them out.

"And so my normal, understandable worries get turned into this big flashing warning sign, and everyone is on red alert just staring at the epileptic girl who's just trying to go about her business. That kind of attention is one of my worst nightmares. So even though I get nervous sometimes, I just..." She trails off. "I just keep it to myself."

"I get that," I say after a second. It's all I can offer her.

"Do you?" she says, sounding relieved. She turns her entire body to face me. "I'm making sense?"

"Yes," I say firmly. "Definitely." And then, even though I remind myself of some self-help text or a walking therapy session, I add, "Those are completely valid feelings."

"Are they?" she says, and the look on her face is almost

desperate. Like no one has ever told her that, and she badly needs to hear it.

"Yes," I say, even as a strange, simmering irritation edges into my gut. Why is no one telling her these things? Why is no one giving her this kind of support? I'm a crotchety, antisocial emotional dunce, and even I know that human beings need to feel understood. That's basic science. Is no one meeting that need for her? Wes, her parents, her friends?

"Look at that," she says softly, pulling me out of my weirdly derailed thoughts, and my stomach flips—because it's the same thing she said in my dream.

"Look at what?" I say, my voice coming out rough around the edges.

A little smile hovers over her features as she points to my face. "You're glowering. Have I mortally offended you somehow?"

"No," I say, some of my frustration leaking into my voice. "I just think it's stupid that no one is telling you these things when you obviously need to hear them."

Molly's head tilts to one side as she looks at me with interest. "Upset on my behalf? I'm touched."

"It's not that," I mutter. This might be a lie. But how do I explain? It doesn't even make sense to me, how I'm feeling. The closest logic I can come up with is the vague idea that if I'm going to use my body to shelter this woman through a storm, her family and friends better be sheltering her too—whatever form that takes.

I know. It doesn't make sense. It doesn't make sense at *all*.

"To be fair," Molly says with a little smile. "I've never really told anybody about feeling that way. So...it's not their fault."

"You haven't told anyone?"

"Nope," she says comfortably. "Just you."

"Why not?" I say.

She shrugs. "No one wants to hear my thoughts on these things. They'll just worry." Then, her eyes dancing, she adds, "And you're *sure* we aren't friends?"

"I'm sure," I say. The words are automatic, rolling off my tongue without thought. I don't *need* to think about them. Because I feel very certain that I can't be friends with this woman. I'm too attracted to her, too drawn to her in ways I don't understand—she's the flame and I'm the moth.

The completely confused moth.

"Ah," she says, her sparkle leaving her eyes as her gaze drops to her lap. "Got it."

I don't miss the hurt in her voice, and regret twists around my rib cage somewhere in the vicinity of my heart. Bizarrely, that feeling of regret only intensifies as I let myself study her—her hair frizzy in its messy braid, her skin smudged with mud, her eyes tired.

"I—it's not—"

"No, I get it," she cuts me off. "Best friend's little sister and all. Nothing in common." The smile she aims at me is bright, but it's too strained, cracked around the edges, and her voice has that same forced quality it had last night when she tried to joke about being stuck here.

"Actually," I say, and I'm speaking before I can stop myself, before I can even think things through all the way. "That's not true. We have plenty in common. So...yeah." I try to take a deep breath without *looking* like I'm taking a deep breath, even as a deep sense of foreboding comes over me. Then I spit out the words I'll probably come to regret later:

"We...can be friends."

ELEVEN
BECKETT

I'M NOT SURE HOW TRUE MY WORDS ARE. I'M NOT SURE I know how to be friends with her.

All I know is I can't stand the look on Molly's face when she's being shot down.

Her eyebrows shoot up now, though, and her feet cease their swinging. "Really?" She shoots me a skeptical look that I frankly don't appreciate. "You're conceding?" Her nose wrinkles. "But you're so...antisocial."

"And you're a perpetual people pleaser," I say with a snort.

"You don't hear me complaining. *You* were the one who wanted to be friends—"

"I'm not a people pleaser!" she says, looking offended.

My jaw drops. "Are you serious?"

"Yes!"

I shake my head slowly, angling my body toward her and ignoring the way our knees brush. "Molly O'Malley, you are one of the biggest people pleasers I've ever met. You are incapable of saying no or imposing on anyone."

"I hardly think you're qualified to make assessments like that about someone you barely know—"

"You stayed here with me on the island even though you didn't want to," I say, holding up one finger. "You walked the perimeter of the astronomy facility because your mom begged you to, even though you originally said no." Another finger up. "You purposefully don't tell people things that you think will worry them." A third finger. "You are absolutely a people pleaser."

Molly glares at me. "Well, you refuse to form relationships with anyone because you don't believe they'll be able to love you or stick around."

My eyes widen, but I don't even have time to respond before Molly is clamping one hand over her mouth, looking mortified.

"Oh my goodness," she says. Then, dropping her hand to play with the hem of her shorts—which she mercifully put back on earlier—she whispers, "I am so sorry. I shouldn't have said that."

I swallow back the tangle of emotions rising in my throat. "Why not?" I say. "It's true." I pause. "That's why you said it, right?"

"Well, yeah," she says miserably. "I mean, maybe. I don't know. I was just—stupid things—just what I noticed—"

It's a combination of mumbling and stuttering, but it gets her point across well enough. And one thought crystallizes in my mind as I listen to her babble: for most of this woman's life, she's probably been severely underestimated, with her quirkiness and the constant fish talk and the lack of filter.

And yet she's saying about me the same things my school-appointed therapist said when I was in the seventh grade, angry at the world and pushing everyone but a select few out of my life.

And she's right.

I *do* avoid relationships, whether familial or platonic or romantic. I avoid most of them. I like to believe that I've been fine on my own for most of my life.

And yet I also can't deny the impact the O'Malleys have had on me. They've been more of a family to me than my real family. Where would I be without them?

"You know," Molly begins, and even though I've only been with her for the last twenty-four hours, I already recognize this tone of voice—she's about to tell me some obscure fact, most likely about fish.

"There are quite a few animals in the wild who are solitary by nature, but even they make exceptions," she says, proving me right. "Most kinds of skunk are considered to be loners, for example, but in extreme cold, they're known to share dens. The black rhinoceros is notoriously grumpy and antisocial—*except* for when it's time to mate. Both male and female snow leopards enjoy being solitary and unmatched, but it's a characteristic that's leading to their endangerment as a species." She pauses, looking thoughtful, and I'm hanging onto every word that spills from her lips. Why? Why am I so interested in antisocial animals?

Or...am I just interested in *Molly?*

"Even those animals, whose behaviors are dictated mostly by instinct, understand that a completely solitary life goes against basic survival."

"So...what?" I say, hopping off the crate and stretching my legs. "You saying I remind you of a black rhinoceros?"

A little smile tugs at her lips. "I'm saying you're lucky you have me as a friend," she says, and she hops off too. "I will cease my people-pleasing ways so that I can tell you all the things you don't want to hear, like how you need people in your life."

Then she smiles at me, and it's a real smile this time. "That way you won't go extinct."

I shake my head. "Don't get ahead of yourself, Baby O'Malley." I look at her, suddenly curious to see what she'll do. I hesitate, then say, "I know you hate that name, but I'm going to call you that anyway. Okay?"

She sighs, her smile dropping. "Yeah," she says. "That's fine."

I roll my eyes. "No." I shake my head. "It's *not* fine, Molly. Say no. Tell me no."

She blinks at me, her smile back, looking halfway incredulous. "You—you're really not going to call me that anymore?"

"Not if you don't want me to," I say, exasperated. Before I think better of it, I put my hands on her shoulders and steer her back to the crate, giving her a little push to get her to sit. "Listen to me, Molly," I say. "Don't settle for things you don't want to settle for. Do what *you* want, not what other people want for you. Got it?"

She blinks up at me, looking dazed.

"Do what I want?" she breathes.

Something about her tone sends shivers racing down my spine—not the creepy kind but the warm, thrilling kind. Her gaze darts over my face, ping-ponging between my features, until—

Until—

Her eyes settle, like they've always belonged there, on my lips.

My stomach flips, electricity humming to life between us, tense and palpable—a rubber band pulled taut.

And it's only then, far too late, that I realize how precarious our position is.

My hands on her shoulders. Her skin soft, warm. Our faces

just inches apart as I stand there, looking down at her where she's seated.

Her body language is unmistakable—she's not leaning away, she's leaning *toward* me. Lips parted, cheeks flushed, pupils dilated.

I swallow, and some sort of disconnect seems to be happening between my brain and my body. My brain is telling me to let go of her, to take my hands off her shoulders, to step back. But all my body does is move closer, my grip on her tightening.

And I've...forgotten her question. I've completely forgotten what she said. That's how lost I am to this moment that strums between us, all tension and rain-drenched silences.

"What?" I manage to get out.

A slow smile curls over her lips as she tilts her chin up, angling her face even further toward mine. "You said I should do what I want," she whispers.

Bad. This is bad. This is the version of Molly that showed up in my dream. Disarmingly seductive and completely self-assured. Clear on what she wants and willing to chase it down.

What is it about her that's holding me in place? I'm attracted to her, yes, but for some reason all I can think of is the way she smiles when she talks about random fish facts, and the way she laughs with her whole being, sunshine incarnate.

"Did I?" I say hoarsely, even as my mind races. It's one thing to be physically attracted to her, but I absolutely *cannot* develop real feelings for this woman.

She nods, her smile widening. "You did." Her gaze moves to play with my lips once more.

Retreat! my mind blares at me. *Snap out of it!*

I blink against the potent force of her stare, trying rapidly to collect my senses. "Stop looking at me like that," I all but growl as the blood hums in my veins.

"Like what?" Her words are breathless, her smile playful.

"You know exactly what I mean," I say as my eyes drop to her lips. "Stop looking at me like you want to kiss me." I can't believe I'm saying this, can't believe I'm actually acknowledging what's happening here, but it's undeniable.

And it needs to stop, *now*.

I remove my hands from her shoulders as though I've been burned; I scramble backward, stumbling over my own feet as I go. Then, with absolutely no dignity left to speak of, I all but hurl myself out the door and into the rainy morning.

WHEN MOLLY EMERGES from the hut some fifteen minutes later, I'm feeling pretty proud of myself.

I don't look like a man whose best friend's little sister was about to kiss him. I *definitely* don't look like a man who would have kissed her back.

I look calm. Cool. Like a master of rainwater collection as I drop purification tablets into our containers of drinking water.

Is my heart back to normal? No. Not yet. Mostly because I keep remembering the look in her eyes, and my pulse spikes all over again. But from the outside, I'm pretty confident she won't know the difference.

For her part, Molly looks completely unfazed. In fact, it seems a little unfair. She's not blushing as she approaches me; her expression isn't sheepish or embarrassed or concerned in any way about what almost happened between us.

Nope; Molly O'Malley looks like this is just another day in paradise.

"So we can drink that?" she says, pointing at the large plastic container that's brimming with water.

"Yes," I say with a nod. If she's going to act like nothing

happened, I'll do the same. "There was a bottle of water purification tablets in there"—I jerk my head at the hut behind us— "but even if there hadn't been, it would most likely still be fine."

"Excellent," Molly says, her eyes shining with anticipation as she eyes the water. "I'm crazy thirsty."

"Drink," I say with another nod. "Take a lot; as much as you want."

She looks at me, her eyebrows jumping briefly with surprise before her face smooths out again. "Are you not having any?"

"I will in a minute. I just need to check a few other things," I say, stalling. Logically my mind knows that there's more than enough water for both of us here, but I'm still going to wait for her to be done. I do my best to tell myself this isn't weird; I just want to make sure she gets enough to drink. That's a normal thing friends do.

Very normal. Very friendly. Not weirdly overprotective.

Molly removes her canteen from her backpack and upends it, dumping the contents onto the muddy ground. Some sort of soda spills out, and I shake my head, sighing. Only Molly would have thought bringing soda rather than water was a good idea. I feel better as I watch her refill the flask, though.

"You got any food in there?" I say as I look at her bag. Last night we didn't eat anything—which was stupid—but I think we both were so tired and drained that it just didn't even register. Now, though, my stomach is twisting, collapsing in on itself like a dying star.

"I do," she says, screwing the lid back on her bottle, "and you're welcome to any of it, but it's not going to be very filling." I watch as she tilts her head back and begins gulping down great mouthfuls of water. Her throat bobs as she drinks, a strangely hypnotizing sight, and I have to tear my eyes away so I can focus.

"Can I get it out?" I say, turning my gaze back to the bag.

She gives me a thumbs up as she continues to guzzle water, which I take as a yes. So I step toward her and reach down, picking up the bag and then beginning to dig. I move past a few bottles and tubes of sprays and lotions before finding a small plastic container that looks promising, as well as a freezer bag with granola bars. One glance inside the plastic box reveals a bunch of little cookies, probably baked by Mrs. O'Malley, and I grab a shortbread Christmas tree before fastening the lid back in place. Then I move to the freezer bag of granola bars and pull two of them out.

"Here," I say, passing one to Molly.

She takes it but wrinkles her nose as she looks at it, holding it with two fingers like it's contaminated. "I don't even like these," she says. "I just wanted to make myself feel better about bringing cookies."

"Eat it anyway if you want to keep up any kind of strength," I advise. "Then we can get going, if you're ready." The rain is starting to slow down, which is promising; if the boat is in okay shape, we might be able to get back to the main island this morning.

"I'm more than ready," she says, and I just nod; I understand the feeling.

We finish eating and drinking, and even though we're scarfing our food down, it still feels like we're moving too slowly; every second that ticks by adds another pound to the weight of anxiety I'm carrying. I try not to let Molly see my thoughts churning in my head—thoughts of seizures and sleep deprivation and the medication she doesn't have—and she doesn't give any indication that she notices. But if there's one thing I'm sure of, it's that people, myself included, probably don't give that brain of hers enough credit.

So who knows? She could be essentially reading my mind at this very moment, and I likely wouldn't know the difference.

I try not to think about that.

It takes us a bit to get from the hut back to the boat when we've finished our makeshift breakfast, and it takes me a full hour of inspecting the speedboat before I'm finally convinced it's in good enough shape to get us out of here. I'm glad I had the presence of mind to cover it before Molly and I left the beach yesterday, because I think that's what's saved us. There's a crack in the glass windshield that I don't remember seeing before, but the cover prevented the interior from sustaining much in the way of water damage—including damage to the inboard engine.

"So," Molly says from behind me, and I jump, steadying myself with one hand on the side of the boat.

"Yeah?" I say, turning around.

"About this morning," she says. She's not quite making eye contact; it's more like her gaze is hovering somewhere around the middle of my nose, and I can't help that but notice the blush staining her cheeks. "It won't happen again."

Finally her eyes come up to meet mine, and when they connect, she smiles impishly. It's not the expression I expected to see, but somehow I'm not completely surprised. Nor am I surprised when she holds three fingers up and says, "Scout's honor."

I don't know how to answer her, or what to do about the faint, sinking disappointment that accompanies her promise. I didn't think she was going to bring this up again; she's been acting like it never happened. So I just nod.

"It's possible that it was just the adrenaline getting to me. You don't necessarily need to read into it," she goes on.

I raise an eyebrow at her, questioning.

"It's a thing!" she says, her eyes wide and guileless as she explains. "It really is. People who are in high-intensity situations together frequently bond more quickly than they would otherwise. It's a phenomenon. It probably has a name and everything."

I nod slowly. "I have heard of that, actually. Maybe that's why..." I let my words fade away as I begin reviewing the past twenty-four hours, seeing my feelings in a new light.

"That's why...what?"

I step closer to her. "That's probably it," I say, the words spilling out of me in an effort to be validated. I ignore my embarrassment as I go on, "I've been feeling kind of—kind of *weird* about you. That's probably it, right?"

She tilts her head, looking curious. "Weird how?"

"I don't know," I mutter, trying to shove my hand through my hair and failing because of how grimy it is now. "Just... weird. Sort of overprotective."

"Ah," she says slowly, and I swear I can hear the gears turning in her mind. It's an infuriating feeling to see her thinking so hard about something, but not being able to tell exactly *what* she's thinking.

"Molly?" I prompt. "That's probably what's happening, right?"

She hesitates for a split second, so brief I might even be imagining things, before giving me a decisive nod. "Very possible."

"Yeah," I say, slightly breathless as relief courses through me. "That's it."

"Either way," she says with a shrug. "This morning won't happen again."

"Yeah," I repeat. "Got it."

"On one condition," she adds, and I freeze. "I have one condition."

I sigh. Of *course* she has one condition. "Fine. Let's hear it."

"We have to be friends," she says. Her voice is completely

matter-of-fact, like she's been thinking about this for a long time.

"I thought we already decided to be friends," I say.

She shakes her head. "I'm talking about *actual* friends. You were just saying that before, because you felt bad. I'm not stupid, Beckett. But from now on, no being weird or standoffish. I'm going to try to be less of a people pleaser, and you can practice forming relationships by hanging out with me. Deal?"

I watch as she swallows and something more vulnerable passes over her face. "I kind of really need someone to be close to right now. It doesn't even have to last forever. Just until we find my family again?"

And I hate the way she's already making concessions—like she's trying to appease me by promising she won't be too much of a pest. Because it makes it crystal clear that she thinks I genuinely dislike her. A twist of guilt tugs at my insides, as well as something warmer—the bizarre desire to give her more than she's asking for, just to see how happy it makes her. It's a tangle of emotions that don't make sense.

But...friends. *Real* friends. With Molly O'Malley, the woman who has me strangely off-kilter.

It's...more appealing than it should be, a tempting prospect. And she's talking about practicing forming relationships, but what worries me is that with Molly, it doesn't feel like the kind of thing I would *need* to force, or to practice. She's one of the most natural, genuine people I've ever met. If I could get out of my head, a true friendship with her would be as easy as breathing.

I study her as she stands there in front of me. There's a smudge of mud on her left cheek, just under her eye. Her hair is desperately trying to escape its confines, reduced to a mass of red that gives off the same feeling as a tornado in a straight jacket. Her eyes are sparkling up at me, her lips tilting at the corners as she waits patiently for me to say something.

"All right," I say. I can't say why, but it's the smudge of mud that seals the deal for me. I'll be friends with Molly, *true* friends with her, so that I can make sure her face is always clean and her smile is always genuine. "Friends. For real this time."

"Excellent!" she says, her smile spreading widely across her pale, mud-smudged face. She moves to stand next to me, so that we're both looking at the side of the boat instead of at each other, and then—to my surprise—she swings one arm up around me.

Except she's really too small to drape her arm around my shoulders. She tries, but after three attempts, I just laugh and push her off. "You're too short," I say, shaking my head. After the briefest of hesitations, I force myself to relax, to treat her like my instincts are urging me to. So I let my arm drape around her shoulders instead.

She melts into my side, and something inside me eases at the contact—a tightness that I didn't realize was there. It's similar to the feeling of sleeping with her in my arms, except *easier*, somehow. Like this is less stressful for my mind and my heart when I'm not trying to force our relationship to fit any specific mold.

And I'm not sure what mold it *would* fit into. I don't have many female friends, but I don't interact physically with the ones I do have. Nor do I treat my guy friends this way. But Molly isn't a girlfriend or a lover or a significant other of any kind, either. It's like she pointed out: she's someone I'm stuck with in this highly unusual, highly charged situation. It makes sense that things will be a little different with her, especially after she's admitted that she needs someone to hold onto right now.

I can be what she needs. Maybe not forever, but for today, and maybe tomorrow too.

I just hope I don't regret it. But I can't let myself think about that now.

"Ready to get out of here?" I say, looking down at her and forcing myself not to obsess about defining our relationship.

"I'm ready."

I nod, giving her shoulder a squeeze before vaulting myself into the speedboat. Then I turn around and hold my hand out to help her up. "Let's go."

TWELVE

MOLLY

You know what would be really great?

A time machine.

So if there are any major corporations out there that are hiding the goods in their corporate research labs, now would be the time for them to speak up. Because there's one clearly-out-of-her-mind crazy lady over here who was absolutely about to kiss the one man she should *not* be kissing.

What's wrong with me? What could have possibly possessed me to act like that? I told myself I wasn't going to make a move on Beckett, and I meant it. I genuinely meant it. He lives in the Virgin Islands; I'm a grad student. He's my brother's best friend. The only thing I wanted from him on this excursion was closure, an endcap to my feelings, so that I could move the heck on.

But *nooo.* Moving on is for normal, emotionally healthy people. And I, apparently, do not fit that bill.

The wind is doing terrible things to my already iffy hair as the boat speeds along, but I don't have the energy to worry about it. All my worries are already booked for the day, and they're all directed at this morning's incident.

Truth be told, I think I'm doing a decent job of acting like everything is okay. Beckett at least doesn't seem to notice that I'm over here drowning in my mortification. But I very much would like to zoom right back in time to the moment when he was being all sweet and nice. I would like to go back to that moment, and I would like to give Past Me a solid *thwack* on the back of the head. Then maybe Past Me wouldn't have started thinking about kissing Beckett when she pondered things she really wants to do. She would have picked something else, like finding a few wildlife funds to donate to, or maybe taking up knitting.

I shake my head and groan, rubbing my hand over my face. *Bad Molly.*

"What's that expression for?" Beckett says, his voice raised so that I can hear him over the wind and the rain. When I don't answer, he goes on, "You have to tell me. We're friends now, remember?" His concerned eyes fly over my face. "Do you not feel well?"

And there's the protectiveness again. It wasn't something I'd picked up on until he mentioned it earlier, but as soon as he brought it up, I started noticing. He asked if maybe he was feeling that way because of the situation we were in together, and I told him it was possible. Probable, even.

In truth, though, I don't know. I just don't know. I'm sure that's part of it, but there's a little part of me that hopes he's growing to like me, too.

"I feel fine," I say, my voice just as loud as his. "I'm just regretting my life decisions." May as well be honest. He's right; we agreed to be friends, and I get the feeling that the last twenty-four hours have changed our relationship permanently, though I don't know how yet.

"Which decision?" he says, his gaze darting back and forth between me and the open sea ahead of us.

"The one where I made a move on you," I say miserably.

I watch as his hands flex on the steering wheel, his knuckles turning white, before he relaxes again. It's a struggle for him to let down his guard; that much is obvious. All I can do, I guess, is be open with him so that he'll see I'm not someone to worry about.

To my surprise, though, when I look from his hands to his face, I don't see that same tenseness. Instead there's a hint of a smile playing at his lips; I wouldn't go so far as to call it flirtatious, but it's definitely real.

"Stop that," I say, poking the corner of his mouth with one finger. "It's not funny. And you didn't think so either. You booked it out of that hut."

He swats my hand away, his smile growing a little. "I mean, it is kind of funny—now, at any rate. I'm not laughing at you," he adds hurriedly. "It's not that. It was just... unexpected."

"What, there aren't women trying to kiss you on the regular out here?" I say, feeling my cheeks burn.

"Despite my outgoing and friendly nature, no," he says sardonically. He hesitates, but he still looks amused when he goes on, "And are you going around making googly eyes at every guy you meet?"

"Only the ones I get stranded on islands with," I say. I press my chilled hands to my warm cheeks before admitting, "I've actually never kissed anyone before." Though I've had a few near misses—guys leaning in clumsily while I turn my head to give them my cheek instead.

Beckett blinks a few times but doesn't look at me. "Do you not date?"

And it hits me what a strange conversation this is to be

having at a yell while on a speedboat after being stuck together all night.

"I date," I say anyway. "I date a lot, actually. But it's just a string of first dates. It never goes anywhere."

I watch his Adam's apple bob as he swallows. "You date a lot, huh? Does your brother know that?"

"I will take this chance to remind you, *friend*, that as a woman in her midtwenties, I do not need to tell my brother everything."

He nods—one short jerk of his head. "That's fair." Then he glances over at me, his smile gone. "Well, I'm honored that I would have been your first," he says, his words coming out awkwardly, like this conversation is completely new territory for him. For all I know, it might be. "Your brother would kill us if we kissed, though," he says. "You know that, right?"

I nod. "Yeah, I know," I say with a sigh. It's on the tip of my tongue to ask what happened to doing what I want to do rather than doing things to please other people, but I hold it in. Even if Wes weren't an issue, there would be other stumbling blocks in our path. Speaking of which..."Hey, you're doing a good job having an entire conversation without glowering at me."

"I'm trying not to overthink anything," he says, and it's such an honest response that for a moment I don't know what to say.

"That's good," I finally come up with. "I can be your safe space. I'm serious," I add when he snorts. "For real. I mean it. If you just need one person you can trust not to judge you or whatever...I'm your girl."

He raises his brow at me, a move that's mostly obscured by the way the wind is flattening his hair over his forehead. "What qualifies you for that position?" he says.

I've been in love with you for years, I tell him in my head. *No one will give you the benefit of the doubt like I will.*

"You're part of the family" is what I say instead.

GRACIE RUTH MITCHELL

His expression fades into something more like concern, his brow furrowing as he stares through the windshield. "Your parents are going to be so mad at me," he mutters.

I blink at him, and my lips purse as I frown. "Why would they be mad at you?"

"For all this," he says, gesturing vaguely around us with one hand. "The storm, getting stuck. All of it."

"Ah," I say slowly, nodding. Then I grab my bag and begin to dig.

"What are you doing?" he says.

"I'm looking for my phone. I'm going to try to get it to work so I can change your name to Zeus, since you're under the impression you're responsible for what the weather does."

He rolls his eyes. "Ha, ha."

"This is exactly what I meant, Beckett," I say, casting my bag aside again. "They won't be mad. You don't need to *earn* my family's love. My parents adore you. They're not going anywhere. Neither am I—are *we*," I correct myself quickly. "Neither are Wes and I. And for that matter"—I'm getting fired up now—"it was not your fault that we got stuck out here. You're not in charge of the weather. If you want to blame someone, blame my mom. She was the one who made us stay behind."

Beckett blinks at me, looking surprised. "I don't particularly want to blame anyone—"

"Then don't blame yourself either," I say.

"Whoa," he says. "Calm down."

"Well, I just think it's stupid," I huff. "You've got this idea in your head that if you make mistakes, people won't love you anymore. And it's not true. It just...isn't."

"All right," he says quickly. "It's not true. I get it. Calm down. Just drop it."

"No," I say, folding my arms over my life-jacket-clad chest.

128

I pin him with a look that says I mean business. "You told me not to say yes all the time, and I don't feel like dropping this yet."

Silence.

"Didn't you?" I prod. "Didn't you tell me just this morning to stop being a people-pleaser?"

"I—yeah," he finally says, scrubbing one hand down his face before placing it back on the steering wheel. "I did. But don't be a bulldozer either. Be considerate."

I nod. "It's a fine line to walk," I concede. "Let me just say one last thing, then, and I'll drop it. Because I can tell this makes you uncomfortable to talk about, but I feel like it might be good for you to hear. Deal?"

Beckett sighs. "Fine."

I clear my throat and then begin. "As the official spokesperson for the O'Malley family—"

"That's not a thing."

"Yes it is," I say, swatting him. "As the spokesperson for the O'Malley family, I would like to tell you, in my most official capacity, that you are henceforth and forever an honorary O'Malley. This means"—I raise my voice when he shows signs of interrupting—"that you will always be invited to Thanksgiving dinner. You will always have a place at our table. You will always be welcome, no matter what you do or say. Our love for you is not conditional. Okay?"

The silence that follows is a little bit awkward—I feel it, and I know Beckett does too. He looks like he'd love to chuck himself over the side of the boat; his tanned skin is flushed pink, his expression hovering somewhere between confused and supremely uncomfortable.

"Oh, come on," I say, trying to lighten things up. "Get rid of that look on your face. It's not like I'm confessing my love to you. I'm just saying that you're a part of our family, and you don't have to worry about us leaving you. That's it. That's all."

"Right," he says after a second. "I—thanks, I guess. Now." I watch him inhale and then heave out a long breath, looking wryly at me. "If you really want to be my nonjudgmental safe space—"

"I do!" I say, delighted that he's going to put this to good use.

"Great. In that case, I could do with some silence right about now," he says. "Introvert, need to focus, so on and so forth."

"Of course," I say quickly, and then I clamp my hand over my mouth, giving him a thumbs up.

He just looks at me and shakes his head, a little smile pulling at his lips. "Thanks, Baby—Molly. I caught myself," he says when I raise one brow at him.

A feeling of warmth trickles through me, ignited by my name and spurred on by his smile. I can't say why, exactly, but this moment in time feels pivotal—like a sign that things are changing, maybe, or a sign that Beckett might see me as my own person rather than a relation of Wes's after all.

And I should shut that feeling down, but I don't. I let it run through my veins, making me feel all warm and gooey, giving me...hope? No. That's stupid. There's no hope for Beckett and me romantically.

Is there?

What would have happened if I kissed him this morning?

I spend the remainder of the boat ride silently thinking about that moment in the hut—his hands on my shoulders, his face close to mine, his eyes dropping to my lips so briefly I might have imagined it.

Maybe he would have pushed me away if I had kissed him.

But maybe he would have kissed me back.

Maybe, maybe, maybe.

OUR RETURN TO ST. Thomas is anticlimactic. I half expect my family to be waiting for us at the pier when the speedboat pulls in, but they aren't. I don't know where they are, or if they realized I wasn't on the ship before it left port. I have to assume they've been trying to reach Beckett and me, but both of our phones are out of commission for good. Beckett pulls the boat into its spot and kills the engine, leaping out and securing it in place. I follow him, and we make our way to where a row of cabs is waiting to ferry tourists around the island.

The taxi driver gives us some serious *looks* when we climb into his taxi, drenched to the bone and covered with all the dirt and grime the rain couldn't wash away.

"Sorry," I say, wincing at him in the rearview mirror.

He just grunts and waits for us to get seated, watching expectantly.

Beckett turns to me once he's pulled the door closed behind him. "I don't suppose we can just go to the drug store and get you some more medicine."

I give one single, humorless laugh as I think of my one thousand-dollar-per-month medication that I can only afford because I qualify for the patient assistance program. "No," I say, rubbing my hands over my thighs as I try not to succumb to my worries. "Definitely not."

"Didn't think so," he says dully, "but I thought I'd check. Is there anything there that might help?"

"No," I say with a sigh. I appreciate his thinking, but the truth is, I just need to get back to that cruise ship.

"All right." He directs his attention to the impatiently

waiting cab driver and directs him to someplace I've never heard of. The driver pulls out of his parking space, and we're off.

Then Beckett turns to me. "We need to pick up phones, or at least *a* phone, so we can get in touch with your family. I'm sure they'll be anxious to hear from you."

"From *us*," I correct.

Beckett hesitates, then nods. "From us," he says. "Then we can go back to my place and get cleaned up and figure out our next steps. Sound good?"

"Sounds good," I say. Then I look at him. "It's not another hut, is it?"

"No," he says, smiling slightly. "It's not another hut."

THE LOOKS the cab driver gave us are nothing compared to the looks we get from the owner of the small electronics shop we enter several minutes later. We look...well. Like we were stranded on an island overnight.

Imagine that.

The selection of phones is limited to several different models in a small glass case, but Beckett doesn't seem bothered. He just points to one of them, an honest-to-goodness flip phone —I didn't even know they still sold those—and hands over a card that he pulls from a soggy, water-laden wallet. He pays for one month of usage and then, before the bewildered salesman can even put the phone in the bag, hands it to me.

"Call," he says tensely. "Wes, your mom, your dad— anyone." He nods once to the guy behind the counter, who looks thrilled to see us go, and then guides me out with one hand at the small of my back.

It takes a second to get the phone on and working like it's

supposed to, but by the time we get to the curb to flag down another taxi, I have service.

My hand hovers over the keys as I think, biting my lip. I'm tempted to bypass my parents and call Wes, just to spare myself any theatrics. My mom does not suffer in silence, and I'm not sure I can deal with her brand of chaos right now.

Ultimately I decide on my dad, though. And it's his calm voice, betraying only a hint of strain, that answers after one ring —a clear sign he's been waiting by his phone. They probably all have.

"Dad?" I say.

"Molly?" he says quickly, and some of his calm seems to dissipate. "Molly, sweetie? Is that you?"

"Yeah," I say, blinking away the hot tears stinging my eyes. His voice is the best thing I've heard all day. "It's me."

"Oh, Molly," he says, and the words are wobbly. "Deb, it's Molly! Are you okay, sweetie? Are you safe?"

"Yeah," I say. "I'm safe."

"And Beckett?" my dad asks. "He's safe too?"

I nod, looking at Beckett who's busy flagging down a taxi. "Beckett is fine too."

He looks over at me when he hears me mention his name, and I beckon him closer before pulling the phone away from my ear and turning it on speaker.

"Dad, you're on speaker phone," I say, holding the phone up next to my mouth as I speak. "Beckett is right here too."

I hear a cacophony of voices on the other end before my mom's voice comes through. "Molly? Beckett? You're okay?" She sounds nothing short of frantic.

"We're both fine," I say quickly. "We both fell asleep on the beach while the storm was rolling in, and by the time we realized, it was too dangerous to come back. We had to stay overnight, but we're back on St. Thomas now. Where are you? Did you get on the ship?"

"This is all my fault," my mom says, and I'm surprised to hear her as she begins to cry. Or really, it's more of a wail. "All my fault! I told you to stay—you've always had a crush on him, and Beckett is such a *dear*, and I thought you two might—might —" But her words die as she hiccups herself into more crying, and I press one hand to my heated cheeks.

Matchmaking. My mother was *matchmaking*.

"Where are you?" Beckett says, and I can't help but notice that his cheeks look a little pink too. "Did you get on the ship, or did you realize Molly wasn't there? She doesn't have her—"

But he breaks off when my hand flies to his face and clamps over his mouth. His brows furrow as he looks at me with outrage, his day-old scruff sandpaper against my palm as he jerks his head back and forth. His hands, warm and strong, come up and wrap around my wrist with a strength that I frankly find very attractive.

"No!" I whisper, holding the phone away from my body so my parents don't hear. "Don't tell them. It won't make them get here any faster, and they'll just worry."

Beckett pulls my hand away from his mouth with ease, but he doesn't speak. He just eyes me for a moment before nodding, and I sigh with relief.

"Where are you?" he says, leaning closer to me and speaking into the phone.

"We're on the ship," my mom says, sounding miserable. "Last night I sent Wes to check and make sure you had come back, and your cabin door was open with sounds coming from the bathroom. He assumed it was you, sweetie, but it was the cleaning service. We're getting off at the next port stop, and they've told us we should be able to find a ferry back to you. It's going to be two days, though. Are you okay for two more days?"

she says anxiously. I can imagine the exact way she's wringing her hands right now, knuckles white, fingers tight.

"Of course," I say, ignoring the way my heart sinks. Two days will put us right at Christmas day. There's nothing we can do, though, and there's no point in worrying them further. "We'll be fine."

I let Beckett take over the phone call from there. I don't have to ask him—he just seems to realize that I need him, his eyes darting over my face as it falls. I try to smooth out my expression, but I know it doesn't work. I've never spent Christmas away from my family before. Maybe I should be more okay with the separation than I am, since I'm in my twenties now, but...

I sigh. All we can do, I guess, is wait. Wait and hope my body and brain behave themselves without my medication.

And try to protect my heart while I'm at it—because every second I spend with Beckett is another second I fall for him even more.

Two days. I can do this. I can still celebrate Christmas here, and I can definitely make it forty-eight hours without caving and confessing my undying love for this man.

Two days.

THIRTEEN
BECKETT

Normally I don't mind a little mess, but as Molly and I step through the front door of my house, I'm keenly and uncomfortably aware of the clutter. A shirt draped over the back of a kitchen chair; a stack of books on the floor by the couch; a stray sock wedged under the fridge, gold toe peeping out. I'm hit with the very unusual urge to run around and pick up, shoving everything into the back of my closet like I'm a teenager again.

I resist. I've never cared about this stuff before; I refuse to change just because a woman is setting foot inside. The *first* woman to set foot inside, actually, now that I think about it.

To be fair, there's not much to the little house. It's maybe six hundred square feet and equipped with only the basics—a kitchenette, a bathroom, and a curtained-off bedroom that couldn't fit a queen bed if I tried. I know because I *did* try, and it didn't work. I had to return the mattress and get a double instead. I didn't bother with a bed frame, either; I just plopped the mattress on the bedroom floor and called it good.

"Right," I say, rubbing the back of my neck as my gaze darts around the room. I dedicated exactly zero dollars to decoration, so the place is pretty bare, pretty bleak, and pretty ugly. Stark white walls, navy Berber carpet, peeling laminate tile in the kitchen. "Uh, the bathroom is there"—I point to the closed door on my right—"so you can go ahead and shower."

"Excellent," Molly says fervently, sliding her backpack off and dropping it on the floor. It was pale yellow when she arrived on the island yesterday; now it's a dingy, yellowish-brown.

She starts toward the bathroom but then stops, looking over her shoulder at me. "What's the hot water situation like?"

"Dismal," I reply.

She nods. "I'll be quick, then." Casting a glance down at her clothes, she adds, "Anything I can wear?"

"Yes," I say, hurrying past the little couch and sliding the bedroom curtain aside. There's no closet—just a narrow set of drawers. I dig through a few of them and emerge with a shirt and some basketball shorts.

Crap. She's wearing a swimsuit. Does she have underwear? Does she *need* underwear? How do I even ask something like that? Should I just give her a pair of boxers and not say anything about it? Would she prefer briefs?

I go through another drawer, my fingers clawing frantically as I search for my least embarrassing pair of boxers, until I find some that are plain black. It's the best I can do, and I'd rather not know she's going commando under a pair of my shorts. I close the drawer. Then I take all the inappropriate thoughts trying to surface, shove them in my brain's little black box, and close that too.

I tuck the boxers in between the shirt and the shorts and then leave the bedroom, heading back to Molly. I won't say anything; I'll just let her find it. That way we can both maintain our dignity—

"Oh, boxers!" she says, not two seconds after I've handed her the bundle of clothing. She holds my boxers up, waving them in my rapidly heating face. "Thanks. I didn't know if I should ask, but I wanted to."

Well. So much for that.

"Yeah," I mutter. "I don't have..." I swallow, gesturing to my chest. "You know. Bras."

Molly nods. "I figured. Do you have a first aid kit?"

I point to one of the four kitchen cabinets. "In there. Why?"

"Ask me no questions, and I'll tell you no lies," she says in a singsong voice as she waltzes over and begins digging through the cabinet.

"Right," I say. I take that to mean she doesn't want to tell me, and I probably don't want to know either. I turn my back and focus my attention on the wall, giving her whatever privacy she needs as she finds the first aid kit. She said there wouldn't be anything at a pharmacy to help with her seizures; what could she possibly find in my cabinet that would work?

I'm hit with a bolt of anxiety as I'm reminded yet again of her medical predicament, but I take a deep breath and force myself not to panic. I listen instead to her every move as I stare at the blank white wall.

After maybe thirty seconds of rummaging, she says, "Okay, got what I need. I'm going to shower."

I nod, turning back around. "Take your time," I say. "I don't need much hot water. So just...yeah. Take your time." I hate to think of her rushing just because of me. Her hair alone will require more water than my entire body probably needs.

She doesn't say anything, though; she just looks at me for a second, and I squirm under her scrutiny. Then she smiles and heads to the bathroom, closing the door behind her.

And look at that—more anxiety. I huff out an irritable

breath, flattening my hair absently. I need to get over this. I can't keep her in my sight at all times. I can't keep a constant eye on her. And judging by what she told me this morning, it would drive her nuts if I tried. She doesn't need someone hovering around her, just waiting for her to start convulsing. No, she doesn't have her medicine—but I'm going to have to trust her to know her own body. It's all I can do.

I spend the next fifteen minutes channeling my anxious energy into picking up—putting a used bowl in the sink, straightening the couch cushions unnecessarily, putting dirty clothes in the hamper. There's no reason for me to be doing this —I don't need to impress Molly of all people—but I can't quite stop myself. I'm just throwing away an old flier when I hear the bathroom door creak open, the hinges protesting. I turn around just in time to see Molly step out.

Her hair is freed from all constraints, hanging long and dark red as she towels it dry. It leaves wet spots on the shoulders of her shirt—*my* shirt—and I watch, fascinated, at the way her curls fall, at tendrils that loop over her ears and the droplets of water that cling to the ends.

My clothes on her are an odd fit; gender differences aside, our bodies are shaped vastly differently. I'm tall and fairly lean, while Molly is short and curvy. As a result, my t-shirt is bordering on too tight but also too long, while the shorts I've given her hang a full six inches past her knees.

I'm just grateful she's out of that swimsuit, to be honest. My sanity can only withstand so much.

The problem is, Molly has so many different kinds of attractiveness. And right now...

"Molly O'Malley," I say, the words falling out of my mouth as I drink her in. "I do believe you're the cutest thing I've ever seen."

"Oh," she says, clearly startled. Her lips form a perfect *o* as her eyes widen to a deer-in-the-headlights look, and though her skin is already pink from the hot water, I can almost imagine her cheeks turn just a few shades pinker.

And something happens then, completely against my will, as I look at her standing there: my stomach flips, electricity sparking somewhere around my navel. And what's more, that flip-flopping, electric stomach is accompanied by a feeling of warmth, faint but unmistakable: affection.

Crap.

I am developing actual *feelings* for this woman. She's not just affecting my body anymore; my heart is starting to get involved. I can sense it, plain as day, though it's been well over a year since I had romantic feelings for anyone.

I'm having them now, though.

For my best friend's little sister.

Crap.

"The clothes are a little long," she says, tearing me away from this horrific realization. She fists her hands in the hem of the t-shirt and pulls a bit at the extra fabric. "It's comfortable, though—"

"Wait," I interrupt before I can stop myself. But I've just seen something—a flash of pale skin where she was playing with the hem of the shirt, and something yellow. "What's that?"

"What's what?" she says, blinking at me with confusion.

I point to the spot I saw, just above her right hip. "I thought I saw yellow. On your skin. Do you have a bruise? Did you get hurt?" I rack my brain, trying to remember if she got hit by anything or fell at all, but I can't recall.

"Oh," she says, her expression clearing. She waves one airy hand and says, "No, that's a tattoo."

My jaw drops as this registers. "What?" I say stupidly.

"A tattoo," she repeats, stepping further out into the room.

"Does Wes know about that?" I say. Because Wes still treats

Molly like a little girl in pigtails; he'd probably freak if he knew she had ink.

"Of course not," she says, completely matter-of-factly. "And he's not going to find out." Then she sends me a look that I think is supposed to be threatening, her eyes narrowing, lips curving into a frown. But all I can focus on is the way her nose crinkles, and how cute it is.

I'm positive she would not appreciate this observation.

"Look at you," I say instead, a smile pulling at my lips. "You little rebel."

"I know," she says, her eyes sparking with mischief. "But I couldn't resist. Want to see?"

I should say no. I should tell her that I'm not interested in whatever was so important that she inked it on her pale, perfect skin. But that little smile of hers, impish and full of glee, makes me too curious.

"Show me," I say.

She nods and then pulls up the hem of her shirt, just high enough to reveal...

"What...is it?" I say, frowning at the tattoo as I step closer, bending over to get a better look.

"It's a yellow boxfish!" she says, pointing. "*Ostracion cubicum*. Isn't he cute?"

"No," I say, shaking my head as I look at the tattoo. "That's not a fish. That's a lemon with polka dots, Molly."

She bursts out laughing, and the sound rings through my tiny house with a glorious liveliness that lights the place up. "It does kind of look like a polka-dotted lemon, doesn't it," she says. "But it's a yellow boxfish. Here's his little tail, see"—she points to the tail— "and his little kissy face."

"Incredible." I shake my head, trying to hide my smile. "I'm going to go get cleaned up, and then please tell me the story behind Mr. Boxfish."

Molly beams at me as she lets the hem of her shirt fall. That joyful look does unwanted things to my insides, but I force myself to ignore it, giving her a nod and then disappearing into the bathroom.

It takes me less than three minutes to wash my entire body from head to toe, but I give myself another five of just standing under the water, staring at the wall. The next two days are going to be full of Molly; she's going to be in my space and in my head. So I take this time to shore up my mental fortitude, reminding myself of all the reasons she's off-limits.

Except...what are those reasons again?

She's Wes's sister, but I'm not super worried about that. Molly's not a child; she doesn't need her brother's approval. I guess there's the whole island thing; any relationship we started would be long-distance.

Yes. That's enough of a reason for me. I live here, she lives there. True, she said she's coming back to this area in a couple months, but I might not even be here then. I've never managed an actual relationship with a woman, anyway; at most we hang out for a few weeks before I get anxious and cut her loose.

It's hard to imagine Molly letting me run away—and I'm man enough to admit that what I do is run—but it doesn't matter. Because the truth is, there's another reason I'd never start anything with her: she's too much. She's just...too much. She's too open, too insightful, too close. She makes me feel too many things.

And I know, without a shadow of a doubt, that she could make me *want* things, too—things I'm afraid to want.

Love.

A future.

A family.

Molly O'Malley would waltz right into my heart and pull all those desires from me with one well-aimed smile, until I could do nothing but beg her to love me. It's already begun—I'm developing feelings for her. I *like* her.

"Friends," I tell myself firmly, feeling the lukewarm water cascade over my face and down my chest. "Friends for two days, and then she's gone."

I nod once to myself; then I shut the water off and step out of the shower. It takes me two minutes to dry off and get dressed, and then I go back out to the living area.

"All right," I say, rubbing the towel over my hair and grasping for a normal, safe topic of conversation. "Tell me about the tattoo."

Molly gives me a sleepy smile from where she's curled up on the secondhand loveseat. Her head is leaning on the armrest, her hair spilling everywhere. She looks like she's five minutes away from passing out.

She answers me, though.

"I went to exactly one party in my college career," she says, holding up her pointer finger. "Just one. And I had too much to drink. So my roommate and I thought it would be a good idea to get tattoos."

"A lot of places won't give you a tattoo if you're drunk," I say, raising an eyebrow and sitting next to her on the loveseat. With irritation I note the anxiety spiking in the pit of my stomach. I don't need to be worried; she's telling a story that already happened, and she's clearly fine. But the thought of a drunk Molly wandering around on her own...it doesn't sit well with me.

She nods. "They wouldn't do it. I guess the alcohol thins your blood, which means more bleeding? You had to have an appointment anyway. But I went in and talked to the guy behind the counter for fifteen minutes about yellow boxfish. I showed him pictures and everything. Told him way more than he ever wanted to know. He gave me a business card and told me to come back when I was sober."

I can picture it perfectly: a teetering Molly, cheeks flushed, hair wild, talking the ear off of a huge, inked man, telling him about the mating habits of her favorite fish. Her eyes were probably shining the whole time, her smile free and potent.

"Anyway," she says, snuggling further into the corner of the loveseat. "I found the business card in my pocket the next day, and then I remembered the whole thing. I thought about it and decided to get the tattoo anyway." She smiles at me, a kitten curled up contentedly in the sun, completely adorable. "And I never touched another drink after that."

"Good," I say immediately. "That's good."

She nods, then shrugs. "That's the story. Not much to it. But Beckett," she sighs, "what are we going to do? Wes and my parents won't be here until sometime on Christmas. I've never done a Christmas Eve by myself."

It takes me a second to catch up to the change in topic. "You won't be by yourself," I say, looking over at her. "I'll be here."

"You don't even have a Christmas tree up," she points out, glancing around the room. Then she turns to me, her eyes lighting up. "Can we decorate for Christmas?"

And because I'm a sucker, because I'm weak, I answer her immediately. "I guess," I say. "We can try, anyway. This is my first Christmas here, so I'm not sure what sort of decorations we'll be able to find on the island, but..."

"But we can look?" she says, smiling brightly.

I hold back my sigh. I know I'm going to regret making this promise when I'm hunting down a Christmas tree or garland or whatever else she wants. And yet, I say it anyway. "Yeah," I tell her. "We can look. We'll do what we can. Okay?"

Her eyes go squinty with the smile she gives me, and I try

to push aside the warmth that hovers in my chest like fog over a city—a hazy glow that has me smiling softly back at her.

"Sleep, sweetheart," I murmur as her eyes drift closed. Her lids flutter slightly. "But I'm not tired," she says, yawning around the words.

"Come on. Sleep," I say again.

I can see the exact moment she decides she's too tired to argue; the last remaining bit of posture leaves her body, and she sinks completely into the couch cushions. "Mm-hmm," she hums.

"Good girl," I say softly, standing up. I tug gently on her feet. "Stretch out."

She complies, her eyes still closed, unfurling her body like the petals of a flower and rolling onto her side. She's cramped, but it has to be more comfortable than sleeping in the position she was in before.

And then I watch as she drifts off to sleep before my eyes. And I'm left wondering, like an idiot, what she's seeing in her dreams—and if she's dreaming about me like I dreamed about her.

What a bizarre alternate reality we seem to have entered; Molly O'Malley is sleeping on my couch, wearing my clothes, and I just called her *sweetheart*. I didn't mean to. It sort of just... happened. And I can't tear my eyes away from her. I can't stop thinking about that ridiculous yellow boxfish tattooed above her hip. And now I'm also thinking about how to decorate for Christmas, despite the fact that decorating is the last thing I want to spend my time doing.

What is this woman doing to me?

FOURTEEN
MOLLY

Ever worn Band-Aids over your nipples because you didn't have a bra handy?

1/10, would not recommend. I need underwire, and I need it *now*.

Which is why the first stop on our shopping trip is not at the grocery store but instead at an overpriced tourist boutique that sells wardrobes full of clothing with the name of the island scrawled across the front. My breasts are now encased in a too-small bra that advertises the Virgin Islands—the humor of which is not lost on me—but at least it's better than nothing, and *certainly* better than Band-Aids. I also walk away with three t-shirts, a pair of shorts, and a flowing maxi dress, all of which cost more money than anyone should reasonably have to spend on six items of clothing. But it feels better to be in my own clothes and out of Beckett's, no matter how good they smelled.

Of course, Beckett is the one who paid for these new clothes, since I didn't bring my wallet when we left the cruise ship. His cash was ruined in the storm, but his card made it unscathed. Small mercies.

It's the maxi dress I've got on now, because it seemed like the best-fitting thing we bought. The fabric is soft and flowy, a rich emerald green, printed with a tropical floral pattern. It has simple straps, leaving my shoulders mostly bare. The belted torso does surprisingly good things for my figure, and on the whole I feel pretty good—especially when I step out of the dressing room and see Beckett's unfiltered reaction. It's subtle, but it sends a thrill through me nonetheless—the tightening of his jaw, the bob of his throat as he swallows, the journey of his eyes down my figure. It's a moment that distracts me from the gravity of our current situation and pulls me instead to a make-believe reality where he looks at me like this all the time.

Exactly how far away is that reality? Because I'm starting to wonder.

I think...I think he might have called me *sweetheart* earlier. But also I might have been dreaming? I was half-asleep, and I'm kicking myself that I can't remember.

After I discreetly fan my face with both hands, we leave the tourist boutique, and I remind Beckett of his promise.

"You said we could decorate for Christmas," I say, rubbing my hands together as I look around the square. The rain has finally stopped, and we're back where we met Señorita and Alfonso, who I plan to visit in a moment. The array of different shops is dizzying. There are several restaurants, clothing places, jewelry stores, and like five souvenir shops. That's four too many, in my opinion, but whatever.

"I did," Beckett says grudgingly, "but I think it's going to be slim pickings. You know that, right?" He looks much better now that he's showered and changed, too. But he has his hands shoved in his pockets, and he looks for all the world like we're

147

discussing an upcoming root canal rather than Christmas decorations—yet he's still willing to humor me.

Two days. Hold your feelings in for two days, I remind myself. *Focus less on the attractive, grumpy, secretly sweet man and more on keeping yourself healthy.*

"It did occur to me," I admit, my eyes falling to our shadows on the paved stone beneath our feet. "But I thought maybe we could...I don't know. Improvise." My shadow shrugs its shoulders.

"We can," he says, and his shadow nods slowly. "Just as long as you're aware this probably won't be a traditional Christmas."

I sigh. "I'm aware," I say, tucking one errant curl behind my ear. Most of my hair is pulled into a braid, but several strands have escaped. I don't have the patience to try to tame them into submission.

Beckett nods again, that same sharp nod he usually does— little more than a jerk of his head.

"Let's look around, then," he says. "These souvenir shops are probably our best bets. They sell knickknacks—so maybe string lights, ornaments, that kind of thing. We might be able to find something there."

"Sounds good," I say. I can picture it now—rows and rows of seashell ornaments with hundreds of different names printed on them. They'd probably have a *Molly* ornament, but I doubt we'd find a *Beckett*. "I just want to visit Alfonso and Señorita first—"

"No way."

Beckett's firm answer has me turning and frowning at him. I'm surprised to see his arms crossed over his chest, mouth turned down stubbornly.

"Just for a second," I say, stepping toward him.

"Those are demon monkeys, Molly," he says, shaking his

head. "They get all up in my space and stick their creepy fingers in my ears. I'm not getting within ten feet of that nonsense."

"Fine," I say, and I don't bother hiding my smile. "I'll go by myself, you little chicken."

"I'm not—it isn't—I'm not *chicken*," he sputters. His eyes narrow as he takes a step closer to me, bringing him near enough that I have to tilt my head to look up at him. "This is basic logic. I don't want to approach the animal that attacked my face."

I nod. "You're right. Very logical," I say. I pat him on the shoulder, doing my best not to focus on how muscular he is.

"Well, now you're just being patronizing," he grumbles, and I laugh.

"I don't know what you want from me," I say, still laughing. "You're not happy whether I agree with you or disagree with you."

"Just go," he says, gesturing across the square to where the dreadlocked man is walking around with the two monkeys perched on his shoulders. "And he'll want a tip; here." He pulls out his wallet and digs around for a second, emerging with a handful of coins. When I give him a skeptical look, his cheeks turn red. "The cash all got ruined in the storm," he mutters.

"I know. Thank you," I say, and I'm still smiling as I shake my head. "I'll be back in a minute."

"Make sure they don't scratch you," Beckett adds. He points to my bare shoulders.

"I'll be careful," I say as I begin to walk away.

"I'm not disinfecting any monkey scratches," he calls after me.

I give him a thumbs up. "Yep."

"Not a single one!"

I just wave over my shoulder at him. He's being a little

ridiculous, but I can't help but find it funny. I can't quite blame him, either; Señorita really did attack his face. Maybe he wronged her in the past and now he's paying the price. Are monkeys vindictive creatures? Do they have the mental capacity for revenge?

I sigh as I cross the square. My brain comes up with the weirdest things sometimes. I make a mental note to look it up anyway; I'd be interested to see the answers to those questions.

I spend ten minutes with Señorita and Alfonso and the dreadlocked man, whose name turns out to be Nilson. Nilson is as mellow as they come, and not a big talker, but with a few well-placed questions, I manage to learn more about him. He's lived here for twenty-five years, and he's had Señorita and Alfonso for the last three. I laugh out loud when he tells me that Señorita is only rude to a select few—Beckett included.

"She can sense when someone doesn't like her," Nilson says, his teeth bright and white in a smile that takes up fully half of his face.

"He's pretty grumpy," I say, turning carefully to look at where Beckett is staring at us from across the square, eyeing the monkeys with way more distrust and suspicion than they deserve. Moving with Alfonso and Señorita on my shoulders makes me feel like an African woman walking miles with a basket balanced on my head, and I keep my motions slow and gentle so I don't startle them or shake them loose as I turn back to Nilson.

"You don't have to be so careful," Nilson says when he notices my movements. "They hold on tight and balance well. They won't fall."

Easy for him to say; his deltoids are the size of human skulls. The man is huge. *I* could probably balance on his shoulders.

"Right," I say anyway, trying to relax. "I'll remember that

for next time. I should get going, though." I point toward Beck-ett. "We've got stuff to do today."

Nilson reclaims the monkeys with ease, and I roll my shoul-ders a few times before giving him a smile and waving to Alfonso and Señorita. I pass him the change Beckett gave me, apologizing that I don't have more, and then stride back across the square toward Beckett. He's still where I left him, glowering unnecessarily in the direction of the monkeys.

"You pointed at me," he says when I'm close enough to hear him.

"I was telling Señorita your address. So she can come visit you in the middle of the night," I say with a grin.

Beckett gives a full-body shudder. "Don't even joke. That's horrifying. Can you imagine? Being woken up in the dead of night with that little rat in your bed?"

"In *your* bed," I correct. "She would snuggle right up to you and wrap her arms around your neck and keep you nice and warm."

Beckett raises one brow at me. "I don't think Señorita and I have the kind of relationship you're picturing, where we keep each other warm at night. Interesting that your mind went there, though—"

"Shut up," I say, laughing and nudging him with my elbow as we walk toward the nearest souvenir shop. Our steps are slow and lazy, and something about it is a nice change of pace from the chaos we dealt with overnight. I slow to a stop, though, when something occurs to me.

"Speaking of beds," I say, looking up at Beckett. "What are the sleeping arrangements for tonight?"

Beckett's answer is immediate. "You're sleeping in my bed," he says.

I frown at him. "And you're going to sleep...?"

He shrugs and starts walking again. "Floor, couch, wherever. It doesn't matter."

"No," I say, shaking my head. There's no way he'll fit on the couch; it was even a tight fit for me earlier. "I've inconvenienced you enough already. You sleep in the bed. I'll take the floor or the couch."

"Nope," he says. "That won't work for me."

"Beckett," I say with a sigh. "I promise it's not a big deal. I'll be absolutely fine on the floor—"

But I break off when Beckett turns sharply to me, leaning down until his face is inches from mine. I gasp at his sudden nearness, my eyes widening as he invades my space.

"You will sleep in my bed, Molly," he says in a low voice. His words are calm, but his tone is steel—he's not asking. "Because if you sleep anywhere else, I will worry about you all night. And then I won't sleep either. So you will sleep in my bed, on my pillow, under my blankets. You will make yourself comfortable there. Do you understand?"

His eyes pin me in place, and he's close enough that I can see the specks of gold in his irises. He watches me expectantly with those eyes, never wavering. When I don't answer, he speaks again. "Molly," he says sharply. "Do you understand?"

"Yes," I breathe. What is my pulse doing right now? It's spiking erratically, tripping and stumbling with every new detail I notice—the curve of his lower lip as he speaks, the cool mint of his breath, his hands braced on my bare shoulders as he holds me in place. "I understand," I manage to get out.

Beckett's eyes roam over my face. "Good girl," he murmurs finally.

"I feel funny when you say that." The words tumble out of my mouth without my permission, but I'm too stuck in this moment to care—too hyperaware of his touch, his palms rough against my skin. Too lost in his eyes. Too close to the lips I've been dying to kiss for years.

The only change in his expression is the slight hitch of his brow. His gaze ping-pongs back and forth between my eyes, growing sharp with interest. "Funny how?" he rasps, taking one step closer to me.

"Like..." I say, feeling dazed. "Like I can't breathe. Like my heart is going too fast."

Beckett's hands clench convulsively on my shoulders, no more than a spasm of movement, but I feel it like it's the only sensation left in my body.

"There are lines, Molly," he says through gritted teeth, "that we shouldn't cross."

"I don't think I'm crossing lines," I say with a hint of defiance. "You asked a question and I answered."

Beckett's hands are still holding my shoulders in a vice-like grip, but now he yanks them away, straightening up and taking a step back. "Fine," he says, his jaw flexing. "That's fair. I won't ask questions like that again."

"You asked because you wanted to know," I say. There's an inexplicable knot growing in my throat, but my words pour out anyway, sounding more and more strangled as I go on. "You asked because you wanted to know, because you—"

"Don't," he cuts me off, raking one hand through his hair. "Just...don't."

I blink hard, swallowing back the tears that are threatening to fall.

He feels something. I really think he does. But he's fighting it, and I don't know what to do with that. Because this situation is so far beyond even my wildest dreams. My initial hope for this port excursion was to see Beckett again and put these feelings to rest once and for all. Even when we first got stranded on Van Gogh Island, that was the plan I wanted to stick to.

But it's hard to keep my distance when he looks at me like he wants me closer.

And yet...he's saying no. He ran from the almost-kiss; he's telling me now not to push this further.

What can I do but listen?

"Let's go," he says, not meeting my eye. His gaze jumps to the single tear that's managed to escape, and he watches its journey down my cheek, looking uncomfortable. "You wanted to find Christmas decorations."

I swipe at the tear, nodding. "Yeah. Go on in. I just need a second." There's no point in lying to maintain my dignity. It's pretty clear this is a rejection.

When he hesitates, I pull out the best smile I can manage. It's bright and cheerful, and it clearly takes him aback, because he blinks with surprise.

"Go on," I say around the smile. "I'm honestly fine. Just give me a second, okay? I'm tired and overly emotional from everything going on. I need to breathe for a minute."

Beckett's answering nod is slow, unconvinced, but he backs away anyway before turning and heading into the souvenir shop we're outside of.

I let my smile fall away as soon as the door closes behind him. Then I wipe at my cheeks and my eyes, forcing myself to take deep, even breaths.

It's better this way, I tell myself firmly. *You'll leave tomorrow or the next day and not see him for probably another ten years.*

One thought cuts through all the others, though, the more I think: Now that I've gotten reacquainted with him, now that I've seen his sweetness and his gruffness and the spark that burns between us...how am I supposed to get over Beckett Donovan?

FIFTEEN
BECKETT

I LOOK AT MOLLY OUT THE WINDOW OF THE SOUVENIR shop I've just disappeared into. She said she needed a minute, and I understand the need for space.

I can't help but watch her, though.

Her smile is gone now that she thinks I can't see her. I'm not surprised; I could tell it was fake. It was too brittle, too sudden. Her mouth is pressed instead into a miserable little line, and she's wiping her eyes again.

It's a physical effort, resisting the urge to run back to her. I hold myself in check, fists tight and body rigid, as I watch her shoulders heave with every breath she takes. My jaw clenches around the words that want to escape me as I fight this desire.

This feeling is...strange. The regret gnawing at my heart, the guilt that hits as I watch her cry—I've felt similar emotions before, of course, but never like this.

She's a ray of sunshine, and I have dulled her light.

I am scum.

And yet I know—I *know*—that it would be unfair to everyone involved if I started something with her now. She's going to be with me for another day; that's it. And who's to say that all these feelings are even real, anyway? Isn't it more likely that they're a byproduct of the super-charged situation we've found ourselves in, and the vulnerabilities we've been forced to share? Yes, I'm attracted to her, but the other, more complex things I've been experiencing...I don't know where those feelings are coming from or how solid they are.

I won't go so far as to make assumptions about her; maybe she really does have feelings for me. But I can't promise her anything, and I can't do a fling. Not with Wes's sister. She deserves more than that by a long shot.

So it's better to stay away.

Easier said than done, I think as I watch Molly square her shoulders, stand up straighter, and then march toward the door of the souvenir shop. I duck my head away from the window and quickly busy myself looking at a shelf of personalized Virgin Island shot glasses, none of which I have any interest in. My glazed eyes trail aimlessly over some twenty different *K* names before jumping to the *M*s, and I'm only seconds away from reaching for the *Molly* glass when I realize what I'm doing.

"Okay, I'm back." Her voice pipes up from behind me, and I whirl around.

Molly's there in front of me, her eyes red but dry. She smiles, another one of her desperately-faking-it smiles, as I do my best to discreetly make sure she's okay. It's on the tip of my tongue to ask if she's all right, but I make myself hold the words in. I'm not sure how she'd react, and it feels like distracting her might be the best option. So I point instead to the back of the shop. "Let's try there," I say, and she nods.

We spend the next fifteen minutes scouring the souvenir shop with minimal luck. All we're able to find are a few rows of island-themed Christmas ornaments. Molly stands in front of the shelves with her lips pursed into a little frown as she looks them over, finally shaking her head and turning to me.

"No," she says. "These aren't worth the money."

I agree wholeheartedly. We exit the shop without buying anything.

And it's while we're on our way to the next store that Molly looks at me and makes an interesting request.

"Help me practice saying no," she says.

I slow to a stop and blink at her, surprised. She looks back at me expectantly, her head tilted to the side, the breeze tugging at her hair. Even though the rain has stopped, it's still a bit cooler out now, and I find my eyes skating over her bare arms and shoulders. Is she cold? Should we go buy her an overpriced sweatshirt?

"Beckett?" she says.

"Do you need a jacket?" is my brilliant answer.

She gives me a little smile, more real than the fake ones she's been handing out. It sends an odd, bittersweet warmth through me.

"No," she says. "I'm not cold."

I nod, my mind going back to her request. "In that case...I'm not sure you need to practice saying no," I say, thinking. "You might do better practicing *not* saying yes. Come on; let's keep moving." I give her arm a little tug, and we begin walking again.

"If I'm not saying no and I'm not saying yes, what am I saying?" Molly says, giving me a confused look. "I think I need examples."

"Well, I'm obviously not a therapist," I say uncomfortably. "But when I don't want to say yes, I put off answering. Like if someone invites me someplace and I really don't want to go, but they're putting pressure on me, I make an excuse about needing to check my schedule. That way I can answer them later when they're no longer standing in front of me, waiting for an answer. It removes the immediate pressure from the situation, which lets me think more clearly about what I really want to do or what I can realistically commit to."

Her expression clears. "Oh, that makes sense," she says, turning mischievous eyes on me. "That's how you get away with being antisocial, huh?"

I smile, relief pooling inside at her easy manner. At least things aren't awkward between us after...whatever that was earlier. "Yeah," I say. "But also...I don't know. Just remember that what you want matters, too." I clear my throat. "Your wants and needs aren't less important than anyone else's. I know you like to be nice or considerate or whatever, and that's great, but don't completely sacrifice yourself."

It's weird to be giving advice like this, and it's even weirder to see how seriously Molly seems to be taking it. Her brows are furrowed slightly as she bites her bottom lip, looking deep in thought. Then she nods slowly. Like she finds value in what I'm telling her.

And it feels...I don't know. Kind of cool, I guess. It feels cool to have someone listening, to have someone value my opinion. I don't have a ton of close friends or confidantes; there aren't many relationships in my life that consist of giving and receiving advice.

"I know what you're saying is true," Molly says, the words halting as she speaks. Her eyes dart to mine, and I watch as the most perfect flush rises in her cheeks. "So I'm not sure why it's so hard to think of myself that way."

I have my own opinions about that, personally; I don't love the way her family brushes her off sometimes. It's not my place to say anything against them, though, especially because I'm far from perfect myself.

"I don't know," I say instead. I nudge her with my elbow.

"Don't stress about it too much. Let's finish our Christmas stuff."

"Yeah," she says, and some of her excitement returns; I can see it dawning in her eyes like the sun just peeking above the horizon. "And you know what we should do? We should buy each other a Christmas present too."

"If you want to," I say with a shrug. "I don't need anything. But if you want to—"

"I do," she says, smiling at me. "And we can put them under our tree."

She's still hanging on to the Christmas tree dream, I see. I'm not sure how that one is going to pan out, but I guess we can look.

She glances around for a second and then points to the path that leads out of the square. "I think I saw a bigger shopping center that way when we were in the taxi. We might have better luck there than in a souvenir shop. They might sell plants at least, right?"

She turns out to be correct. We give the second souvenir shop a try, but it lasts all of ten minutes before we both decide we'd be better off elsewhere. We don't need Hawaiian shirts or water bottles shaped like coconuts.

It's at the shopping center that we finally find something of use. "Look!" Molly says, grabbing my hand and pulling me toward one of the side aisles. My eyes catch a brief glimpse of green and terra-cotta before I emerge into a small row of decorative items, including one shelf of plants. I've barely gotten a look at them when Molly hurries over and stops in front of one.

"It's perfect," she says, her eyes shining when she looks over her shoulder at me. I move to stand next to her so I can see the tree she's picked. Except...

"This?" I say, shooting her a look. "This is what you want to use as a Christmas tree?"

It's a cactus. A three-armed cactus—fake, judging by the plastic sheen—maybe eighteen inches tall and resting snugly in a yellow pot.

"Yes," she says, once again smiling dreamily down at the cactus. "He's so cute! Look at his little arms! And these seem pretty sturdy," she says, pinching one of the spines and giving it a tug and a wiggle. "We can hang ornaments from these."

"I—it's—okay," I finally sigh. Who am I to say a cactus can't be a stand-in Christmas tree, especially when Molly is looking so fondly at it?

We look for packs of Christmas ornaments, but there's nothing Molly likes. Instead she chooses a packet of colorful pom-poms and a needle and thread. Not sure what she's going to do with those, but I don't ask. I just do as I'm told when she tells me I have ten minutes to find her a gift. I watch as she hurries off in the opposite direction, her steps lively and excited, and then I begin my hunt.

Finding a present for Molly is significantly more fun than finding Christmas decorations. It needs to be something small, but I want her to really like it, too. I scour the aisles for something that speaks to me, finally stopping when I reach the aisle that sells island-themed gifts and decor, much of it labeled with our Virgin Islands location. I slow down, my eyes scanning the shelves until they snag on the perfect gift.

I hesitate for just a moment. I think she'll love it, but will it send the wrong message?

Those worries vanish, though, when I think of everything Molly has been through in the past thirty-six hours. I pull the little box off the shelf and then carry it to the front of the store, where I meet a flushed-looking Molly holding something behind her back.

"Don't look," she says as we head for the register. "It's a surprise."

"I wouldn't dream of it," I say, a smile tugging at the corner of my lips.

We pay for our things and then leave, flagging down a taxi to take us back to my house. Molly cradles her Christmas cactus the whole time, looking at it every now and then with a little smile on her face.

Keeping distance between us would be so much easier if she weren't so cute.

We spend the afternoon doing a whole lot of nothing. I sit on the loveseat and watch while Molly painstakingly threads each pom-pom onto the thread she bought, until she has a garland of colorful little poofs. She winds it carefully around the cactus, singing under her breath the whole time. She's not a particularly gifted singer, but I vaguely recognize "Joy to the World" and "Winter Wonderland."

And something about this scene tugs at my heart in a way that's almost painful. Growing up my home was never very festive during the holidays; my dad worked long hours, and my mom split when I was still a kid. I have very few memories of decorating for Christmas or Thanksgiving or anything like that. All those memories come from spending time with the O'Malleys.

But here I am, decorating my own home with Molly O'Malley. It's so...domestic. And it's impossible not to think about the future when I see a scene like this—a woman who makes me smile, wrapping a pom-pom garland around a makeshift Christmas tree, all but glowing with that inner light she has.

Is this how it would be? Is this what a life with Molly would look like?

I sigh, shoving one hand through my hair. I'm being stupid. I'm not going to have a life with Molly. My feelings for her aren't real; they're just a product of our situation. I'll forget all about her when she and her family leave the island.

"Do you have wrapping paper?" Molly says, pulling me out of my thoughts.

I give her a flat look. "What do you think?"

She cocks one brow at me. "Don't give me attitude," she says.

My laugh sounds unnaturally loud in my tiny home. "Sorry," I say. "But you have to know I'm not the kind of guy to keep wrapping paper on hand, right?"

"Meh," she says, but she can't stop her smile. "That's fine. I don't need it, I guess. I'll just keep your present in the bag."

"I won't hold it against you," I say, nodding.

"After all," she says. "The *true* Christmas gifts are the friendships we've made along the way—"

My snort of laughter interrupts her, and she grins.

"Do you remember that Christmas when my dad was in charge of buying the wrapping paper?" she says.

"But he waited too long, so by the time he got to the store they only had *Happy Birthday* paper left? Yeah," I say, smiling. "I remember that." I went over to the O'Malleys' house Christmas afternoon, and I found that they had waited for me to get there to open presents. "That was the Christmas your brother and I got in trouble for hand-delivering mistletoe to all the girls in the neighborhood."

Molly laughs. "I forgot about that," she says, looking at me. She scoots her body around so that she's facing the loveseat. "Who came up with that plan?"

"Who do you think?" I say with a roll of my eyes.

"Wes," she says.

"Definitely. If anyone would come up with a way to kiss multiple girls on Christmas, it's your brother."

Molly sighs, but she's still smiling, and there's a faraway

look in her eyes. "I remember being so upset," she says. "I was—
I mean—" Her gaze darts to mine, and I'm surprised to see her
cheeks turning pink. "I kind of had a crush on you back then,"
she says. "When I was in middle school."

I move quickly past my surprise—not that she had a crush
on me, but that she's bringing it up. "I know," I say, grinning at
her. "I could tell."

"Could you?" she says, pressing her hands to her cheeks.
She gives me an impish little smile. "I guess I wasn't very good
at hiding it."

"You were not," I say. "But it's okay. I knew you'd get over it
eventually." Of course, now part of me—the weak part of me
that wants what it can't have—wishes she *hadn't* gotten over it.
"I'm sure you moved on to bigger and better things, huh?"

She doesn't respond; she just drops her gaze to the carpet,
keeping her hands pressed over her cheeks.

Why isn't she answering?

My pulse jumps in my veins, my heart starting to beat more
quickly as I study her. She's still staring at the carpet, and even
though her hands are still on her cheeks, I can spot the
increasing flush of her skin—pink and freckled and so soft-
looking I want to reach out and touch her.

And I shouldn't ask. I should not vocalize the question
that's playing on repeat in my head. But...I need to know. Don't
ask me why; all I know is that if I'm left wondering about this, it
will haunt me until I go crazy.

"Molly?" I say hoarsely. "You moved on, right?"

"From this conversation? Yes," she says. She stands
abruptly, teetering until she throws her arms out for balance.
"I'm going to use the restroom, and then let's find something to
eat. I'm hungry."

"Yeah," I say. I'm barely paying attention to what I've
agreed to, but I'm still stuck on her refusal to answer.

There's no way. Right? There's no way she's liked me this whole time.

My anxiety spikes the second she's out of my line of sight, but I force myself to stay calm. Her medicine situation has me on edge; no matter what else I'm thinking about, that worry is always hovering in the back of my mind.

Which is why, when we're getting ready for bed later that evening, I fill her in on some of my thoughts.

"All right," I say, taking a deep breath and letting it out slowly. "Here's the deal. If it's okay with you, I'd like to sleep on the floor in here." I point to the spot of carpet next to the mattress on the floor. "Because I'm worried you'll have a seizure in the middle of the night. *However.*" I hold one hand up before she can interrupt. This next part kills me to say, but I know I need to. "If you truly do not think I have to worry about you having a seizure in the night, I will trust you. So"—another deep breath, another rough exhale—"can you look me in the eye and tell me honestly that you're confident you'll be all right?"

I know what answer I want to hear; I know what answer will make me feel better. But I also know that Molly understands her body and her triggers better than I ever could.

"No," she says quietly, and though my heart sinks, I'm not surprised. It's what I expected her to say. "I can't promise nothing will happen. I'm sleeping in a different bed, I'm stressed, I don't have my meds. So...no." She fiddles with the hem of one of her new t-shirts as she speaks, and she's back in my basketball shorts from earlier.

I nod. "I'll sleep on the floor here, then." I toss the pillow from the loveseat onto the floor and then dig my one spare blanket out from under my bed. There's no point in genuinely trying to get comfortable; my carpet feels like the equivalent of felt stretched over marble. It's going to be a rough night no matter how many blankets or pillows I use. I lie back anyway, resigning myself to my sleepless fate as Molly turns out the light and gets in bed.

The cool night air drifts in through the cracked window as we lie there. In the distance I can hear a dog barking. But the only sound I'm paying attention to is the sound of Molly's breathing, a soothing hypnosis in the dark. Every time I close my eyes, they snap right back open. I end up just staring at my ceiling, my ears straining as I listen to make sure she's okay as the minutes bleed on.

Some time later—maybe half an hour—I hear something.

"Beckett."

I startle at the sound of my name, whispered but audible.

"Yeah," I say immediately, sitting up in the dark. I glance over at Molly; all I can see without light is the rough shape of the mattress and some dark, blobby shapes on top.

"You can't sleep?"

I sigh. "No."

"Because of me?"

"I—it's—no," I say. "I'm just—"

"Worried," she says, and she sounds sad in a way I don't understand. "Yeah."

I don't want to lie to her. So I don't say anything.

"Here," she says a moment later. "Hold my hand."

I swallow. "What?"

"Hold my hand," she says tiredly. "That way you'll be able to feel if something happens."

And from the darkness I feel a soft, warm touch on my arm—searching, hesitant, then more sure as her fingers glide over my skin. I flip my palm up to meet hers when she reaches my hand, threading our fingers together in silence.

She gives my hand a squeeze, and I reciprocate, my heart thudding.

When's the last time I held a woman's hand like this? It's

intimate in a way I didn't expect. But in this room so dark and this house so lonely...I like it. I like having her here with me.

I lie back down, waiting for her to get comfortable so I can adjust accordingly. The mattress she's on sits directly on the floor, so she's only elevated a foot or so above me; that makes it easier to hold on.

So I keep her hand clasped in mine, small and warm, and I listen to her breathe. And it's only when her breaths even out, some twenty minutes later, that I let my eyes flutter closed.

SIXTEEN
MOLLY

I WAKE UP WITH MY HAND HANGING OVER THE EDGE OF the mattress, curved toward Beckett's. We look like God and Adam in the Sistine Chapel, reaching for each other, our fingertips inches apart—though the figures Michelangelo painted never looked like me. His models, from what I remember, were mostly devoid of freckles and wild red hair.

Beckett, on the other hand, could model for any sculptor he wanted, and they'd all be happy to have him. I look at him for a moment, my eyes scanning over the details I don't normally get to stare at when he's awake. His face is more relaxed in sleep than it ever is otherwise; he's a worrier. Those creases in his forehead are all smooth now, and there's no hint of a frown on his lips. He's nothing but serene.

I roll over onto my back and stare at the ceiling. It's Christmas Eve today. And I'm with Beckett Donovan, in the Virgin Islands, without the rest of my family. I'm not sure what I pictured for this Christmas season, but it wasn't this. I wish I felt as serene as Beckett looks. But instead, my insides are a riot of emotion—splashes of excitement and worry and sadness all running together until I'm nothing but a tangled mess of feelings.

"Molly?"

I jump, yanked out of my thoughts by Beckett's groggy voice.

"Yeah?" I say quickly, looking over at him. He stretches languidly, like a big cat bathing in the sun, his shirt riding up and offering me a glimpse of tanned, muscular perfection.

"Are you...humming?"

"Huh?" I say, blinking and yanking my gaze away from that strip of skin. When his words register in my brain, I realize he's right; I have been humming. I've been humming "Deck the Halls," to be exact. "Oh," I say. I sit up. "Yeah. Sorry. I didn't realize I was doing that."

He shrugs. "It's okay," he says. Then he runs one hand over his hair, which is sticking up in the back. "Did you sleep okay?"

"Yeah, I did," I say. Surprisingly well, actually. "Did you?"

Another shrug. "It was fine."

A twinge of guilt plucks at me. "You can have the mattress tonight," I say.

He gives me a look that plainly says *Don't start this again*, and I hold my hands up to placate him.

"Or not," I say. "I can take the mattress."

He nods. "Good." Then he stands up, stretching once more. After a wide, gape-mouthed yawn, he says, "Do you need to shower?"

"I'm good for now," I say.

"I'll use it, then." He goes to the chest of drawers against the wall and begins rifling through them, pulling out a shirt and some shorts. Then he leaves the room, and two seconds later I hear the bathroom door close.

I sigh, looking absently around as I think. What are we going to do today? We should do something Christmasy, right? There's a Christmas Eve show on the cruise ship that I was looking forward to; I guess that's not in my future anymore.

But there's no point in focusing on the things I'm missing. "Focus on the positive!" I tell myself, forcing a smile onto my face. I read somewhere that smiling can trigger the release of dopamine and serotonin, so I push my muscles a little harder, until I look like a cavewoman baring her teeth at her prey.

I can't say I notice any dopamine or serotonin action. My cheeks hurt, though. I let the smile drop.

It only takes me a couple minutes to get dressed and braid my hair. At this point I'm a walking Virgin Islands advertisement, but it's better than being stuck in my swimsuit. Then I leave the room to examine what we've got to work with in the living room.

One loveseat. One small table. Two wooden chairs. I glance over my shoulder back to the bedroom, my eyes narrowing on the blankets as I think.

I can make it work. It should be enough.

First I drag the blankets off the mattress, along with the blanket Beckett slept under. Once they're all in a nice pile in the middle of the living room floor, I begin moving furniture.

Beckett joins me halfway through the wrestling match I'm having with the loveseat.

"Why is it so heavy?" I gasp, looking at him as he stares, bewildered, at my progress. "It's small. It should not be this hard to move."

"Are you..." he says slowly, "trying to make a fort?"

"Of course," I say, giving up on the loveseat. I slump against it so I can catch my breath. "It's my favorite Christmas Eve tradition."

He nods, and I do not appreciate the skeptical look on his face. But then he points to the loveseat. "It's because of the feet at the base," he says. "That's why it's heavy. They're pretty solid. The cushions are dense, too."

I bend over to look at the bottom of the loveseat. Sure enough, it's being held off the ground by four wooden cylinders, each roughly the size of two Roombas stacked on top of each other.

"Oh," I say, nodding. "Right. That makes sense." Then I look at him. "Are you going to help me?"

"I—yeah, I guess," he says. He seems to realize fighting about this will get him nowhere.

Smart man.

"Great," I say happily. "So what we want is the couch over here"—I point to the middle of the room—"and we'll drape the blankets from the back of the couch over the table. The chairs will go on either side of the table. Got it?"

Beckett does in thirty seconds what I couldn't do in five minutes. He gets the furniture moved, and then we drape the blankets strategically until we're standing in front of a roughly made fort.

It's nothing like the ones my family makes at Christmas every year, but it has its own kind of charm—especially since only two of us need to fit inside. O'Malley forts are a go-big-or-go-home affair, and we have more furniture and blankets in our house than Beckett has in this temporary little place.

"It's not like at your house," he says, echoing my thoughts.

"It's perfect," I say with a smile. It doesn't need to be big or fancy. "Thanks for helping."

He nods. "I assume we're watching Christmas movies in there?"

"If that sounds good to you," I say. I'm clinging to my Christmas traditions, and I'm clinging hard. Except...maybe I should ask him what he wants to do. "Unless you want to do something else?"

"It's fine with me," he says with a shrug. "Your family's forts are one of my favorite parts of Christmas anyway. It's not like my parents ever did much."

I swallow, searching for words, but I can't find any. "I'll grab some snacks," I say instead.

We reconvene inside the fort a few minutes later, and then we spend a lazy morning watching movies and eating the remainder of the Christmas cookies I packed, as well as stale pretzels and bread with butter and honey. It's a hodge-podge potluck provided by Beckett's sparse pantry, but something about the entire experience feels almost magical. I'm not sure why; our Christmas cactus is cute but not awe-inspiring, and there are no twinkly lights or Christmas carols playing in the background. Everything I would have listed if asked about what makes Christmas magical—none of those things are here.

It's just me and Beckett in a blanket fort with some random snacks and *White Christmas* playing on his laptop.

"I've always wanted to be a good dancer," I sigh as I watch Vera-Ellen.

Beckett gives a little snort of laughter. "I'm not sure that's in the cards for you," he says. Then he turns to me. "But I will support you in all your dancing endeavors." His voice is gentle, his eyes soft.

And how is this man even real? Yes, he's grumpy on the outside, but he is pure marshmallow fluff on the inside. I'm just about to respond when an embarrassingly loud sound comes from my gurgling stomach.

He grins at me. "I guess the snacks aren't cutting it?"

"I could use some lunch," I admit.

"We're limited on supplies, but I do have...hmm." He gets on his hands and knees before crawling out of the fort. I follow, and by the time I make it out, he's shuffling around in a kitchen cabinet.

"Got anything?" I say.

"I have canned soup," he says, pulling out two cans and holding them up. "Tomato bisque."

I nod, because I'm pretty sure *tomato bisque* is just a fancy way of saying *tomato soup,* and I can get behind that. "Tomato bisque sounds perfect."

We're mostly quiet as we heat the soup, but it's a nice sort of silence—the comfortable kind, where no one has to force conversation. We divide the soup into two bowls and then clear the blanket off the table and chairs, effectively dismantling over half of our fort.

We eat in silence until our new phone rings. Beckett has a mouth full of soup, so I answer it.

"Hello?"

"Molly?" It's Wes's voice.

"Hi," I say, pulling the phone away from my ear and turning it on speaker so Beckett can participate in the conversation too. "How are you guys doing?"

"We're fine," Wes says. "We just wanted to check on you all. We should be there tomorrow morning sometime."

"Well, we're alive," I say as Beckett continues to eat. "We're just making the best of things."

"Good, good," he says, sounding distracted. Then he goes on, "And look, Molly. You're not—you guys aren't—you remember what I said, right?" he finally gets out.

I tense at his words. I have a feeling I know where this is going, and it sends something sharp and irritable through me, prickling at my insides like I've swallowed our Christmas cactus. "Remember what you said..." I say, tapping my chin and pretending to think. "Oh! That I'm ugly?"

"What? No—when did I say that?" he says, and I picture him frowning, his glasses sliding down the bridge of his nose.

172

"At the waterfall. When I was talking about seeing my reflection in Dad's shiny head."

"Oh, right." He snickers, then says, "But I was obviously joking. No, I'm talking about—"

"About when you said ichthyology was stupid?"

"Well, it kind of is. It's just *fish*, Molly—"

"It's not just fish, Wes," I say, trying valiantly to rein in my temper. I shouldn't be picking a fight. "But even if it were, what's it to you?"

"Fine. Fish are cool. Now can we please get to the point?" I hear him take a deep breath, exhaling and blowing static into the phone. "Look, I know you've had a crush on Beckett for pretty much your entire life."

I clear my throat uncomfortably, my eyes darting to Beckett just long enough to see his head snap up, his gaze zeroing in on me, his spoon suspended in the air halfway between his bowl and his mouth. It's dripping steady droplets of soup on the table in front of him, but he doesn't seem to notice; he just stares at me while Wes keeps running his stupid mouth.

"But you and Beckett aren't a good match, Moll," he says reasonably. "And I don't want you to get hurt."

"What makes you think I'd get hurt?" The words are past my lips before I can stop them.

"You just would, Molly," he says impatiently. "Come on. Promise me."

And it's crazy—it's insane—how my mouth automatically opens to promise him. Without even thinking about his request, my mind is ready to jump in and promise him something I don't want to promise. Is this what I've become?

I snap my jaw shut. Clear my throat. Swallow. Clear my throat again. Then I say it.

"No."

Silence. Then Wes's voice, bewildered. "What?"

"I said no," I say again, my voice stronger now. "I can't promise you that. I don't want to promise you that."

"Molly, come on. Beckett has baggage—"

"There's nothing wrong with his baggage," I say, irritation spiking deep in my gut. "Everyone has problems. It's not just him."

"And he wouldn't want to hurt your feelings," Wes goes on, "but you're not his type. You're great, of course, but you're not his type."

I can feel the heat flooding my cheeks—no, not even just my cheeks. It's my whole body. My whole body is hot with embarrassment, from my face to the tips of my fingers to my toes. I want to lean across the table and drown myself in Beckett's bowl of soup, just to get away from this humiliation. Death by tomato bisque seems like a great option at this point.

And the stupid thing is, Wes isn't even trying to embarrass me or humiliate me. He loves me; I know he does. We bicker, but it's all in good fun; we get along well.

I guess I just never realized before that some of his jokes hurt. Why didn't I realize that? Why haven't I said anything? Am I just so used to it that joking putdowns are what I expect?

Even though I dread what I might see, I find my gaze being pulled up, up, up until my eyes clash with Beckett's again. I blink, and it's not until I feel something trickle down my face that I realize there are tears in my eyes. I blink again, squeezing my lids shut and wiping my eyes.

"Hey," Beckett says.

And at first I think he's talking to me. But then he reaches out and takes the phone from my hand, speaking into it. "Why are you only telling Molly this? Why aren't you warning me off too?"

"Beckett?" Wes says, clearly surprised. "Oh, hey. I didn't realize you were there—"

"Why aren't you warning me off, Wes?" Beckett repeats. His voice is calm, but his face is a mask of stone, the only movement a muscle jumping in his jaw.

"Because," Wes says after a second. He must be able to tell something's up; his voice is warier now, more tentative. "I'm not worried about you. Molly's not a girl you'd be interested in."

"She's not a girl at all," Beckett replies, rolling his eyes. "She's a woman. And I *am* interested in her, you idiot. So don't call her ugly or make fun of her fish. It's pissing me off."

A deafening silence falls over the tiny kitchen, broken only by the steady *drip, drip, drip* of Beckett's soup.

"Dude," Wes says finally. "Are you serious?"

"Yes," Beckett says, sounding more frustrated still.

"I...don't know what to say to that." Wes's voice is utterly bewildered.

"Well, you're in luck; your opinion is not required," Beckett bites out. "We'll see you tomorrow, Wes." And then, without another word, he hangs up.

For one long, tense moment, we stare at each other. Beckett's spoon is still dripping soup all over the table, a puddle of orangey-red tomato bisque. Like Wes, I, too, don't know what to say to Beckett's announcement that he's interested in me.

My heart, on the other hand, has *plenty* to say.

It's a riot down there in my chest. That fleshy chunk of muscle is beating against my rib cage with celebratory fervor, wearing a party hat and blowing on a kazoo. There's confetti flying everywhere and music blaring through my veins.

My heart is celebrating, even as it pulses against the walls that are still sore from Wes's words.

"Sorry," Beckett says, finally putting an end to our weird stare down. His gaze drops to his spoon, and he frowns when he sees the puddle of tomato bisque pooling on the table. He puts his spoon back in his bowl with a little *clink* and then scoots his chair back away from the table. The loud scraping sound echoes through the tiny kitchen, and I watch as he moves to a cabinet and rummages through it. He emerges a few seconds later with a wad of napkins, brown and slightly crumpled.

I smile at this; I didn't take him for the kind of man who saves the napkins when he orders take-out, but I do the same thing.

He cleans up the tomato bisque with hasty impatience before tossing the napkins in the trash. Then he looks at me.

"Sorry," he repeats, rubbing the back of his neck. "About that, I mean"—he gestures to my phone—"and going off on Wes and stuff."

I shrug. "He's your best friend. You're allowed to tell him off." I hesitate before adding, "I appreciated it, actually. Thank you."

Beckett sighs and then takes his seat again, slumping back down. He looks tired; not just physically but emotionally. Like he needs a nap and a hug.

And you know what? I can help with part of that.

I get out of my chair, leaving my bowl where it is and rounding the tiny table. Then I move to stand next to Beckett.

He cranes his neck around, looking at me with confusion and wariness. His brows are pulled low over his eyes, the corners of his mouth turned down.

I reach out without thinking, smoothing my thumb over his forehead. "Such a frown," I murmur. "Relax."

And then, almost as though I'm in a trance, I lean down and kiss him.

Don't ask me why—I truly do not know.

No, that's a lie. I know exactly why. I'm kissing him because I've wanted to kiss him since I knew what kissing was. I'm kissing him because he's been so incredibly kind to me over the last couple days. I'm kissing him because not ten minutes ago he admitted, out loud, that he likes me.

So I press my lips to his, my hands firm on his face. He gasps right before our lips meet, but I gobble the sound up. It only lasts for a second, though, because he doesn't respond. Not at all. He doesn't kiss me back; his hands come to rest on my shoulders before he pushes gently, separating us.

"My first kiss," I murmur.

Through my haze of determination, I'm vaguely aware of the sting of rejection. That sting is soothed, though, by the look on Beckett's face, still only inches from mine.

His brown eyes are wide and blazing, his gaze zeroed in on my lips. His broad shoulders rise and fall as his chest heaves, choppy bursts of breath puffing against my mouth. His Adam's apple bobs as he swallows, and I follow the motion greedily.

"No," he breathes. "That doesn't count as your first kiss."

And then, faster than I can even process, he reaches up, grabs the back of my neck, and yanks my mouth back down to his.

He kisses me.

He *kisses* me.

Hands in my hair, fingers twisted through curls, grip so tight my scalp stings.

Sandpaper stubble against my skin, rough against smooth.

Lips hungry, devouring—push and pull, give and take, the nip of my teeth and our stilted breaths in the silent kitchen.

And perhaps most notable of all: the beat of my heart, the rhythm of my pulse, the fire in my veins that roars *finally, finally, finally—*

"No," Beckett gasps suddenly, and the next thing I know I'm stumbling backward, my steps horribly loud on the linoleum tile. I bump into the refrigerator, but the collision barely registers in my mind; I'm too focused on the man in the chair in front of me.

"No," he says again, his eyes wild. He runs his hands through his hair, making it stick up like a mad scientist's. His gaze darts around the kitchen until finally it comes to rest on me, at which point I realize I'm dealing with a cornered animal.

"All right," I say gently. I hold my hands up in surrender. "I won't do it again. Okay?"

"Crap, Molly," he says. He rakes his fingers through his hair again. "Crap. Look." He exhales roughly before going on. "It's not that I don't want to, all right? I obviously do. But—"

"It's okay," I say, keeping my voice slow and calm. "It's truly okay. You don't need to explain." Then, because his eyes are still a little shell-shocked, I add, "Just relax, all right?"

Beckett slumps back in his chair. "I can't relax with you," he says. The words are croaky, like they've been stuck in his throat. But I just smile.

"Yes, you can," I say softly. Then I lean down, over the back of his chair, and wrap my arms around him from behind, resting my chin on his shoulder. "I'm a safe space for you."

"You're not, though," he sighs. His hands come up to rest on my forearms, his thumbs rubbing my skin back and forth, back and forth, in a way that sends shivers through me. He lets his head drop back. "You're dangerous, Molly O'Malley. You're doing things to me that I can't make sense of."

And it clicks, then, the truth of this situation. Bits and pieces of the puzzle I've already had begin floating around in my mind's eye, rearranging themselves and then snapping into place until the full picture appears.

He likes me. But he's scared.

"I understand how you feel," I say slowly. My voice is barely above a whisper, but with my chin propped on his shoulder, I know he can hear me just fine. "And it makes sense that you feel that way. I know you're not big on forming relationships or getting close to people, especially with how you grew up." The words keep spilling out of me, but I don't stop them. It feels important to validate him, somehow; to let him know that what he's feeling is normal and okay. At the same time, though...I clear my throat. "But just because something is new or scary doesn't necessarily mean it's bad or dangerous."

Beckett sighs again. "I know that," he says. He continues to trail his hands over my forearms where they're wrapped around his shoulders, his palms calloused and rough and perfectly warm. "My mind knows that."

"But it doesn't change how you feel," I say.

"Yeah."

I nod—or I try to, anyway. It doesn't work that well, since my head is resting on his shoulder. "I get that," I say. "And I won't push."

Beckett's hands stop their trek over my arms, and without warning he turns his head toward mine. Our cheeks smoosh together, his chin bumping into my mine. "Your whole life?"

I blink. "What?"

"That's what Wes said. That you've had a crush on me for pretty much your whole life."

"Oh," I say. I move to unwrap my arms from around his shoulders, but his hands tighten on them, holding me in place. I give in, slumping back against him. "Um. Kind of? I guess?" There's no point in denying it, I guess. I'm going to take it as a blessing in disguise that he can't actively look at my face right now, though. Otherwise he'd see that I've probably turned the same red as his tomato soup.

"I guess I am a pretty incredible male specimen," he says.

"Modest, too," I say with a little smile.

His voice is more serious, though, when he speaks again. "I can't promise you anything, Molly. I really can't."

"I know," I say as my smile fades. "I'm aware."

"I barely understand how I'm feeling. And—" He breaks off, and his hesitation hangs in the air around us, heavy on my skin.

"Just say it," I say, resigning myself. "You won't hurt my feelings."

He sighs. "It's just that...I think a lot of what I'm feeling has come from this situation. So I don't..." He trails off. "I don't know how sustainable my feelings for you are. That's why I really can't start anything right now."

"I know," I say again. "I told you I won't push. I won't kiss you again, either."

"Sad," he murmurs, "but probably for the best."

I ignore my wilting heart and my desperate pulse, laughing instead. "Promise me one thing?" I say.

He only hesitates for a second before he nods. "Anything."

"If you change your mind, will you let me know?"

A little smile carves itself over his lips. "You'll be the first," he says.

That will have to be good enough for me.

SEVENTEEN
BECKETT

Oh, how the mighty have fallen...

Me. It's me.

I'm the mighty. And I have fallen.

Hard and fast.

Not in love—I haven't fallen in love. There's no way anyone falls in love over the course of two days. But...Molly O'Malley kissed me. She kissed me, and I pushed her away. Then I pulled her right back and kissed her again.

And now I can't stop thinking about it.

Molly kisses with absolute abandon. She's inexperienced—she told me as much—but she more than makes up for it with reckless passion. I wouldn't have expected anything else from her, honestly. She was all lips and tongue and hands fisted in my shirt and—

"Snap out of it," I mutter to myself. If I keep reliving that memory, it's going to be impossible to stop myself from kissing her again—especially because I know she would probably welcome it.

Unbidden, Wes's words ring through my mind. *Look, I*

know you've had a crush on Beckett for pretty much your entire life.

How is that possible? How is it possible that she's had feelings for me all these years? I haven't seen her since I graduated from high school. She was barely a blip on my radar.

That's another strike against us, one I have no choice but to acknowledge: whatever Molly feels for me probably isn't based on who I actually am as a person. How could it be? She doesn't know me—not really. Whatever version of me that's been living in her brain for the last ten years—that's the person she has feelings for. Some idealized version of me that she's built up in her mind.

"You're doing an awful lot of thinking over there." Her voice snaps me out of my thoughts, and I turn to see her looking at me with one brow raised. "Want to share with the class?"

I sigh, leaning back into the cushions of the loveseat. We've dismantled our fort and settled for sitting here instead. It's a departure from the O'Malley fort tradition, but it's also more comfortable. Time is doing strange things in my mind; the rest of Molly's family will arrive tomorrow, which means my time with her will be over. I don't know what that will mean for us. I only know that things will change. That fact makes me want to pull her close and soak up every last second.

"Nah," I say finally. I glance over at Molly, who's still giving me that look. "Just thinking about what to do for the rest of the day."

"How about we nap?" she says. She snuggles into the same corner of the loveseat she favored yesterday, yawning and making me yawn too. "Watching movies makes me sleepy."

I can't help the smile that tugs at my lips—she's just so cute. I hesitate for just a second before patting my lap. "Lie down," I say.

Her mouth forms a little *o* of surprise. "I—is that okay?"

"It's fine," I say with a laugh. What is it about her that makes me feel so light, so buoyant? "Rest. Close your eyes."

The smile she gives me is nothing short of blinding. "That would be nice. Thanks."

She turns so that her back is to me and moves to lie down, but I stop her.

"Wait," I say. "Your hair." I reach for her braid, hesitantly at first, before removing the hair tie from the end. I comb my fingers through the braid, loosening it and marveling at the feeling of her curls. Her hair is softer than it looks—something I noticed when I kissed her—and I fight the bizarre urge to rub it against my cheek. She lays her head gently on my legs, draping her own legs over the arm of the loveseat. Then she looks up at me, her mint hot chocolate eyes sleepy. I think I could spend the rest of the day and into the night exactly like this—with Molly, soft and warm, her hair spilling into my lap.

"Sleep," I say, my hand moving of its own accord to stroke her hair.

"I don't want to," she murmurs with a little smile. "I want to stare at you."

I shake my head, smiling back as her lids flutter in an effort to stay open. She's so tired, and that makes me nervous. The best thing she can do now for her health is to rest. "Close your eyes, sweetheart."

"Mmm," she hums. Her eyes finally close, light lashes fanned over pale skin, perfectly lovely. "I like when you call me that. What should I call you? Babe? Honey buns? Sexy pants?"

"Don't call me anything right now," I say softly. "Just sleep."

She nods, sighing happily.

"Good girl," I whisper.

"Thought you weren't going to say that anymore," she says in a dreamy, vague voice that tells me she's already half-asleep.

"You're right," I say. "I'll do better. Sleep now."

"Bossy," she mumbles, but she falls silent after that. Her breathing slowly evens out as her face and body relax, until she's fast asleep in my lap.

I let my head rest against the back of the couch. It's not very comfortable; I'm too tall, which puts my neck at a bad angle, my chin jutting toward the ceiling. I close my eyes anyway, letting my body chase the sleep it couldn't find last night. Because it was a lie when I told Molly this morning that I slept fine—I did not sleep fine. I didn't sleep even *sort of* fine. I tossed and turned and had weird snippets of dreams that left me with a vaguely ominous sense of anxiety.

So despite the awkward angle of my neck, I drift off almost immediately. Molly is warmer than any blanket, and something about having her right here is calming.

I enter dreams filled with her—dreams of soft skin and warm lips and things I can never, ever tell Wes. I'm pulled from these blissful moments, though, by an odd sound. I jerk awake, and for one wild moment I think there's an animal in my house before I realize that's not possible. But it's a keening, groaning sound that humans don't typically make—

Except they do. Because when I look down at Molly's head in my lap, I realize that sound is coming from Molly, from her pale, parted lips.

And something is wrong. Something is very wrong. Her body moves, her arms and legs straightening—and then the seizing starts—

And everything turns to ice.

Ice in my veins, the frosty grip of panic curling my insides, my head spinning frantically as bizarrely, insanely, I'm yanked back to a moment from years ago.

I played intramural soccer in college, and there was one game where a guy on the opposite team twisted on his leg wrong and ended up breaking it when another guy then landed on top of him. A compound fracture, his shin bone sticking right out of his skin. I'm not ashamed to say that when I clapped eyes on that protruding bone, I dropped like a bag of rocks and started shaking so hard my teeth chattered. The goalie doubled over and vomited; more than one guy started crying.

The brain *knows*. It knows when it's seeing something so horrible, so unnatural, and it rebels.

And that's what it feels like to be watching this seizure. Molly's skin is gray and clammy, her lips turning rapidly blue, and for a second all I can do is stare, completely in shock. I know, without knowing how I know, that I will remember this moment forever; the press of her head still in my lap, the soft fabric of her Virgin Islands shirt brushing against my fingertips, the faint scent of tomato soup in the air.

Because this is Molly, *my* Molly, and it's wrong, it's all wrong—her limbs, locked and jerky, her eyes rolled back in her head, her teeth gnashing wildly. This is wrong, so wrong—

I shake my head violently, because I'm spiraling, and there's no time for that. Why, *why*, did I not think to ask her what I should do if she had a seizure? Isn't that the first thing I should have done? What was I thinking?

With trembling arms, I lift Molly off my lap and lay her gently on the floor. She's not easy to move—her body is rigid and seizing rhythmically—but I manage. Then I grab the phone and dial Wes's number, the only one in his family I know off the top of my head. I misdial the first time because my fingers are shaking, but I get it the second time around, punching the keys with more force than normal, worrying the whole time.

What if he doesn't answer because he's mad about our conversation earlier? What if he doesn't hear his phone ringing? What if—

But the phone clicks as he picks up. He begins to speak, but his first word doesn't even make it out of his mouth before I interrupt.

"Molly's having a seizure," I blurt out. "She doesn't have her medicine. What do I do? Tell me what to do. Should I call 911?"

Wes swears loudly. "All right. First off, stay calm."

"I'm trying," I say.

"Good. You're doing good," he says, and I can tell he's switching into nurse mode. I've never appreciated it more. "Don't call 911. She doesn't need that. Turn her on her side if you can. She might throw up, and we don't want her to choke. Can you do that?"

"Yes," I say immediately. "Yes. I can do that. Hang on." I punch the button for speaker and then get down on the floor next to Molly, setting the phone down on my scratchy carpet. With one hand on her shoulder and one at her hip, I manage to get her on her side. "Okay," I say. "What now?"

"Can you cushion her head?"

"Yes," I say. There's a weird sensation in my eyes, and a second later I realize that hot, stinging feeling is tears. Actual *tears*. I squeeze my lids closed impatiently; I don't have time for this. I grab a pillow from the couch and lift her head as gently as possible, placing it underneath. Then I look breathlessly at the phone. "Now what?"

"Now we wait," Wes says gravely. This is the most serious I've ever heard him in our many years of friendship, but I can picture the tight set of his mouth and the crease in his brow. "Stay on the phone with me. I have a timer going. It should be over soon."

"Yeah," I say, my body sagging. "Okay."

"She might wet herself," Wes warns. "Or throw up—"

"I don't care," I say. "I can clean up. I don't care." I swallow, my eyes glued to her as panic continues to rise in me. "Wes, it *really* doesn't look like she's breathing—"

"She is," he says quickly. "I know it doesn't look like it, but she is. And her breathing will go back to normal when she's done with this phase."

"Her lips are blue, man—"

"I know," he says. "I know. I need you to breathe, okay? I know it looks scary. It looks bad. But she's going to be okay. All right?"

"Yeah," I say, forcing myself to take deep breaths. "Is she— is she conscious right now?"

"Not at all. She won't remember any of this."

I nod. A second later I notice a wet stain seeping over the crotch area of her shorts; like Wes said might happen, she's lost control of her bladder. I sit up straighter as her body begins to relax, her limbs going limp as the seizing stops. "Oh, she's done. She's done."

"The seizing is over?"

"Yes," I say. "What now? Do I need to call an ambulance?"

"No," Wes says. "If this were her first seizure, maybe, or if it had lasted an abnormally long time. But the only thing you can do now is wait. She's going to be unconscious for a little bit— maybe five minutes, maybe ten. Something like that. When she comes to, she's going to be confused. She'll be completely out of it, and probably still unresponsive even though she's conscious."

"How long will that last?" I say.

"Maybe thirty minutes. Now listen up. After she opens her eyes, I want you to wait ten minutes. At that point I want you to tell her she's had a seizure."

Through the surreal haze of everything that's going on, another emotion pierces my panic: confusion. "Won't she know?" I say, frowning.

"No," he says. "That's how disoriented she'll be; she won't even know what's happened."

"Okay," I say, committing every word he says to memory. "Ten minutes, tell her she had a seizure. What then?"

"Try asking her to follow a simple command. Maybe give her your hand and ask her to squeeze it. Don't try to make her talk yet."

"Simple command," I mumble. I'm still paying attention to Wes, but most of my mind is focused on the slight bit of color that seems to be returning to Molly's skin. Her breathing is becoming more apparent too, her chest moving up and down. Some of my icy panic melts when I see this, and I exhale roughly, my body slumping as some of the tension leaves my shoulders.

"Even once she's back to herself, you need to stay with her until we get there," Wes says, snapping me out of my thoughts.

I nod. "I planned on it."

"I'm talking pee with the door open, Beckett."

"I'll make it work," I promise, my eyes darting over her unconscious form.

I'm kneeling at her side, a desperate man praying at the altar. My hands hover over her body, and I let them rest on her upper arm. I need to touch her, even just the tiniest bit—I need to feel that her skin is still warm, that she's still here with me. That she's alive.

I don't know how long I sit like that, on my knees next to her, Wes silent but present on the other end. It might be twenty minutes. It might be twenty years. In that time warp, I become an expert on Molly O'Malley's face, because my eyes never move.

I count the freckles on her nose; twelve.

I calculate the area under the curve of her lips; pure beauty.

I make a mental list of all the places I want to kiss; every freckle. This one and this one and this one. All of them.

I watch her, and I make reckless deals with the gods of this world if only they'll keep her safe.

And then I wait.

EIGHTEEN
MOLLY

Skin. Rough. Dark. Noise. Bright. Wet. Dark.

"Molly?"

Me.

"Molly, baby. You had a seizure."

Seizure.

Skin. Warm.

"Here's my hand. Can you squeeze my fingers?"

Skin. Hand. Follow.

"Good girl. She squeezed, Wes. She opened her eyes but closed them again. What now?"

Him.

No.

No.

"Oh—no, what's wrong? Molly, what's wrong? I think she's crying, Wes—"

"Calm down. Give her time. Her brain needs time to bounce back. Just wait." Silence. "And dude. I need you to cut out the *baby* crap. That's my sister—"

"I'm gonna hang up now. I'll call you in a little bit, okay? I just want to focus on her right now."

"Ugh. All right. Just breathe and stay calm. She'll be fine. She's going to be weak for a bit, and she might be a little emotional, so just be prepared. Call me later. I need to go tell my parents anyway."

Wes.

Parents.

Eyes. Hot. Wet.

"Shh, sweetheart, you're okay."

Him. Warm.

Dark.

Dark...

"NO, Molly—don't get up. What do you need?" Beckett is kneeling on the floor next to the couch where I'm stretched out, but now he jumps to his feet, a blur of long limbs and tan skin.

"I need to change and get cleaned up," I say. I don't look at him; I can't. I peed on his carpet. I had a seizure right in front of him. All I want right now is to run away.

Instead I press my palms to my warm cheeks, which I'm positive are flushed and pink with humiliation, and stare at the floor.

This is so much worse than the hives.

"Right," Beckett says. From the corner of my eye I see him rub the back of his neck. "You have more clothes, yeah?"

I nod. "I bought some. They're in that bag." I point to the plastic bag on the floor by the bathroom door. "Can I have another pair of boxers though?"

I heard my mom say once that after you give birth, you lose all sense of modesty or shame about your body; having a seizure in front of Beckett seems to have had the same effect on me. I wet myself in front of him—there's no point in being embarrassed about underwear.

I can sink no lower.

The hot prick of tears stings my eyes, and I blink a few times to dispel them.

"Yeah, hang on," Beckett says. I can feel his eyes on me, but he doesn't comment; he just disappears into his bedroom and returns not five seconds later with a pair of boxers, probably the first ones he could find. Then he grabs the shopping bag and returns to the couch.

He doesn't want to leave me alone.

My cheeks burn hotter; my eyes well with tears again.

"You can stay," I say as he hands me the boxers and the bag. I know he's going to ask. "Just turn around, please."

My voice sounds horrible—monotonous and dull, devoid of emotion or inflection. I sound like a zombie. But I don't know how to make that stop, and right now I don't care. My mind keeps coming up with new realizations, new ramifications, and a new awareness of what's happened.

"I'll probably need to hold onto you for support," I say, prying the words out of my mouth. They're sharp in my throat and bitter on my tongue, but if I don't tell him, I risk falling over and having him turn around to see it. "The seizing usually makes my muscles shaky and then sore for a couple days."

"Yeah, of course," Beckett says immediately. He steps closer to the couch before turning around, giving me his back. "Am I close enough? Just grab on wherever you need to."

"Thanks," I say. I do the best I can to stand, but my legs shake enough that I end up clamping one hand around Beckett's upper arm.

"Two years," I murmur as I strip out of my shorts and the

boxers I had on. I let them fall unceremoniously to the floor, my shame bunched tangibly around my ankles.

Beckett is silent for a second before he speaks. "It's been two years since you had a seizure?" His posture is rigid, but he sounds normal enough.

"No," I say. "Two years in the state of Florida that I have to be seizure-free before I can drive again. Although..." I bite my lip, thinking. "I think after six months I can apply for an exception to that. I'm well-controlled on my medication." I sigh as I pull the new pair of boxers up—black with a pattern of red chili peppers, something I certainly would tease him about if the circumstances were different—and then follow with my new pair of shorts. "I'm done," I say.

Since my dignity is already gone, I let myself fall back onto the couch in a tangled heap. Truthfully, as much as I hate just lying here, it feels like I've been through a full-body workout. My muscles are tired. Maybe this wouldn't be happening if I exercised regularly, but that definitely doesn't happen.

I walk past a yoga studio when I go to the bakery on Saturday mornings. Sometimes I peer in the window and think it might be nice to learn. Does that count?

I move clumsily back into a reclining position on the loveseat, letting my head rest on the arm of the couch. Then I close my eyes, mostly so I don't have to look at Beckett.

"Molly."

Hmm. Can I pretend I don't hear him? That would be weird, right?

Yeah. It would be weird. Crap.

"Molly."

I open one eye to a slit, just to scope out the situation. When I see Beckett looking at me, one eyebrow raised as he kneels next to the loveseat, I sigh and open both eyes.

"What?" I say, fixing my gaze to my hands. My voice is still doing that terrible dead-sounding thing.

Beckett sighs next to me. One second later he places a finger under my chin, tilting my face up until I have no choice but to look at him.

"Molly," he says—the third time now—as he moves one hand to cradle my face, his thumb tracing circles over my jaw. His voice is gentle, impossibly kind and full of emotions that I've only ever dreamed about from him. "What do you need from me right now?"

And that question, it seems, is my undoing; I burst into tears. There's no in between, no escalation period—it's zero to sixty in no time flat. I'm calm one second and bawling the next.

"I need you to forget everything that just happened," I sob. "I peed my pants in front of you and I really like you and I'm so embarrassed." I had no intention of telling him these things, but the dam has opened, it seems—and I can't stop it. "I never meant for any of this to happen. I just wanted to make a good impression and maybe get some closure but I *like* you, Beckett, and I want you to think I'm pretty and cool and instead I peed on your carpet and that's not sexy and seizures aren't cute—"

"Whoa, whoa," he cuts me off, looking startled. "Whoa. Hang on. Breathe, sweetheart." He scoots closer, resting his elbows on the loveseat and taking my hand in both of his. "Breathe."

I drag in one large breath, and it does help some; a few more stuttering breaths let me stem the flow of tears until I'm able to gulp myself into silence.

"Good girl," Beckett murmurs, moving one hand to my head. He strokes my hair for a second, his eyes darting over my face. "Better?" he says. "Can you breathe okay?"

I nod hesitantly, pulling my hands out of his and swiping my eyes.

"Good. In that case," he says, and a steely glint enters his eyes as his gaze zeroes in on me, "listen up."

I blink at this sudden change in tone, but I don't get a chance to ask him what's going on—because a second later his hands are on my face, his eyes are burning, and he's kissing me.

It's not gentle or sweet. It's the hard press of his lips against mine, a chasing, demanding kiss that pulls the air from my lungs and sends warm shivers cascading down my spine. An assault on my senses, the slide of his hands to my jaw and the tangle of our breaths.

And then, as quick as it began, the kiss stops; Beckett wrenches his lips away from mine, breathing hard, his eyes still blazing.

"I do not care about you wetting yourself. I do not care about the seizure. I *do not care*." His voice is as fierce as I've ever heard it. "All I care about is that you're safe. My opinion of you has not changed, and it *will* not change. You are not broken. You are not defective. Do you understand?"

"I—I don't—" I say.

But my words are lost as he presses one finger to my lips, warm and calloused. "I need a yes or a no, baby. Do you understand?"

And look. When Beckett called me *Baby O'Malley*, I hated it. But when he calls me *baby*?

Sign me up now. Sign me up *yesterday*.

"I understand," I breathe, my insides fluttering like a leaf in the wind. My words are slightly garbled since I'm speaking past his finger, and I look pointedly down at his hand. He lets it drop, taking hold of my hands again.

"You can't ask me a question and then cover my mouth," I say. I really hope my voice isn't betraying how flustered I am right now. "How am I supposed to answer?"

"You've figured it out fine so far," he murmurs, his gaze fixed on me.

"Still," I say, sniffing. "That alpha male crap might fly in romance novels, but it won't work here."

The corners of his lips twitch. "Noted," he says. "I'll try to tone it down."

"I mean, you don't have to tone it down *that* much," I say, blushing. "Just be reasonable when you ask me a question. Don't get impatient for an answer when you're covering my mouth. And let me talk."

"That's a valid request," he concedes, that little smile still on his face.

"Of course it is."

His smile fades, and something remarkably like curiosity enters his eyes as he looks at me. "What are you doing to me?" he says. His voice is musing, and that little crease appears on his forehead. "I go out of my way not to feel big feelings, especially attachment to other people—"

"Very healthy—"

"But here I am, making an absolute fool of myself."

I swallow all the words that want to escape—declarations of love and propositions about forever—and rein myself in. "You're pretty great," I say instead. More tears spring to my eyes as I watch the emotions play over his face.

"Are you crying again?" he says quickly.

"These are good tears," I say, my voice quiet.

"Wes said you might be emotional," he says. "Do you remember hearing us talk?"

"I remember that he was on the phone, but I don't remember anything you guys said," I say.

"That's okay," he says. "It wasn't anything important." Then he reaches up and wipes my tears from my cheeks.

Ugh. I want to date this man. I want to be with him so badly. I know he has baggage, but the raw materials are ready to be polished into high-quality gemstones. He would be an incredible boyfriend, husband, father—all of it.

We would have to get to know each other better, and we would probably have some speed bumps as we unpacked his relationship hang-ups. But I have a feeling it would be worth it.

"You know," I say, trying and failing to hold back a yawn. "You're relatively closed off, and I think you're probably a runner, but you're also way more communicative than I would have expected."

Beckett is quiet for a second before nodding. "I am a runner," he says. "And I usually am closed off."

"But you talk about things," I say. "And you're reasonable. I like that." I pause. "I like *you*."

He sighs. "I like you too. But..."

"I know," I say. "And I understand." I search quickly for a new subject. "It's still Christmas Eve. Should we watch another Christmas movie?"

I can tell from the way he hesitates that he's not ready to drop the subject, but thankfully he nods anyway. There's not much more to say; not yet, anyway. He can't make me any promises right now. "Yeah," he says. "Pick something and I'll pull it up on my laptop."

I decide on a movie while Beckett makes us two mugs of mint hot chocolate, served in red Solo cups. I last maybe half an hour before I can't keep my eyes open anymore; the last thing I'm aware of is Beckett carrying me bridal-style into the bedroom, where he settles me onto the mattress with impossible gentleness.

"Merry Christmas Eve," he says softly, pressing a kiss to my forehead and then draping a blanket over me.

And my last thought before drifting off is that even though it's been an iffy day, I wish every night could end like this—with Beckett next to me, his lips on my forehead, his hand in mine.

Maybe in a few months. Maybe in a few years.

Maybe, maybe, maybe.

NINETEEN
BECKETT

I DO NOT SLEEP ONE WINK ALL NIGHT.

I stay awake, alternating between staring at the ceiling and staring at Molly, and watch as the Christmas Eve hours fade into Christmas morning hours. I listen as my heart performs its rusty dance every time I let myself think about kissing this woman, about making her mine—a pounding rhythm in my chest that pushes at my rib cage until I'm sure Molly will hear.

These feelings are absolutely absurd. They've sprung up out of nowhere. And yet I can't deny that they're real—and they're strong.

Maybe it's because I've been so deprived of female companionship for the last eight months. Is that possible? Heck, I don't remember the last date I went on, and I'm not the kind of guy who does one night stands. So maybe that's it—maybe I'm just lonely.

Something deep inside rebels at this idea, though, and when I try to imagine falling for some other woman, my stomach turns unpleasantly. That feeling only intensifies when

I try to picture the mattress next to me being occupied not by Molly but instead by one of the most gorgeous women to ever exist: Marilyn Monroe.

Marilyn was stunning, but did she ramble about fish when she got nervous? Did she look adorable with mud caking her skin? Would she have told me in no uncertain terms that I was part of the O'Malley clan—that their love for me was unconditional?

I doubt it. And if I'm not interested in *Marilyn*, I'm not going to be interested in anyone else, either.

That settles it. I don't think I like Molly because I'm lonely. I think I like Molly because she's Molly.

I like her, and she's leaving. Today, in fact; the wan sunlight peeking through my curtains tells me that morning has come, and today is the day that the rest of Molly's family will arrive to pick her up. It's the reason I'm hanging onto by a thread, the single fact I keep reminding myself about: I cannot promise Molly anything, and I cannot start anything with her, because she's leaving. And as much as I want her now, I need to be sure that these feelings are sustainable—that they're not going to fade in a week once the craziness of the last few days has been put behind us. At this exact moment in time it seems like they'll last forever, but her words keep ringing through my mind—that people in extreme situations often bond more quickly because of their shared experiences. It makes sense, then, that once those extreme situations have passed, the extreme emotions might lessen as well.

It would be irresponsible to give Molly hope, only to back out a month from now. I can't hurt her like that. Especially because I can tell that however transient my feelings might be, hers aren't; she admitted that she's always had a thing for me.

There's a picture forming in my mind of what I'm going to have to do, and it sends a sour feeling to the pit of my stomach.

I'm going to have to let her go. I'm going to have to cut her off, even if only for a little while. But it's the only way I can know for sure if what I'm feeling has any potential to last in the real world. When I lessen my exposure to Molly, will the Molly Effect remain? That's the experiment I'm going to have to run.

Because I'm going to have to be all in with Molly O'Malley if we're going to be together.

My pulse jumps as that image unfolds before my eyes with almost supernatural vividness—like a movie screen on the blank white wall in front of me, our future begins to play. Grocery shopping together, standing by the crate of produce and arguing over which apples look best. Carefully applying a Band-Aid to her finger when she cuts herself chopping vegetables. Donning matching pajamas with the rest of the O'Malley clan next Christmas, two Christmases from now, ten Christmases from now. A *family*, one that doesn't leave or consider me as only an afterthought.

People who accept me unconditionally.

I wrench my eyes away from the wall and that future, swallowing the sudden lump in my throat. This is completely ridiculous. It's like I've leveled up—like Molly has unlocked an entire new set of emotions in me that now come out to play whenever they feel like it, with no regard for what I want. I'm in bed on Christmas morning, for goodness's sake; what is this tightness in my throat? What's this stinging in my eyes?

Crap. Speaking of crying—Mrs. O'Malley is going to sob. There are going to be *so* many tears. She's the kind of woman whose emotions are not restricted by little things like social convention or proper public behavior. She's loud and over-the-top, and most of the time I love that about her.

But despite Molly's assurances that her parents won't be mad about what happened...well. I'll believe it when I see it.

I sigh, my eyes jumping away from the ribbons of daylight

playing on the carpet and moving instead back to Molly. She's asleep facing my direction, her face squished to the side by her pillow, so that her cheeks are bunched and chubby, her lips puckered slightly. Her hair is absolutely wild, several corkscrew curls falling over her forehead and a few strands stuck at the corners of her lips. The rest falls to the pillow all around her head with a volume that's almost gravity-defying. There are no Sleeping Beauties here.

I smile anyway as I look at her. She's cuter than she has any right to be. And I'm going to miss her.

As though my dopey, lovestruck staring is a physical touch on her skin, Molly suddenly swats at her cheek in her sleep— like she's swatting a mosquito. Her puckered lips turn down immediately afterward, her brow bunching, and I have to stifle a laugh. A second later she shifts her body, rolling onto her back, lifting her arms, and stretching herself into wakefulness. Her eyes flutter open, and she looks around for a moment before turning back to face me.

A little smile curves her lips when we make eye contact. "Hi," she says. Then she curls more tightly into a ball and lets out a contented sigh. "Isn't a warm bed when you wake up the most comfortable thing in the world?"

"It is," I agree, and I can't help my returning smile. I think I might give my right foot to be curled up under those blankets with her, holding her close.

I keep this thought to myself.

"How are you feeling?" I say instead.

She sighs, propping her head up on her elbow as she looks at me. "This is the only time today you get to ask that question. Are you sure you want to use it now?"

"I'm sure. It will be the first and the last time I ask. I promise," I say. I take in the cascade of hair that's falling to the mattress now that she's propped up a bit, and I have to force myself to pay attention to her answer instead of those curls. It's just that they're perfect for running my fingers through—

"I feel fine," she says, pulling me out of my curl-induced reverie. "My quads feel a little sore, maybe, but that's it."

I nod, sitting up and turning my body to face her. "Still shaky at all?"

She sits up too, then shakes her head. "Nope," she says.

"Good." There's another question I want to ask, but I'm not sure she wants to talk about the seizures anymore, so I tuck it away into the back of my mind. Maybe later.

"Just say it," she says into the silence that's fallen between us.

I blink at her in surprise. "How did you know—"

"It's written all over your face," she says, pointing. "You have something you want to say, but you don't want to upset me. It's fine; just say whatever you want to say."

"I—it's not—" I sigh. "It was just a question."

Even though the room is still dim with the curtains closed, her answering smile is bright enough that it seems to light the place up. "It's fine, Beckett. Truly. Just get it out of your system. I'm giving you permission."

"It's just—" I clear my throat before going on. "You say you're well-controlled on your medicine, but you were talking yesterday like your seizures happen a lot. You said you're always sore and shaky afterward. And that made it sound like this happens regularly. So—"

"No," she cuts me off. "Yesterday was the first seizure I've had in years. But I've tried...four? Five? Yeah, five," she says, nodding. "My seizures started when I hit puberty, and since then I've tried five different seizure medications. It's always trial and error for those. Sometimes you break through; sometimes the dose is wrong. Sometimes a certain medication just doesn't work. So I'm well-controlled now, but I've still had a decent number of seizures over the course of my life." She looks at me. "Does that make sense?"

"Yes," I say. I'd been confused and a little worried when it sounded like she was having seizures on a regular basis, but now relief spreads through me at her explanation.

"And that was your question?"

"That was my question."

"Great," she says. "Any more?"

"None," I say. I smile a little. "Should we forget about yesterday, then?"

"Yes," she says fervently. "We should. It's Christmas!"

"It is Christmas." My smile grows as I watch the excitement dawn on her face. There's something almost childlike about the way she claps her hands and smiles at me, her eyes shining.

"It's Christmas, and I'm hungry. Let's eat."

That freaking smile of mine grows even more. "Let's eat," I say. I'm going to make this the best Christmas I can for her.

BECAUSE TOURISM IS the number one source of income for the island—followed closely by trade and rum production—we're able to find somewhere to eat breakfast with ease. It's a little café I've never actually been to, despite the fact that it's located prominently in the square where Señorita and Alfonso hang out. We're only inside for three seconds before it becomes apparent that this place has leaned heavily into the island theme; there's some sort of tropical music playing in the background, and the tropical flower motif is incorporated pretty thoroughly everywhere, from the tablecloths to the wallpaper.

A cheerful man with a wide smile greets us and then leads

us to a tiny, two-person table next to the large front window. Then he hands us two menus, takes our drink orders, and promises to be back shortly.

Molly opens her menu right away, but I let my gaze wander out the window for a few minutes first. As always there's a steady stream of people, and people-watching is one of my favorite things to do. I'm not sure why; I don't know what I get from seeing random crowds going about their business.

"It's because you're lonely," Molly says when I tell her this. "You don't feel socially fulfilled, so you like to watch other people being social."

"I'm socially fulfilled," I say. It's a knee-jerk response more than anything; considering her words for even two seconds leads me to the conclusion that she's right.

"Are you?" she says skeptically. "Didn't we establish just a few days ago that you're a chronic avoider of relationships?"

I swallow. I do remember that conversation. "All right, fine. Yes. I could stand to be more social," I say.

Molly smiles, radiant and beautiful. "Don't worry; you have lots of chances to practice. You like the people you work with, don't you?"

My shrug is halfhearted. "I guess, yeah. They're fine. They're good."

A snort of laughter escapes her, and then she says, "Such a convincing character recommendation." She points to my menu, which is still folded on the table in front of me. "Have you decided what you want to eat?"

Oh. I should probably do that. I open the menu, scanning quickly over the items. "Eggs, breakfast sandwich, fruit—" But I break off when Molly suddenly begins to laugh.

"Do you remember how that first day Wes and I were late?" she says through her giggles.

"Yeah," I say, wondering where this is going.

"It's because I had an allergic reaction to the tropical fruit they served on the breakfast buffet," she says. "At least, I think it was the fruit; that was the only thing I ate that I hadn't had before. I had these splotchy pink hives all over my face, and I was so worried because I was going to see you for the first time in years." She's still smiling, a faraway look in her eyes. Her gaze turns to me as she goes on, "I wanted to make a good impression on you."

She laughs again, and it's a contagious sound; I find myself laughing too. Except there's something about our laughter that's tinged with desperation, a sharp edge to the sound that slices at the space between us. I think I know why, too—it's because this is our last day together. And even though we haven't talked about what will happen when she returns to her family, we both know.

She'll continue to do her own thing, gobbling up the world in greedy, pleasureful bites; I'll do my own thing, merely existing day in and day out. We'll go our separate ways while we wait to see if our feelings die.

And we will never get these moments back.

By the time our food comes—a breakfast sandwich for her, eggs Benedict for me—the desperate laughter has died, and we're much more subdued. We eat mostly in silence, although I am faintly amused to learn that I was right the other day; when she's eating food she really enjoys, Molly does indeed make borderline obscene sounds. My smile is short lived, though, overshadowed by the knowledge that our time is almost up. We pay for our meal and then leave, heading back to the curb outside the square where we can find a taxi. Despite our moods, the sun is bright in the sky, the cheerful hum of tourism all around us.

"I want to hold your hand," Molly says as we walk, dropping her words abruptly into the silence that's fallen between us.

I look over at her, surprised. "What?" My hand flexes seemingly of its own accord when her words register.

She stops in place, her footsteps dying on the paved stone. The look she gives me is the closest thing to heartbreaking I think I've ever seen; somewhere between desperate and hopeful. "I want to hold your hand," she says again, louder this time.

My arm moves before my brain can even formulate a response; I reach out and grab her hand, interlocking our fingers as our palms meet. My entire body sighs at the contact as a pleasant warmth rushes through me. It's an overly enthusiastic response to such a simple touch, but I guess this is who I am now: a man so captivated that his heart explodes from even the tiniest things.

"I know you can't promise me anything," Molly says as she looks at our linked hands. "And I know this doesn't mean anything is going to happen. I just..." Her voice is small as she goes on, "I just want to make the most of the time I have left with you. Before all this is over."

"I understand," I say after a beat, squeezing her hand. It fits perfectly inside mine, but that's not surprising. *Perfectly* is the only way our bodies could possibly fit together—of that, I'm convinced.

"I guess...do you think we should keep our distance for a while after I've gone?"

I hate that she's come to the same conclusion I have.

"It might be best," I say, wrenching the words from my tongue. "Just for a month or two, to see how we really feel away from all the life-and-death situations."

"My work study starts in early February," she says, and I catch her peeking over at me before she looks away again. "Not here on St. Thomas but close enough. We could meet up in February. Or we don't have to meet if we don't want to," she adds quickly. "We could—"

"Yeah," I cut her off. "Let's do that. Let's meet when you come back." I don't know how I'll feel when that time comes, but if it's anything like now, I'll definitely want to see her.

She nods. I nod. And that's that. I know that's the one and only time we're going to talk about what will happen; neither of us want to dwell on it.

We resume our walk, and I keep her hand tightly in mine the whole time, smoothing vague circles over her knuckle with my thumb. The pads of my fingers are a little rough, a little calloused, but everything about her is soft, and I love it. She's a mass of contradictions that all come together to create the most intoxicating woman—energetic but gentle, soft but loud, selfless but hungry for life.

And suddenly holding her hand isn't nearly enough. So I untangle our fingers before wrapping my arm around her shoulder and pulling her close, pressing a kiss to the top of her head as we continue to walk. Her arm snakes around my waist, her grip on me just as tight as mine is on her.

We would be the annoying couple that both sat on the same side of the table at a restaurant. And we would laugh about being those people, but we would do it anyway.

We don't speak again until we arrive back at my little house. I talked to her parents yesterday while she was still coming to, and they'll arrive at about eleven; that means we've got about two hours left. So as soon as we get inside, I steer her straight to the loveseat.

"Sit," I say, pressing gently on her shoulders. "I'll get your Christmas present."

"I have to get yours too," she says, shrugging my hand off. "Just remember it's not wrapped at all. Normally I would wrap it up and put a cute bow on top. So you'll have to use your imagination and pretend all that stuff is there."

I gesture to our Christmas cactus, which is stationed unceremoniously against the wall across from the loveseat. Both her present and mine are tucked around the base of the flowerpot, each of them wrapped in their plastic shopping bags. "I'll grab both of them and bring them over," I say. "Get comfortable."

She concedes, plopping onto the couch and watching as I retrieve our gifts.

"I wish I were wearing my Christmas sweater," she says, looking ruefully down at her Virgin Islands t-shirt and shorts. Then she glances up at me, her eyes running down my body. "Do you have any Christmas clothes?"

I give a snort of laughter, which makes her smile.

"No," she says, answering her own question. "Of course you don't."

"Not so much as a Christmas sock," I say. I return to the loveseat and pass her the bag with her present in it, taking a seat on the floor next to the couch.

"I'm not surprised," she says, still grinning. Then she points to the bag in my hand. "Open it!"

"Right," I say. It's some sort of book, I think, based on the shape and the feel. But when I pull it out of the plastic bag, I'm surprised to find that I wasn't quite correct.

"I know you're probably not a journaler," she says, looking hesitantly at the notebook I'm holding. It's simple and black, no frills or adornments, and very much my style if I were to pick out a journal on my own. "I figured you weren't," she goes on. "But you're so isolated and closed off that I thought...I don't know." She shrugs, and a delicate pink blush stains her freckled cheeks as her eyes dart up to me and then back down to her hands again. "I thought it might be good for you to express yourself somehow. Write down what emotions you feel or what you wish you could talk to people about or something. You can use it for anything, though—make to-do lists or grocery lists or sketch the people you see when you people-watch. It can just be a pad of paper if you—"

"Molly," I cut her off gently. "It's perfect. And you're right; it would be good for me." She's correct in her assumption that I've never used a journal before, and yet I know that I've just changed. The second she bought this for me, I became a journal user. I'll use every single page, even if it takes me years. "So people just write what emotions they feel?"

She smiles at me, a relieved, happy smile that sends warmth through my veins. "Sure. Or the things they wish they could say. Anything."

I nod, tucking those instructions away for the future. "Here," I say, passing her the plastic bag that has her gift inside. "Open yours."

It's stupid how nervous I am as she pulls the little box out. I shouldn't be. But I want her to like it, and I want her to remember everything that's happened in a good way rather than a bad way.

She looks at the box, one of those gold, sparkly cardboard boxes that jewelry always comes in, and then turns her curious eyes to me. I just jerk my chin at the box, silently telling her to open it.

"Oh," she says softly when she pulls the lid off. A smile spreads across her lips as she gazes fondly down at the contents —a delicate silver necklace with a tiny fish charm, inlaid with mother-of-pearl. "He's so cute."

I clear my throat, feeling suddenly embarrassed. "You like fish," I say—like an idiot.

She laughs, and her eyes sparkle at me when she looks up. "I do," she says.

I nod at the necklace. "What kind is that?"

"Mmm," she hums, lifting the box and inspecting it closer. "Some kind of angelfish, maybe." Then she holds the box out to me. "Put it on me?"

"Oh," I say, taken aback. "Yeah. Of course." I take the box and watch her turn her back to me. She lifts her hair out of the way and twirls it onto the top of her head, holding it in place.

I swallow as I stare at her smooth, pale skin—at the wisps of hair curled at the nape of her neck and the smattering of freckle constellations. I've never thought about the back of someone's neck before, never anticipated that it could be beautiful, but it is; the back of Molly's neck is perfect.

"Do you need help?" she says after a second, turning her head and looking at me over her shoulder.

"No," I say quickly, yanking my eyes away. "Sorry. Here; I'll get it." I remove the necklace from the box and then fumble with the clasp for a second before I manage to undo it. Then I stand up so that I can reach her. I put the necklace in place, fastening the clasp once more. It settles delicately against her neck, resting just over the neckline of her shirt.

I hesitate just briefly before making one last allowance: I lean down and touch my lips to the skin above that little silver clasp. It's the last time I'm going to kiss her—for now, definitely, but maybe forever. I can't kiss her on the lips again today, at any rate; my self-control is too threadbare for that, worn thin by her smiles and the laughter in her eyes. So I put everything I can't articulate into this press of my lips, lingering just a moment before standing up straight again. "There," I say.

Molly releases her hair, letting it tumble down her back. Then she smiles up at me. "I love it," she says, and I can tell she means it. "Thank you."

"Merry Christmas," I say.

Her smile widens. "Merry Christmas," she replies.

It's incredibly tempting to kiss her again, especially when

she's looking at me with that expression on her face—happy, content, dreamy—so I wrangle what's left of my self-control and nod to the window. "It's nice outside. Let's go sit on the porch."

THE ARRIVAL of the rest of the family is a loud affair, mostly because of Mrs. O'Malley.

"I'm so sorry, you two," she sobs, throwing one arm around my neck and one around Molly's as she drags us closer to her. "I'm so sorry. It was all my fault. I shouldn't have been match-making, and I promise I'll never do it again—"

"Here," Mr. O'Malley cuts in, prying his wife gently off of us. Then he passes something to Molly. "Take your medication."

"Yes," Mrs. O'Malley says in a warbling voice, flapping her hands at Molly. "Take it."

I go immediately inside to grab her a glass of water, and a minute later she's gulping down the first dose of seizure medicine she's had in days. Something eases inside of me as she swallows that pill, a tension I didn't realize I was carrying. My body relaxes slightly, and I nod gratefully to Mr. O'Malley.

There are still tears in Mrs. O'Malley's eyes, but she's calmed down some; she's sniffling now instead of blubbering and wailing. Mr. O'Malley drapes his arm around her shoulder and looks fondly at her.

"The kids are okay," he says to her. "They're fine."

"Yeah," Wes says, speaking for the first time after his initial greeting. His gaze is suspicious as it bounces back and forth between Molly and me. "They seem...good."

"Let's go inside," Mrs. O'Malley says to us. "Just for a

minute. I need a tissue, Beckett, sweetie. And I need to use your restroom. My bladder isn't what it used to be."

"Mom," Molly and Wes groan in unison, but she waves away their protests and marches right on inside without waiting for the rest of us.

We follow her, Molly and Mr. O'Malley sitting on the loveseat while Wes prowls the room, examining everything. He's never been to this house, but I have a sneaking suspicion he's not curious so much as looking for signs that Molly and I have been getting cozy. I don't know what he expects to find— couples' mugs in the sink? His and hers towels in the bathroom?—but I let him do his thing.

We chat for a few minutes, the conversation driven mostly by Mrs. O'Malley after she returns from the bathroom, until she stands up and announces that they need to leave to get back to the ferry and then from there back to the cruise's port stop. Her words send a weird bolt of panic through me, my head snapping to look at Molly.

This is happening. She's leaving. And while she is coming back to a different part of the Virgin Islands roughly a month from now...will I see her then? Will she want to see me? Will *I* want to see *her*?

"So...you two."

I jump guiltily, like Wes has caught me doing something wrong instead of simply staring at his sister.

He points back and forth between Molly and me. "You didn't...you know." He clears his throat. "Nothing happened here, right?"

Molly rises from off the couch and rolls her eyes. "Shut up, Wes. It's none of your business what does and doesn't happen." Then she looks at me. Her head tilts to the side. "You," she says, her voice cracking.

I'm vaguely aware of an excited-sounding Mrs. O'Malley

telling Wes to give us some privacy—so much for never match-making again. But even when Wes grumbles and turns his back to us, I only have eyes for the woman in front of me.

"You," she repeats as she steps closer, closer, closer, until there's no more than a few inches of space between us. She presses one finger into my chest, tears coursing down her cheeks. "You don't have to fall in love with me," she whispers brokenly. "And distance doesn't have to make your heart grow fonder. But you'd *better* not forget me."

And then, with no warning except her searing gaze, she surges up and kisses me.

And I'm helpless to do anything except respond. My arms band around her waist immediately, eliminating what little space is left between us as I pull her as close as I can. She must be on her tiptoes, but I still have to lean down to reach her. I don't care; I'll take that pain. Her hands slide up over my chest, over my shoulders, until they're locked around my neck—her tears on my cheeks and the taste of salt on my tongue as she cries. Every stroke of her lips against mine opens a yawning, gaping chasm inside, an electric desire in my veins, and this is why I couldn't kiss her when we were alone—because I *want* this woman, body and mind and soul, and I can't have her.

Not yet, anyway.

With one last press of her lips to mine, fierce and full of unspoken words, Molly releases me, and the arms that hugged my neck move to hug herself around the waist instead. She just looks at me for an eternal moment, and then she's gone—out the door that's left swinging on its hinges as she passes. I hear a distant sob from somewhere outside, and it shatters something deep in my heart.

I hug the rest of the O'Malleys and promise to take care of myself, barely paying attention to a single word that's coming out of my mouth and ignoring the sympathetic looks of Mr. and

Mrs. O'Malley. Wes looks for a second like he's going to say something to me, but he must be able to tell that now isn't the time; he just claps me on the shoulder and tells me he'll talk to me later.

And then they're gone, all of them, and I'm alone again.

Just me, a Christmas cactus, and a house that's haunted by the ghost of Molly O'Malley.

TWENTY
BECKETT

JANUARY 1

Emotions I feel: sad, weird, hungry

Something I wish I could say: I want to ask her if she thinks hungry is an emotion.

JANUARY 6

Emotions I feel: Lonely because my house is quiet. Frustrated because I almost caved and asked Wes how she's doing.

Something I want to say: I want to tell her I decided hungry isn't an emotion. I think it's just a physical state.

JANUARY 8

At some point I have to stop thinking about her. Right?

JANUARY 10
-*eggs*
-*bread*
-*tomato soup*
-*pepperjack*
-*deli ham*
-*maybe some of those cheap plastic plates they sell in the bargain aisle*
-*cups from bargain aisle*

JANUARY 14
January is a stupid month. I don't see any reason it needs to last this long.

JANUARY 16
Today I initiated a casual, social conversation with a guy at work. We talked about the weather. It was painful. I hated every second. I wish I could tell her.
She'd be proud of me.

JANUARY 20
One of the pokey things broke off the Christmas cactus. It's been sitting on the table but I accidentally knocked it off, and one of the spike thingies snapped off. I tried to tape it back on because I don't have any glue, but obviously that didn't work. Tape isn't meant for fake cacti. It's too late to go out and buy glue since the stores are closed now, so I'm going to have to get

some tomorrow morning and hope it works. Superglue is probably what I need if I can find it. I'll google the best kinds of superglue and see if I can find that. There's a little hardware store a couple miles down the road; I think they open at 9:00.

I'll be there at 9:01.

JANUARY 21

I fixed the cactus. It's a little messy, but it's better than the tape. I turned the side with the glue toward the wall so you don't see it anyway.

New couch came today. I'm happy about that. It looks pretty good. It's secondhand, but there are no weird stains or anything.

Work at the job site is going to start wrapping up in a few weeks. I need to figure out my next steps. I think I've been waiting for word from her, but what if she's waiting to hear from me? Her work study thing starts in February, but if we're going to meet up we'll need to talk before that.

My emotions are weird these days. I've been trying to figure out how I feel about her now that she's not around. But whenever I try to delve into all that, I end up putting it off, because thinking about her makes me...sad, I guess. It doesn't help that Wes keeps asking me what's going on between the two of us.

I don't know. I don't have answers or magical insights to all of my feelings.

I just miss her.

JANUARY 22

I went over to the hut after work today. First time I've been back. I shouldn't have gone. I remembered that dream I had *while we slept on the floor and I remembered how she looked all covered in mud, glaring up at me after I dropped her.*

I don't think Molly is the kind of woman who leaves your life quietly. She leaves a gaping hole in her absence, one that screams and makes creaking noises in the middle of the night, like footsteps on rickety stairs.

I want her to come back.

JANUARY 27

So close to February. As soon as the first of the month hits, I'm getting her new phone number from Wes. If he won't give it to me, I'll ask their mom instead.

I'm coming for you, Molly O'Malley.

JANUARY 27, *later*

Except you don't think she's changed her mind, right? Or met any amazing men and fallen in love with them? Crap.

"HEY. YOU WERE LOOKING FOR ME?" The words come from behind me, spoken in my coworker's unmistakable voice. *Unmistakable* because I've never met a man whose voice is as nasally as Vlad's.

"Yeah," I say, only half paying attention. I turn around, notepad in hand, my eyes narrowed on the sea of wooden chairs in front of me. Then I look at Vlad. As usual, my pulse jumps at the first glimpse of his red hair—hair that always makes me think, for the tiniest second, that I might be seeing Molly. I

219

don't know why my brain keeps mistaking this scrawny, thirty-year-old Russian man for the woman I've fallen for, but I guess I really must be that desperate.

"We're supposed to have forty of these," I say, pointing to the chairs and putting aside thoughts of red hair and bright smiles.

"Uh-huh," Vlad says, rubbing his hand over his wispy hair. It's thinning to the point that he really would do better just shaving it all off, but to each their own, I guess.

"But we don't have forty."

Vlad frowns, and his hand stops mid-hair-rub. Then he begins to count, pointing at each chair as he does so.

"It's thirty-two," I say, because I'm not patient enough to wait. "But we have forty dorm room desks. We're eight short. Can you double-check that you ordered forty?"

"I definitely ordered forty," Vlad says. Despite his nasally voice and his underwhelming looks, though, he's a good worker; if he says he ordered forty, I believe him.

So I nod. "In that case, can you get in touch with the suppliers and ask what the holdup is for those last eight?" I'm not too worried; field studies won't start here until next term, sometime in August or September. We've got a bit. But I don't want to get stuck here waiting on nothing but chairs.

"I'll email them," Vlad says. He shoves his hands in his pockets, rocking back and forth from his heels to the balls of his feet and then back again.

"Something else?" I prompt, because he's got that nervous look on his face that people usually get when they want to say something but don't know how.

"We were just...gonna go for drinks..." he says, thumbing over his shoulder to where a few other guys are standing around, waiting. "If you wanted to come."

I blink at him, surprised. This is the first time they've ever invited me out with them, though I know they usually get together a couple times a week. I've been (grudgingly) trying to be more social—which, in my case, means I make eye contact sometimes and speak in full sentences rather than monosyllabic grunts. It's not natural for me to reach out, but I guess it's working.

"Sure," I say after a moment of internal debate. I'm tempted to say *no thanks*, despite the fact that invitations like this are what I've been striving toward. There's something intimidating about hanging out with people you don't know well; I know these guys from work, but I have no idea what they're like in other settings.

Still, I told Molly I would try to be more social. And, even more than that—hanging out with her made me realize how lonely I've been.

I doubt Vlad and his friends are going to make me miss her any less, but it wouldn't hurt to be out and doing things, distracting myself.

Vlad nods easily, then thumbs over his shoulder again. "You ready, then?" he says.

"Uh..." I say, looking around and pushing my hand through my hair. "Yeah, I think so. You'll get in touch with the suppliers about the chairs?"

"I'll contact them before I come tomorrow," he promises. "Now stop thinking about work." Then he claps one hand on my shoulder. I jump, unused to the contact, and I try to play it off like I'm just moving rather than being a weirdo. Not sure it works.

I trail behind Vlad and the other three, all of whom are chatting with each other. I slow to a stop when we leave the building and pass the place where Molly and I huddled together during the storm. The first time I came back to Van Gogh Island, I looked at this spot to see if there were any

remnants of her left. I don't know what I expected to see—
MOLLY WAS HERE etched into the brick? Her shape permanently darkening the wall like the Hiroshima shadows, left
eerily behind after the city was bombed?—but there was
nothing.

It's just a stretch of brick, plain and unassuming. Anyone
who looked at this wall would never know it was our only
shelter through the worst of an island storm, and I'm suddenly
hit with the bizarre urge to mark the spot, to leave a little x with
leftover paint or carve our initials—

"You coming?" Vlad calls from up ahead, and it's only then
that I realize they've almost left me behind completely; they're
almost to the paved drive, while I'm still moping around next to
this wall.

"Yeah," I say, hurrying my step and giving the brick one last
glance over my shoulder. "Sorry." Then I sigh, steeling myself
for an hour or two of socialization.

I can do this.

TWENTY-ONE
MOLLY

As of ten minutes ago, according to the clock on my phone, it is officially February. The month of love, the month of lingering winter, the month when everyone is starting to get sick of snow.

And, now, the month when I get to see Beckett again.

Hopefully, anyway.

I've been good. I've been *so* good. I have not contacted him once. No emails, no calls, no texts. No carrier pigeons or snail mail. Lots of attempted telepathy, but I pretty much knew that was a bust ever since my eleventh birthday, when no acceptance letters to Hogwarts showed up.

So yeah. Beckett has not heard one single word from me for the entire month of January.

A little twang of nervousness ripples through my gut. One month is a long time—long enough for his feelings to fade. Knowing him, I doubt he's miraculously fallen in love with someone else during this time, but that doesn't mean his feelings for me have stuck around, either.

That's kind of what January was about, though—a chance

for us to find out if our feelings for each other were real, or if they were just byproducts of the things we went through together.

There was never any question on my end. Until we got stuck on that island, I was head-over-heels in love with the version of Beckett I had been building up in my head for years. That version of him was based on the real thing, but it wasn't quite true to life. The real Beckett—especially the current version of him—is a little grumpier than I imagined, a little more antisocial. More protective than I would have imagined, definitely, and unexpectedly softer, too. Vulnerable. Caring.

My feelings for him have not faded one bit. I'm just crazy about the real Beckett now, rather than the version of him I'd been holding onto.

Who knows how he's feeling about me, though? I want to believe that he still likes me as a person, at the very least. I want to believe that I'm no longer just Wes's little sister. But it's hard to know for sure.

Until now, that is.

I bite my lip, looking at the time again. Yes, it's officially February now, but I shouldn't call him at midnight, right? That's bad manners. Also it sort of reeks of desperation.

So I settle for texting him instead. That doesn't reek of desperation so much as it just *slightly smells* like desperation. And I'm fine with that. I wet myself and had a seizure in front of him. I have no room for embarrassment anymore.

It takes me a stupidly long time to formulate a text, considering my message ends up being exactly eleven words. But I hit send, my heart pounding in my chest like fists banging against my rib cage.

ME: *It's Molly. Still want to meet up now that it's February?*

. . .

I FORCE myself not to sit and stare at my phone, waiting for a response. He's probably asleep, so I'll mostly likely hear back in the morning. And I'm okay with that—

Except my phone buzzes, startling me. That thudding in my chest grows louder, picking up speed until I start to think my heart is just going to leap out of my gaping mouth.

Did he really text me back already?

BECKETT: *Yes. When will you be here?*

I CAN'T HELP the smile that spreads across my face as I look around me—at the row of shops, all dark windows and locked doors; at the stretch of paved stone where Nilson carries Alfonso and Señorita during the day; at the port entry on the other side of the square.

In truth, I've been on the island for about twenty-four hours now. My work study starts next week, a few islands over. Call me presumptuous, but I wanted to get here early enough to see Beckett before I had to go get settled in the dorm.

I turn on my phone's flash and take a picture of myself, turned so that the port entrance is clearly visible in the background. Then I send the photo to Beckett with shaking hands. I'm not a big selfie girl, and I'm definitely not one to send selfies to the guys I like. But this feels like a good time to respond with a photo rather than words.

My phone buzzes thirty seconds later, and I take a deep breath before reading it.

. . .

BECKETT: *Stay where you are. I'm coming to you.*

"WHAT?" I squawk, jumping up. I figured he would ask to see me tomorrow. He might even ask to see me in the morning, if I was lucky. I didn't think he'd come to me right this very second.

I'm about to text him back and tell him to wait—because I for sure need to shower before I see him again—when my phone rings.

"Yeah," I say breathlessly. I don't even look at the caller ID; I know it's him.

"Molly, you can't just wander around by yourself in the middle of the night," he says. "Can you go inside? Is anywhere open?"

"No," I say, looking around at all the darkened shops. "But—"

"Of course not," he mutters. I can hear faint sounds in the background, and I imagine him rushing around his little house, putting on shoes, grabbing his wallet, getting out the door. "Look, just sit somewhere and—I don't know. Try to turn invisible."

"Hmm," I say, a smile pulling at my lips. "A solid plan." Something giddy and full of sunshine is bubbling up inside of me, and I bizarrely feel like laughing. "What should I do if I can't manage the invisibility thing?"

"Keep your eyes peeled and try not to get mugged."

"Are you gonna stay on the phone with me until you get here?" I say, still smiling.

"Obviously. You're in the square?" From what I can hear on the other end of the line, it sounds like he's outside now; catching a taxi, maybe.

"Yep," I say, looking around again. I spot two or three

couples, strolling along, keeping to themselves. "But I'm not the only person here. It's not like I'm by myself."

"That makes me feel worse," he groans.

"You know what?" I say, biting my lip as my smile threatens to float right off my face. "It's been a month, but you're still pretty overprotective."

A grunt is the only response I get.

"And you're dropping everything in the middle of the night to come see me."

Another grunt, and then, "Yeah, because you're wandering around by yourself." There's a beat of silence before he speaks again. "And..."

"Because you missed me?" I say, the words popping out before I can stop them. I can't stop the hope in my voice, either.

"Because I missed you," he admits. "When does your study start? I was going to call you in the morning to see when you would be here."

"It starts next week," I say, sitting back down on the bench once more. I swing my feet, scuffing them against the paved stone as I talk. "I just wanted to come here first and see you once January was over."

"Well, I'll be to you in about two minutes," Beckett says— and maybe I'm imagining things, but he almost sounds anxious, or nervous. "Just talk to me until then. How was January?"

"Meh," I say after a second.

He snorts. "Yeah. Mine too."

"Did you socialize?" I ask him. "Because I'll have you know, I've been working very hard on not being a people-pleaser."

He hums, a low, pleasant sound that runs down my spine and makes me jittery. "Details, please."

"Well, I told a guy at the aquarium that I couldn't cover his shift because I had some prep work I had to get done—"

"Good."

"And when Wes kept trying to bug me about you, I told him to back off and mind his own business," I say. "Which he eventually did."

"I told him the same thing," Beckett says. Once again I can hear the sounds of the night in the background; he must be close. "And I think I was probably ruder about it than you were."

"Probably," I agree, smiling. "So what about you?"

"What about me?"

"Did you socialize?" I say.

"Kind of. I guess. Yeah. I've been trying. I got food with some guys after work earlier this evening."

"Good for you!" I say. "I'm proud of you."

He doesn't answer; he just gives a little snort of laughter.

"So have you cut down on the glowering?" I say. "Because that's a bit off-putting. I bet a lot of the other kids would want to be your friend if you didn't look so grumpy all the time."

"I don't look grumpy all the time!"

"Okay, but you don't look cheerful all the time, either," I point out. "You sort of have resting grump face, I think."

"No one looks cheerful all the time," Beckett says.

"That's true," I admit. Then, because I'm impatient, I say, "Are you almost here?" I suddenly remember my appearance, though, and I add, "Except okay, Beckett, I fully did not expect to see you tonight. So I am gross, okay? Like my hair is gross from traveling and my clothes aren't cute and I'm not wearing any makeup or—or—" But I break off, stuttering into silence when someone across the square catches my eye.

A shadowy figure, visible mostly from the bright light of the phone he's holding to his ear. He's moving directly toward me with surprising speed; he passes the little café where we ate breakfast on Christmas day and then the spot where Alfonso and Señorita usually hang out, moving ever closer. I watch him, breathless, my heart almost painful as it pounds in my chest.

And then he's in front of me, five steps away, four steps, three steps, two steps, one step, but he doesn't stop—he just keeps walking until he runs right into me, his arms encircling me and holding me tightly to his chest.

"Molly," he says in a broken whisper. His hands smooth over my hair, up and down my back, over my shoulders and down my arms—like he wants to touch everything and doesn't know where to start. Like he's making sure every part of me is in place.

"Could you even see me?" I say. My words come out muffled, since my face is squashed against the hard planes of his body, but in what universe would I ever move from this position of my own free will? "It's dark. What would you have done if I were just some strange woman you randomly mauled?"

"You knew it was me," he points out, his lips brushing my ear as he speaks. I shiver and fist my hands more tightly in the soft fabric of his shirt. "Why wouldn't I know it's you?" Then he releases me, his hands gripping my shoulders as he holds me at arms' length and lets his eyes trail over me. I don't know how much he can see out here, but I let him look his fill; it gives me a chance to do the same thing.

White t-shirt, some sort of neutral shorts. I can see vague shadows of his hair, slightly messy, and the general features of his face. I smile up at him.

"Hi," I say softly. I was so self-conscious about how I looked, but now that he's here in front of me, I'm not even thinking about that. I just want to be with him. He doesn't care if I'm a mess. He's seen me covered in mud.

"Hi," he says, exhaling loudly. He reaches up with one hand and brushes his knuckles down my cheek. "Let's date."

I blink, my jaw dropping a little. "I—let's what?"

"Date," he says again. "Let's date. You and me." His voice is calm, matter-of-fact, but the hand that's still on my shoulder is gripping me too tightly to hide how he really feels. He's trying not to come on too strong, but...

"You...want this. Want...me," I say slowly. Tasting the words on my tongue. Savoring them.

He nods, one sharp jerk of his head. "It's possible that I have become unreasonably attached to you."

I burst out laughing. "It's possible? *Unreasonably* attached? Sweet-talker."

In the darkness I can just see the outline of his smile as he grins. "And there's more where that came from."

I want to jump right in; I want to take him at his word. But the part of me that's wanted this for so long is harder to convince. What if he changes his mind? What if long distance gets too hard?

I sigh. "Are you sure, Beckett? Don't say yes if you aren't completely sure. I can't be a fling for you. And if we dated, we might have to do long distance—"

"Yes," he says breathlessly, stepping closer. "Fine. To all of it. Long distance, short distance, whatever. I just—" I sense rather than see him swallow. "I just need you to be mine. I want to call you whenever I want. I need to take care of you and make sure you're happy. I want that person to be me."

His words sound so perfect—so *right*. "You're *sure* sure?" I say, my voice bordering on desperate.

"I bought a new couch while you were gone, Molly. One that pulls out into a bed so you'll have someplace to sleep when you stay with me," he says patiently. "I accidentally broke a spine off the Christmas cactus and freaked out. I went to the hardware store first thing the next morning to buy glue. I haven't stopped thinking about you. And I..." He trails off, taking one shuffling step closer. "I'm gonna kiss you."

He bought a new couch for me? Does he even have room for a couch? His place is tiny. "What?" I say, dazed.

"I'm going to kiss you," he repeats, his hand sliding up my neck and into my messy hair. His other hand moves to my waist, pulling me toward him until there's no more space between us. "Molly."

"Huh?" I say.

"Need to hear you say yes."

"Yes," I say quickly. "Kiss me. Date me."

And against my lips, he murmurs two words: "Good girl."

And then he's kissing me. Hands in my hair, at my waist— lips chasing the taste of our future.

I inhale this moment.

I exhale the past.

And then I wrap my arms more tightly around him and kiss him back with everything I have.

EPILOGUE

MOLLY

"OKAY, EVERYONE, SMILE!" MY MOM BUSTLES INTO THE room with her phone in hand, already holding it up to take another picture.

"Mom," Wes and I groan.

"Every year," he says, looking at me as he nudges a few crumpled balls of wrapping paper with his foot.

"Every year," I agree. I try to smile, but I think it looks more like a grimace—here's hoping nobody notices. Wes doesn't, at least; that's for sure. He's the least observant person I know when it comes to his family members. I think if I showed up bald, he'd tilt his head to the side and ask if I'd done something new with my hair. My parents aren't as bad as Wes, especially my dad, but he doesn't seem to notice anything off, either. He just smiles indulgently at my mom as he throws one arm around Wes's shoulders and drags him forcefully to stand in front of the Christmas tree.

No, the only person who appears to know something's up is my husband. He's been watching me with a keen eye, his gaze trailing after me all morning. He's been suspicious for days, in fact.

Now I jump as I feel his arms encircling me from behind; I turn my head to see him leaning over the back of the couch, his arms draped over my shoulders, his lips brushing my ear as he whispers something meant only for me to hear.

"You gonna tell me why you're being so weird?"

I turn my head toward him again, trying to hide my smile. We've been married for three years, but Beckett still takes care of me the same way he did when we first fell in love. He makes sure I'm okay, makes sure I'm happy, and I do the same for him.

"These look much better on you than they do on me," I say to distract him, plucking at the fabric of his sleeve. The designated O'Malley Christmas pajamas this year are a shade of red that clashes horribly with my hair, decorated with a little pattern of candy canes and mistletoe. I wanted ones with little fish wearing Santa hats, but I was outvoted.

"And that's why you're being weird?" he murmurs in my ear, sounding amused.

I grin. "Could be."

"Come on, you two," my mom says, flapping her hand at Beckett and I and then pointing to the Christmas tree where Wes and my dad are waiting—my dad smiling genially, Wes still trying to escape the borderline headlock he's got him in. "Christmas morning pictures!"

I heave an exaggerated sigh and force my tired body to stand up. Beckett's hands brace on my shoulders from behind as he helps steady me. Then he rounds the couch and joins me next to Wes and my dad. Wes's eyes catch on Beckett's arm around my waist before darting away again.

Things were a little patchy between them for a while when

Beckett and I started dating, but it wasn't long before Wes realized how serious we were about each other. After that he mellowed.

"All right," my mom says, squinting at her phone and holding it way closer to her face than she needs to. "I'm turning on the self-timer. It's going to count down from five, and everybody needs to smile, all right?" She turns around and slides her phone into the slot on the phone tripod she has set up on the top of the fireplace. We got it for her several Christmases ago for this very purpose. "All right," she mutters again. "Here we go...it's starting! It's counting down! Everybody smile!"

I grin as my mom begins to count.

"Five!" she says, bustling over to the group of us. "Four!" She stands next to Wes, slapping my dad's hand so that he and Wes stop tussling. "Three! Two! One—"

"I'm pregnant!" I shout.

Click! The camera makes its little shutter sound as it takes the photo, but no one is looking at it anymore. Everyone is looking at me.

My mom's eyes are wide, her jaw dropped comically. My dad has a massive smile beginning to stretch across his face. Wes is looking back and forth between me and Beckett, looking dazed.

"You knocked up my sister," he says faintly to Beckett.

I ignore him. The only reaction that really matters is Beckett's. So I turn to my husband, wrapping my arms around his waist and studying his face.

His mouth is gaping open, his expression a picture of stunned surprise. Then, slowly, a smile appears—huge and glowing and so genuine it makes the corners of his eyes crinkle in a way they rarely used to when we were growing up.

"You're pregnant," he breathes.

"I am," I say with a nod.

"I knew you were being weird!"

"I've been pretty nauseated," I admit.

He smooths his hands over my hair. "Here, sit," he says, steering me back to the couch. "Sit down. Do you need something? Are you hungry? Thirsty? Do you need ginger tea—"

"Beckett," I say, laughing. "I'm fine." I anticipated this rush of overprotectiveness, one of his most endearing qualities. Maybe someday I'll get tired of it, but that hasn't happened yet. "I'll sit, but I'm good." I return to the couch, settling in comfortably.

"You got my sister pregnant," Wes says, and I start; for a moment I forgot that there were other people here. When I look at Wes, he still has that same dazed look on his face—the look that clearly tells me he's been in denial about what his sister and his best friend get up to when they're alone.

"Apparently so," Beckett says, plopping next to me on the couch and then grinning up at Wes. "And I enjoyed every single second—"

I clap my hand over his mouth before he can say anything else.

"Boys," my mom says disapprovingly, waving her hands at them. "Cut that out." Then she bustles over to the couch, kneeling down next to where I'm seated. She reaches up and pulls me into the kind of hug that can only come from your mother—warm and comforting and full of memories. "Congratulations, sweetie," she says, and I'm not at all surprised to hear her sniffle. I *am* surprised to see the glossy sheen to my dad's eyes, though.

"What about your medicine?" Beckett asks suddenly, turning to me. "Is it safe for pregnancy? You still have to take it, though, right?"

"Definitely." I don't resent him asking; the seizures are always going to be part of our life. It's something we just have to work around in every situation. "I've already talked to my epileptologist. She'll monitor me more closely to make sure my levels stay high enough. As for it being safe for pregnancy..." I shrug. "Ideally you wouldn't take anything during the first trimester, but you just have to weigh what's safest. There are some anticonvulsants that are specifically dangerous to a developing fetus; mine isn't."

"So it's okay," Beckett says anxiously. "For you and for the baby. It's okay."

"It's okay," I say, nodding.

"Good," he says. Some of the tension drains out of him, and he relaxes back into my side. "Good."

I rest my head on his shoulder and smile at my family—at my crying mother and my brother and dad, who are bickering about what grandkids should call my parents—and my heart swells with happiness.

There's snow on the ground outside, with more flurries falling from the blanketed, gray sky. It's warm inside, and I'm surrounded by the people I love. That first Christmas on the island was one I'll always remember and treasure, but I'm glad to be here now.

With my people.

With my Beckett.

"Just another day in paradise," he murmurs to me, pressing a kiss to my cheek as Wes insists loudly that *Grandpappy* is the best option, while my mom turns to them and says she refuses to be called *Grandmammy*.

"Just another day in paradise," I say, smiling.

He's right.

Paradise.

THANK you for reading A NOT-SO HOLIDAY PARADISE! If you want access to free bonus content and occasional updates about what I'm working on next, you can join my newsletter here! Please also consider leaving a review if you loved this book; it means the world to your favorite authors!

READ THE NEXT BOOK IN THE SERIES!

The next book in the Christmas Escape series is Later On We'll Conspire by Kortney Keisel.

Everyone loves a Christmas surprise—just not when it's a spy in disguise.

ACKNOWLEDGMENTS

I write this page for every book I publish, and it never gets any easier. Every time I sit down and think about all the help I've received and the people who've supported me, I'm overwhelmed with gratitude. A page of thanks will never be enough, but it's a start!

First and foremost to the six other authors in this amazing series—I am still starstruck and fan-girling that I get to work with you. You guys rock.

To Scribere Ferro: thanks for helping me understand what it's like to be a large-bosomed woman, and specifically what it's like trying to shop for swimsuits. This is one area I have no personal experience in, seeing as how I'm flat as a board. Also, thank you for being awake at two in the morning when I need plot help.

To Kiki and the rest of RomCom Plot Talk: you all get a solid A+ in supportiveness and brainstorming genius.

To our incredible cover designer, Melody Jeffries—thank you for capturing Molly and Beckett so beautifully!

To the Bookstagram community: what an amazing corner of the internet. Special mention goes to Molly from the.bookish.mom, who named Wes and who coincidentally also shares a name with my main character!

To my family, of course, go all my most fervent thanks. My tribe supports me through writing retreats, getaways, and long days spent holed up in my bedroom, typing furiously to meet my deadlines.

And to my God. I have no words, but You know what I'm trying to say.